THE BEDEVILED

THOMAS CULLINAN was born in Cleveland in 1919 to an Irish Catholic family. He was a playwright, novelist and television screenwriter whose best-known work is the gothic Civil War novel *The Beguiled* (1966), which was filmed in 1971 starring Clint Eastwood and remade in 2017 in a version directed by Sofia Coppola and starring Colin Farrell and Nicole Kidman. His other works include a second Civil War-themed novel, *The Besieged* (1973), *The Eighth Sacrament* (1977), a murder mystery set in a convent, and the occult horror novel *The Bedeviled* (1978). He died in 1995.

D1081659

Thomas Cullinan

THE BEDEVILED

VALANCOURT BOOKS

Dedication: For my sister Betty

The Bedeviled by Thomas Cullinan
Originally published by G. P. Putnam's Sons in 1978
First Valancourt Books edition 2019

Published by Valancourt Books, Richmond, Virginia
http://www.valancourtbooks.com

ISBN 978-1-948405-43-0 (*trade paperback*)

Also available as an electronic book.

All Valancourt Books publications are printed on acid free paper that
meets all ANSI standards for archival quality paper.

Set in Dante MT

Book One

Chapter One

I spend much of my time lately watching Franny, and wondering what she's thinking about. If she's in bed when I visit the nursing home, she just stares at the ceiling. If she's in her chair, she stares at the wall.

Is this a good way to begin a journal? As good as any, I suppose. The motel manager gave me an unused ledger. I presume he thought the work might persuade me to turn off his television set that has been on day and night when I'm in my room. I don't watch the programs, but I'm hoping the sound will cause certain people to think I'm taking an interest in life.

I went to the farm a few days ago, although Father Jackson disapproved. He loaned me his car to drive out there, but he didn't offer to go along. I'm sure he was afraid to go. I was afraid myself, more so after I got there, and I didn't stay after dusk.

I don't know what to do with the place. There seems to be plenty of money—all that Franny and I will need for years, since my husband, Jack, had a lot of insurance—but I'm just not ready to make any definite plans to leave. One of the reasons, I guess, is the fact that two members of my family are buried in the graveyard behind the Caine house.

New beginning. I suppose it was Jack's second heart attack that started it all, that followed by the loss of his job at Marks and Chapman. They gave him a year's salary and maybe that was generous enough, since he'd been creative director for only three years.

Then in the middle of June the real estate man telephoned. The four of us were having a late breakfast—one of the advantages of Jack's unemployment and the kids' school vacation—when Jack took the call.

"Does anyone here realize that we're living in a ninety-five-thousand-dollar house?" he asked after hanging up.

"Far out," Franny said and continued eating her grapefruit. Duff was reading a new flute score, I remember, and he didn't even look up.

"It's probably worth more than that," I said. "You haven't been reading the ads. But where would we live if we sell? We'd need ninety-five thousand and maybe more to buy another house around here."

"We could move to that farm of Dad's in Ohio," Duff said. He mentioned it first, I remember, although I'm not sure that's of any significance. He still didn't look up from his flute score.

And Franny said, "Why not?"

Franny was an outgoing, gregarious child, something Duff had never been. He had his music and his books and he didn't seem to want anything else. He was a good swimmer and tennis player and a half dozen strokes better than his father at golf, but he just wasn't very interested in competitive or social activities.

"Do you think you'd like it out there in the sticks away from your friends?" I asked Franny. I wasn't taking the matter seriously at that point.

"I haven't any friends," she said. She was suffering from not being invited to a fifth grade end-of-term party, apparently the fault of the post office and not the party giver's mother.

"Maggie, it isn't exactly wilderness country anymore," Jack said to me irritably.

He hadn't seen the farm for years, except for the time last fall when he went there for his Aunt Hannah's funeral. She was his great aunt, his grandfather's sister, a spinster who had lived alone on the place for many years. After a crippling stroke, she had employed a housekeeper-nurse who stayed with her until she died.

Jack had inherited the property, but he was unwilling to sell it because it had been in his family for so many years. A real estate company in the area had tried to rent it for him, but with no success.

"It may not be wilderness," I said now, "but it must lack something, if no one wants to live there."

"It's out of the way," Jack said. "It's a good distance from any large city and there aren't many jobs around there. Anyway we're not all that attached to this place, are we?"

"I'm not," said Franny.

"What about you, Mozart?"

Duff looked up from his score and considered it. "I guess I'm not," he said.

"What about his music?" I wanted to know.

"There must be music teachers around there somewhere. And the Cleveland Orchestra isn't too far away."

"What about schools?"

"I'm sure the schools in Ashland and Cainesville are as good as those in Scarsdale."

"You don't believe that any more than I do. And Duff's in his last year here."

"But he has credits enough to graduate now, hasn't he? And he's already practically accepted at Yale for the year after next."

"We'd need quality medical care too, a good hospital and good doctors. Also, that house is probably a wreck."

"It isn't," Jack said. "At least it wasn't last fall. And the furnishings are pretty good too. What will I tell the man? I said I'd call back."

"I'll never agree to sell this house until we've made definite arrangements for another place," I said firmly. "And I won't commit myself to a farm in Ohio until I've seen it and the facilities around it."

Jack agreed to that and a couple of days later—with plenty of misgivings on my part—we flew to Cleveland and rented a car to drive to the farm. Jack wanted to drive all the way in the Oldsmobile station wagon, but I felt he wasn't up to it.

It took about an hour from the Cleveland airport to reach the Ashland real estate office where a Mr. Siebold gave us the keys to the Caine house.

"If you decide not to stay, I'll be happy to try and rent the place again," he told us. "I'm sure I can eventually, especially if you'd be willing to come down a bit in what you're asking."

"It seems to me that two hundred a month is little enough for a furnished house that size and a hundred and fifty acres of land," Jack said.

"Farms are going begging around here, Mr. Caine, especially rental farms."

"Has anyone even considered renting it?" I asked.

"Three or four families have looked at it," Mr. Siebold said.

"And turned it down because of the price?"

"They didn't say, but I assumed that's what it was. I don't know of any other reason, do you?" He ushered us to the door, seemingly anxious to be rid of us. "If any problems come up, you might want to talk with Mrs. Reddy, your aunt's house-keeper. She lives with her daughter and son-in-law, the Emil Webers. They're a mile and a half or so down your road on the same side."

"What sort of problems would you expect to come up?" I inquired.

"Oh, I just mean that Mrs. Reddy could probably give you the names of reliable repair people, if you ever need them. Incidentally there's no telephone on the place. I guess your aunt wouldn't have one. If you want one installed, you'll have to make arrangements with the company here in Ashland."

"We won't bother about it right now," I said.

Mr. Siebold wished us luck and we started off with the hand-drawn map he had given us. Jack wasn't sure he remembered how to get to the farm, which was located on a secondary road about ten miles from Ashland.

When I saw the road, I was even more discouraged. It was gravel and I wondered what it would be like in winter, although I was determined then never to see snow on it. On each side the fields were overgrown and seemingly abandoned, with patches of what I took to be second-growth timber here and there.

"Didn't the Caine family have any neighbors?" I asked.

"Not too many close ones." Jack was trying to steer around the washed-out places in the road. "There are more farms on the other side of our place and the road is paved there too. A lot of these places were abandoned years ago."

"Why?" Duff asked from the back seat. Jack had offered to

let him drive, but Duff had never been much interested in driving.

"To tell you the truth, some of the people around here didn't like your great-great-grandfather. He wasn't a very popular fellow."

"You never told me that," I said.

"I guess the subject never came up. Anyway, the old man was hard to get along with, as I understand it. He had a lot of disputes over property lines and water rights—there's a creek that borders the farm—and his dogs killing neighbors' chickens or their dogs killing his chickens, things like that. He was just plain cantankerous, I guess. Of course, on the plus side, he was a Civil War hero."

"A hero?" shrieked Franny, who had just begun to take an interest in American history.

"Well, he was a general anyway."

"An army general?"

"Yep, a brigadier. I've told you about him, haven't I, Duff?"

"I think you may have," said Duff diplomatically. Duff could never work up any enthusiasm for warfare more recent than Greek or Roman.

"You were named after your great-great-grandfather. I'm sure you knew that."

"What battles was he in, Dad?" Franny wanted to know.

"Let's see. Shiloh, I guess. Chickamauga maybe. There are books at the house that will tell you all about his career."

We came upon the farm suddenly then, coming up to the Caine mailbox and the lane from a dip in the road. The lane was narrow and rutted. Not many cars had ever driven over it, I thought, as we bounced along. It had been made for wagons and carriages and never improved.

The house was a surprise. It was half hidden behind a grove of trees and we didn't get a good look at it until we were almost on it. I don't know what I expected, but it wasn't what I saw. Maybe I thought it would be a Victorian monstrosity, with towers and turrets and shutters creaking in the wind.

Well, it looked Victorian all right, but not like a Victorian house. It looked like a nineteenth century factory or warehouse.

It was built in unequal parts of brick, stone and wood, as though the builder, having run out of one material, made do with another.

Jack shut off the motor. "What do you think of it? It's supposed to look like Libby Prison."

"What's that?"

"A Confederate prison in Richmond. The old man was captured and confined there during the war. I guess his stay made such an impression on him that later he built this house to look like it. The first house was a log cabin."

"I've seen pictures of Libby Prison and there is a resemblance," Duff said.

"I'm sure General Caine would be pleased at your approval," said Jack grinning. He seemed happier than he had been for weeks.

The house had been painted recently and the slate roof was in good repair too. Grudgingly I admitted that the building wasn't all that ugly. It could be taken for a large school or a meeting hall of some kind.

The front door was of heavy planks bound with iron—I suppose like a prison door. Jack opened it with the large key and we entered a dark hallway and an even gloomier parlor. It was like something out of a turn-of-the-century Sears Roebuck catalogue.

There was a horsehair sofa, a smaller settee with leather cushions, a couple of rocking chairs with cane seats and, in the center of the room, a pot-bellied stove. The two small, high windows were covered with heavy double curtains.

"What do you think?" Jack asked. He spread the curtains on one window and coughed as the dust flew.

"Charming," I said. "For a museum."

"Come on. Aunt Hannah lived to be ninety-two here. That says something for a place, doesn't it, if a person can live to be that old in it. And, heck, if you wanted to change anything, it would be no problem. We could put in central heating—"

"There's no central heating?" I hadn't considered that the stove might be necessary.

"Not now, but it would be easy to install it. Also, we could put a big picture window in the front here, throw out all of this old furniture—"

"Some of it might be worth a lot of money to collectors," Duff said.

"That's right," said Jack. "We could probably make enough on it to pay for the renovation. Anyway, let's take a look at the rest of the house before we turn around and go home."

He didn't want to go, I knew that. He wanted to live here, maybe because he felt that in this place he could put aside all the defeats he had suffered and make a fresh start. Also, maybe he thought that if he stayed on the farm, some of his aunt's longevity would pass on to him. On the other hand, maybe he sensed that his end was approaching and he had some primeval urge to be near the place of his ancestors when it came.

Chapter Two

Franny was examining a framed photograph on a table. It was a tintype of a little girl in ruffles standing beside a seated woman who was holding a baby.

"That's Aunt Hannah," said Jack, "and that's her mother, my great-grandmother. The baby is my granddad, John Caine."

"And those kids were the son and daughter of the General?" Franny asked.

"That's right."

"Do you have a picture of the General?" asked Duff.

"I don't think I've ever seen a picture of General Caine, but there must be one around here somewhere," Jack said. "By the way, there are electric lights." He flipped the wall switch and grinned.

"Thanks," I said. "I wondered."

We toured the rest of the house and I must admit my antipathy lessened a bit. There was a fairly large dining room, as well as two small bedrooms and a bathroom downstairs, and the kitchen was a complete surprise. It was dominated by a huge wood-burning stove, but near it stood a modern electric range, and next to that a seemingly almost new refrigerator and freezer.

Upstairs were two more bedrooms and another bathroom. The rest of the second floor area was an enormous storeroom. It would have been an antique dealer's heaven. Piled on top of one another were pieces of eighteenth and nineteenth century American furniture, as well as a number of items that must have been imported. There were certainly some Louis XV chairs and a Queen Anne chest and a long oak table that looked positively Elizabethan. Taking up a lot of space between the articles of furniture were a great many old trunks, as well as piles of newspapers and books, including scrapbooks.

Duff opened one of these and started to read some yellowed clippings.

"What's all that stuff?" Franny asked him.

"Newspaper stories about the Civil War mostly. May I take some of these books downstairs and read them, Dad?"

"Later," Jack said. "There will be plenty of time later."

I didn't agree with that, but I held my peace. Then we went out to the back yard, where we found a sizeable barn with cow and horse stalls and lots of rusted farm equipment. From the appearance of the overgrown fields, no farming had been attempted here in many years.

Next to the barn was a wagon shed, containing a collapsed wagon and an even more decrepit two-seater buggy. Beyond, a weed-grown path led toward a woods maybe three hundred yards away. Halfway to the woods was the family burial plot. It was perhaps fifty feet square and surrounded by a rusted iron fence.

"I wonder if Aunt Hannah is buried here," Jack said. "You remember there was a dispute about where she was going to be buried?"

"Something about a local priest."

"Right. He'd been visiting Aunt Hannah occasionally and he evidently thought she wanted to become a Catholic. I think he wanted to bury her in the Catholic cemetery near Cainesville. Mrs. Reddy insisted that Aunt Hannah had told her that she wanted to be be buried here with the family. Anyway, I left it for Aunt Hannah's lawyer to decide. When I flew home, the body was still at the funeral home."

Franny opened the gate and went into the graveyard. "Aunt Hannah's here now," she reported, "or somebody new is." There was an apparently new grave near the fence on the far side.

"I suppose I should arrange for a stone to be put up," Jack said. "I probably should've done it before this."

The engravings on some of the stones had worn away, but most were still legible. The oldest stone was on the grave of Thankful Caine, who had been born in 1775 and died in 1825. Near Thankful were the graves of her husband, Hosiah, and her infant children, Charity and Bountiful.

"They must have come here from the East," I said. "Those are New England given names."

"They did," Jack said. "The Caines along with some other families moved west from Cape Cod around the turn of the nineteenth century."

"There must have been Indians here then, Dad," said Franny.

"There were. In fact, I remember a stone here for one of Hosiah's sons who was killed by Indians."

We looked for it among the graves of Thomas, William, Patience and Rebecca. There were many graves of children, pitiful evidence that only the most hardy could survive the diseases and perils of early America.

In a corner was the stone of Brigadier General Duffin Hadley Caine who had been born in 1825 and died in 1890. The inscription also revealed that he had been commander of the Second Ohio Cavalry Brigade from June 5, 1863 to October 26, 1863.

"That date in 1863 must have been when he was captured," Jack observed. "It's strange, but I don't remember the placement of some of these stones. That's Ada, the General's wife, next to Aunt Hannah. Now where's my grandfather's grave?"

We finally found it, almost hidden by weeds, beside the grave of his wife, Martha. They had both died in the 1930s and theirs were the most recent stones in the plot.

"My father never lived here and my mother didn't want him buried here," Jack said. "My grandfather left here as a boy and didn't return until he was shipped back in a coffin."

"Why did Aunt Hannah live here then, if nobody else wanted to?" Franny asked.

"Maybe she didn't have anywhere else to go. Or maybe she found a secret charm in the place, as we will too."

"I doubt that I'll ever find it," I said. I was ready to head for the nearest telephone to make reservations on the next flight back to New York.

"Let's stay here tonight anyway," Jack said.

"Here?"

"Sure. Where else?"

"If anywhere, I suppose a motel. There must be something around Cainesville or Ashland."

"But why? We have a perfectly good place here with plenty of room."

"What about food?"

"We can go to a restaurant—or, better yet, get some steaks in Cainesville and bring them back here."

"What about towels, soap, bed linen?"

"The beds are all made—you saw them—and there must be towels in the cupboards. Soap we can buy, if we have to. Let's go see Mrs. Reddy."

We found the Emil Weber place without difficulty. The house and small barn were newly painted and the fields were freshly mowed. In the drive was a station wagon with tools and ladders in it, seemingly indicating that Emil Weber was some sort of handyman rather than a farmer. A small boy on a dappled pony came up to greet us, then dismounted and ran to tell of our arrival.

Mrs. Reddy and her daughter came out and invited us into the house. We sat in a pleasant, sunny living room, furnished in Early American style, and Mrs. Weber served lemonade and cookies.

Mrs. Reddy was plump and jolly, like a little old Mrs. Santa Claus in a starched housedress. I took her to be in her mid seventies, while Rose Weber, blonde and equally plump, was perhaps a little more than half that age.

"So you've come to live in the family home," said Mrs. Reddy.

"To visit it," I said.

"That house needs to be lived in. It needs children in it. It was an old folks' home too long."

"That's right," Mrs. Weber agreed. "It's a good farm and it's a shame to see it deserted."

"We're not farmers," I said.

"You could get help to work it. There's plenty of young fellows looking for work around here." Mrs. Reddy poured more lemonade and passed the cookies again.

"But no one willing to rent the place?" Jack said.

"That's something different. That takes cash and there's a shortage of that nowadays."

"The kitchen seems to have been modernized," Jack said—to change the subject, I hoped.

"Your aunt spent a packet of money on that. And my son-in-law, Emil, installed the dishwasher and the rest of it. He put in that new shower upstairs too. If you need any other work done, just let us know. Emil is very familiar with that house."

"We're planning on going back to New York tomorrow," I said.

"Oh, that's not fair—not to the house or your aunt," Mrs. Reddy protested. "I don't mean to interfere in your affairs, but your aunt always hoped you folks would come and stay in the house after she was gone. Of course, if you've got pressing business elsewhere . . ."

"It's not that," I said. "It's just that our home is in the East."

"On the other hand we've been considering selling that," Duff said. While eating cookies he had been staring as though fascinated by Mrs. Reddy. She in turn was watching him and smiling and nodding in grandmotherly fashion.

"Please, Duff," I said sharply, irritated as much by his manner as his words. Then to Mrs. Reddy: "Aunt Hannah must have realized it would be impossible for us to stay here, considering my husband's work."

"Oh, yes, but she thought Mr. Caine would be retiring from that one day. He has retired now, hasn't he?" The old lady paused after what seemed to be a warning glance from her daughter. "Though I suppose it's hard to cut ties you've had a long time. Maybe you could do it gradually. Just stay a month or so this time and get used to the place."

"We can't stay a month," I said flatly.

"Well maybe a couple of weeks then to start."

She was beginning to irritate me, although I felt that she meant well. I managed to turn her to the subject of towels and linen and the location of the best supermarket in Cainesville (tell the butcher you're a friend of Mrs. Reddy's) and we got up to leave.

While we were standing at the door, Mrs. Weber's daughter, Stephanie, came into the room. She seemed to be in her early twenties, tall and rather sleepy looking. She could have been rather attractive, I thought, but like her mother and grandmother she was overweight. It seemed that she had completed two years of nursing training at Ashland Hospital, but had to drop out of the program because of an allergic condition. After greeting us without really looking at us, Stephanie began nibbling cookies.

Mrs. Reddy's last words to us were a reminder that her son-in-law could do any sort of work that needed to be done at the Caine place. As we drove away, I wondered aloud if that was why she wanted us to stay so badly—to provide work for Emil.

Jack pooh-poohed it. He thought maybe Mrs. Reddy just missed Aunt Hannah and hoped to be consoled by having some of Aunt Hannah's relatives near her. Also, he thought it only natural for any property owner to want responsible people as neighbors.

It was a ten-minute drive to Cainesville, a one-commercial-street town. The recommended supermarket turned out to be the only supermarket. It was well stocked, however, and the prices seemed lower than those we had been used to paying in Scarsdale.

I had intended to buy only enough food for dinner and perhaps breakfast, but Jack and Franny loaded up the cart, and Duff got into the spirit of the thing too, contributing crackers and other snacks that, he explained, we could take back with us if we didn't use them at the farm.

Instead of four steaks Jack bought a dozen and three pounds of ground sirloin as well. I didn't try to stop him. If he wants to stay three or four days, just keep your mouth shut and put up with it, I thought. It's not going to kill you. Of course, it never occurred to me that it might eventually kill him.

"Everything looked so good," he said lamely as we put the bags in the car trunk.

I kissed him lightly on the cheek. "You've been mesmerized by Mrs. Reddy."

Duff had wandered off as we were loading the car. Franny and I went looking for him and found him on the other side of the parking lot talking to three burly motorcyclists.

It was impossible to tell whether they were much older than Duff or not, considering their sunglasses and beards. They were wearing the customary sleeveless denim jackets and no shirts and their arms were tattooed from their wrists to their shoulders.

Duff was conferring earnestly with them. When I called to him, they all turned to stare at me, and then one after another they roared out of the parking lot.

"Who were they?" I asked, trying to keep it casual.

"Some local guys."

"What were you talking about?"

"Oh, I was just checking on the local scene—where the action is around here."

I thought he was kidding, although his expression was serious. I would have been willing to bet plenty that he had never before in his life had words with such people. Not that he would have been afraid of them. He would just have considered them to be of subhuman intelligence and wouldn't have wasted his time.

But then I thought, maybe the boy is just making an effort to come out of his shell, and I said no more about it. I didn't even ask what advice the bikers had given him. I think now he might have told me. He might not have reached the point of lying to us yet. And what the bikers said to him very likely led to much of what happened later.

Anyway we went back to the farm. Jack drove up to the barn and we carried our bags of groceries into the house. While I prepared dinner, the others did some more exploring and chose their bedrooms.

Duff and Franny decided to take the upstairs bedrooms and Jack and I would sleep in the rooms downstairs. Jack and I had been sleeping separately since his last heart attack. Dr. Raphael had suggested that he go easy on the sex for a while—not that he had been much interested in it for the past year or so anyway—and we decided that he could rest better in a room by himself.

We had a very nice dinner of broiled T-bone steaks, fresh peas, and corn on the cob, with ice cream for dessert—even a smidgen of the latter for cholesterol-watching Jack. Then, to fill out the evening, Franny found a pack of playing cards in a cupboard and we played bridge, hearts, poker, using a collection of Aunt Hannah's buttons for chips, and several other games that Franny introduced to us, some of which I think she invented.

Around ten we all went to bed. About two hours later, Duff had a nightmare. His screaming awakened all of us, including Jack, who, after scrambling out of bed and trying to run through a dark and unfamiliar house, fell and broke his hip.

Chapter Three

By the time I found the wall switch at the bottom of the stairs, Duff had stopped yelling. Jack was on the floor, clutching the stair rail and trying to pull himself up.

Franny came down to report that nothing was wrong with Duff except he was feeling rather embarrassed. She and I stupidly tried to help Jack to his feet until I realized how much pain we were causing him. Then Duff came downstairs, putting on his glasses.

"I'm sorry," he said. "Gee, I've never done anything like that before. Is Dad all right?"

"I'm OK," Jack said. "I've sprained something, that's all."

"I'm going to call a doctor," I said.

"We don't know any doctors here. And we don't have a phone."

"We could go to Mrs. Reddy's and phone," Duff suggested. "I'm sure she'd know a doctor."

"At this hour of the night?"

"She'll realize it's an emergency," I said. I ran to my room and put on a sweater and a pair of jeans.

"You're not going out alone at this hour of the night," Jack yelled.

"Franny can go with me. Put a coat on, Frances."

"I'll go too," said Duff.

"No, stay with your father. Don't let him move from that floor."

"You're not blaming me for what happened, are you?" Duff asked plaintively.

"Of course not." I hugged him briefly and Franny and I ran out to the car.

Maybe this is where I should report that I never loved my husband. As a matter of fact, I didn't even like him very much in the early days of our marriage.

He was a copywriter at Marks and Chapman, and I was a secretary to an account executive. I had never paid any particular attention to Jack (I was trying to captivate one of the agency artists at the time) but then we got chummy at an office Christmas party and went off in a taxi to a westside hotel.

A few weeks later, during which Jack asked me to lunch and dinner a number of times and I refused, I found I was pregnant. The next time he invited me to lunch I accepted and told him about my condition. He offered to marry me and after three martinis I accepted.

There just wasn't any other answer, since an abortion was out of the question. I just couldn't forget my Catholic upbringing that much, or my ethical convictions either. And I wasn't about to go home to Hartford to my widowed mother, who was a pillar of her parish church and a great one, besides, for the old "I told you so" about the evils of the big city.

On the positive side, Jack was presentable, if not exactly handsome. He made good money and was on his way to making more, according to restroom gossip. Of course he was as dull as a rusted butter knife, with few interests other than his work. He did have a certain competence as a copywriter, and an even greater one as an administrator, which Marks and Chapman soon recognized.

And so we were married and Duff was born seven months later. I used to wonder if he would someday find out the date of our wedding and compare it with his birth date. On the other hand, I suppose such things don't matter to kids nowadays.

I tried to be a good wife, but I don't think I ever reached the level of Jack's hopes or even his expectations. I never cheated on him (maybe because no one attractive ever asked me) but I ignored him a lot. We never quarreled much, but we were never very friendly either. Then after his first heart attack, I began to feel guilty about it. I suppose that was the main reason I went along with the idea of the trip and then staying at the farm.

I was feeling particularly guilty that night as I drove to Mrs. Reddy's. One additional thing that was nagging me was the fact that I had intended to leave a lamp lit at the bottom of the stairs and was too lazy to get up and attend to it when I remembered it later in bed. I confessed that to Franny.

"If anyone should be blamed it ought to be Duff," she said. "If he hadn't started yelling, the thing would never have happened."

"He was dreaming. He couldn't help it."

"I've never heard of anyone dreaming while walking around."

"Wasn't he in bed?"

"Lord, no. He wasn't even in his bedroom. He was in that big storage room where all the junk is, or at least that's where he was coming from when I saw him."

"He was walking in his sleep then."

"He sure didn't look like he was asleep, although he did seem frightened. Lord Almighty, I was certainly scared enough myself."

"It was probably the result of his being in a strange bed, or maybe it was something he had for dinner."

"We all ate the same things and none of the rest of us had nightmares," said Franny.

We turned into the Weber drive. I was hoping that someone would still be up, but the house was dark. I rang the bell and when that didn't bring an immediate response, pounded on the door. After a minute or two, a light came on and a man opened the door to the length of chain and peered out.

"I'm sorry to bother you at this time of night," I said, "but my husband had an accident. I'm Mrs. Caine."

"Caine?" For some reason that seemed to alarm him.

"We're from New York. We're staying at my husband's family home."

"Oh, yes. I was out in the barn when you came before." He unloosed the chain and opened the door. He was stocky and balding, wearing pajamas.

"My husband fell and injured his leg. I'd like to use your phone to call a doctor."

"Come in, come in." He ushered us into the living room just as his wife came down the stairs, followed by Mrs. Reddy, both in their robes but seemingly wide awake.

"Mrs. Caine's husband got hurt. She wants to call a doctor," Emil Weber said.

"It's his leg," I said. "I think he may have dislocated something or maybe it's broken."

"I'll call Dr. Fowler," Mrs. Weber said. She went to the telephone stand in the corner, dialed and waited.

"That's one thing we have here that I'll bet you don't have in New York," said Mrs. Reddy. "A doctor who's willing to come to your house at any time of the night."

"It's hard to find a doctor like that," I agreed.

Dr. Fowler answered the call, seemingly almost immediately. Mrs. Weber identified me and then put me on the phone to describe Jack's injury. I also mentioned his heart condition.

"Your husband almost certainly needs to be x-rayed, and he may also need to be hospitalized for a while. I'll be there in half an hour," the doctor told me.

"Your man will get the best of care from Dr. Fowler," said Mrs. Weber after I hung up. It seems to me now that she and her mother exchanged brief glances when I mentioned Duff's nightmare, but I thought nothing of it at the time.

"And if your husband needs nursing, we've got a first-class nurse right here in Stephanie," said Mrs. Reddy.

Stephanie hadn't impressed me very much, but at that time I didn't think we'd have need of her services. I drove back to the Caine farm at a reckless speed, the more so since I wasn't familiar with the curving, uneven road. Then Franny and I rushed into the house and found Jack, sitting on the floor now with his back against the wall, playing gin with Duff.

"You'd better start looking sicker before the doctor comes," I said.

"The leg honestly doesn't hurt as much as before," Jack said. "It's kind of numb now, although it hurts if I try to put any weight on it."

Dr. Fowler arrived within ten minutes. He was a small, spry seventy or so, wearing an old-fashioned white linen suit and glasses with a ribbon. He knelt and examined Jack's leg quickly.

"Fractured coxa—broken hip," he said laconically, then took a stethoscope from his bag and checked Jack's heart. "Ticker's OK, near as I can tell, but he'll have to go to the hospital to have that hip repaired. Ashland is the nearest and it's where I'm affiliated, not that that matters."

"Couldn't we take him back to a New York hospital?"

"You could, I suppose, but I wouldn't—not if it was my hip."

"How long will I need to be hospitalized?" Jack asked. He had turned paler, but he was trying to smile.

"Not too long, I should think, once the hip is reduced. We can get you into surgery and do that early on the schedule today." He took a vial out of his bag and shook a few capsules into my hand. "Give him two of these with a glass of water. Now we need an ambulance and a stretcher."

He said he would telephone for the ambulance from the Weber house. I went out to his car with him, wondering if he had any more alarming information to give me out of Jack's hearing.

He didn't. He assured me that he saw no reason for Jack's not making a complete recovery from the accident.

"How soon *can* he go back to New York then?"

"I suppose he *could* go as soon as the bone is repaired and immobilized, if there's a real necessity for his going."

"I guess there's no immediate necessity."

"Maybe you think he can get better care in New York. I can guarantee you we have the most modern facilities here and, although I won't know until I see the X rays, I think your husband's fracture is a relatively uncomplicated one."

"Well, whatever is best for him."

"That's the way to look at it. And I'll be glad to consult by telephone with any New York medical man you like."

He gave me a courtly bow and got in his car. Then he lowered the window and said, "If your son has any more trouble sleeping, give him a couple of those capsules."

"He won't have any more trouble," I said. "Duff has always slept like a log."

Dr. Fowler nodded and drove off. When I went back into the house, Jack had taken the medicine and within minutes he was feeling better. We all sat on the floor and played four-handed rummy until the ambulance came forty-five minutes or so later.

The two attendants put Jack on the stretcher and carried him out, while I packed his toothbrush and shaving equipment. Then Franny got in the ambulance with her father and Duff and I followed in the Chevy to Ashland Hospital.

There Jack was whisked into a gown and onto a table and rolled down to the X-ray room, where he spent about half an hour. Then he was brought back to a cheerful looking room and given some more medicine that put him to sleep almost immediately.

He was scheduled for surgery at eight o'clock and, at Dr. Fowler's suggestion, the staff orthopedic surgeon was going to put a pin in his hip. The X rays had shown the fracture to be of such a nature that the cast could be a simple one, allowing him some degree of mobility on crutches. Also, a cardiologist would be checking Jack before the operation and would stand by during it. If he deemed it advisable, the cardiologist would get in touch with our Dr. Raphael in New York before anything was done to Jack.

So all seemed well, or as well as could be expected. I intended to stay at the hospital until after the surgery, but I saw no reason for Duff and Franny to lose a whole night's sleep, even though they both pleaded to stay. I can still swear that I saw tears in Duff's eyes then.

Even though he didn't have a license, I felt that this was an emergency that justified his driving the car home. As I have indicated, I wasn't concerned at all about his ability to handle the Chevy or even about his driving judgment. He had shown himself to be skillful as well as cautious behind the wheel.

As he and Franny got in the car I asked him, "What were you dreaming about anyway a while ago?"

He looked at me very seriously, his blue eyes, as always, seeming oversized behind his fairly thick glasses. "I thought I saw a crazy-looking man on a horse," he said. "He tried to ride over me."

Franny laughed and I laughed and Duff drove away. On the way home—I learned much later—he tried to sexually molest his ten-year-old sister.

Chapter Four

Shortly after seven, Jack was trundled off to the operating room, and I went to the coffee shop and brooded over why, even now, I hadn't been able to show him more affection. I had squeezed his hand a couple of times and told him not to worry, but I could've done as much for a comparative stranger.

He was brought back from the recovery room around eleven, and Duff and Franny returned shortly after that. I noticed no change in their relationship toward each other then, but later I remembered how unusually quiet Franny had been.

Dr. Fowler and the surgeon, a Dr. Vincent, came to see us and reported that the operation had been a complete success and Jack was doing splendidly. They also said they'd like to keep him in the hospital for about ten days.

"He'll need nursing care when he goes home then, won't he?" Duff asked.

"It probably would be good to have professional help for a short while, until he can shift for himself," Dr. Vincent said.

"We can get someone in Scarsdale," I said.

"We could get someone to take care of Dad here too, couldn't we?" said Duff. "Mrs. Weber's daughter is a nurse, isn't she?"

"Stephanie Weber had two years of training at this hospital,"

Dr. Fowler said. "I would say she could serve as a good practical nurse, which is all you need in this case."

"We won't discuss it now," I said.

Jack was coming around, although he was still pretty groggy. We talked with him for a few minutes, and then, on the advice of Dr. Fowler, let him go back to sleep while we returned to the farm.

There I cooked bacon and eggs—I was starved by then, with the worry over Jack abated—and we all ate heartily and went to bed, or at least I know that Franny and I did. I'm not sure what Duff was doing then. Anyway, I was just dozing off when the front doorbell rang. I put on my robe and went to the door, fearful that it might be someone with bad news about Jack.

It was a telephone serviceman. "I came to install the phone," he said. "John W. Caine?"

"Yes, but we didn't order—"

"Somebody ordered it." He showed me a piece of paper. "And the order was confirmed by your neighbor down the road. Let's see . . . Emil R. Weber. We generally try to get a confirmation before we drive any great distance—just to avoid the practical jokers."

Duff came downstairs and to the door. "I ordered the phone, Mom," he said. "I thought we'd probably need it because of Dad."

"But we're not going to stay here!"

He was very patient. "But while we are here, we'll want to phone the hospital, won't we? And Dad may want to phone us."

I was still angry, mainly because he hadn't asked my permission. "Go ahead," I told the man, "since you're here."

"It'll be a twenty-five dollar deposit."

"All right."

"It will take a while. I'll have to run a line in here from the road."

"We're in no hurry." I closed the door and turned to Duff. "Where did you make the call to the telephone company?"

"From Mrs. Reddy's. I went down there this morning before Franny and I went to the hospital."

"Very convenient. Mrs. Reddy and the Webers were right

there to confirm the order when the telephone company called back. And did you discuss our hiring Stephanie as a nurse too?"

"Mrs. Reddy mentioned it. She says that Stephanie knows all about taking care of patients with broken hips. She had a case just like Dad's last spring."

"Shut up."

"Yes ma'am."

"Go to your room. You're supposed to be sleeping."

"Yes ma'am." He started up the stairs, then paused. His eyes really were tearful now. "If Dad should get worse, Mom, and the hospital wanted to reach us quickly . . ."

My eyes were filling too. "You might at least have told me about it," I said.

"I forgot."

Duff forget? I had never known him to forget anything, but I didn't doubt his word then.

"All right, we have a telephone and let's be grateful for it. Even if it's only for a few days, it's worth whatever it costs."

"That's the way I felt." He sniffled a little, took off his glasses and wiped them with his shirttail and went up the stairs.

The telephone was installed by mid-afternoon. Our first caller was Mrs. Reddy, who wanted to express her joy at our being able to communicate with the outside world. The next caller was Jack, sounding a bit weak but definitely in good spirits. It seemed that Mrs. Reddy had taken the liberty of telling him the good news about the telephone. We also learned that we should be grateful to Emil Weber who had a friend at the telephone company. Otherwise several months might have elapsed between the request and the installation.

We had a late lunch and then went back to the hospital and spent the rest of the afternoon with Jack. Franny had come out of her shell somewhat (although I remembered later that she never engaged in any direct conversation with Duff) and Duff was positively gabby. I think he must have talked more to us on that afternoon than he had for the entire previous month.

He told us about books he had read, music he had heard, movies he had seen. He gave us an elaborate rundown on his past-year school experiences, going over all his classes and rating his teachers. He was getting on to Ohio history and Indian activities in the Ashland area when I realized he was wearing Jack out. Later I also realized that while Duff was talking, Franny by necessity was silent.

On the way back to the farm I asked Duff where he had learned so much about the area.

"Reading," he answered vaguely.

"In school?"

"School and other places."

"Also in that rubbish room at the farm," Franny said viciously.

I was surprised at her anger. She and Duff almost never quarreled.

"He surely hasn't had much time yet to spend with those old books," I said.

"He didn't go to bed when we got back from the hospital this morning," Franny said.

"I did so," Duff insisted. "I looked at some books for a few minutes, but then I went to bed. You were supposed to be asleep, Franny, so how would you know what I did?"

Franny didn't pursue the matter. She lowered her gaze and sulked for the rest of the ride home. I told myself that both she and Duff were suffering from the strain of the past day and thought no more about it.

We had dinner—steak and packaged french fries again—and Franny and Duff helped with the dishes, although Franny still wasn't talking to her brother. Then Duff announced that he was going alone to the hospital to see his father and that Franny and I were going to stay home and get a good night's rest.

I suppose I shouldn't have allowed it, especially since he was breaking the law in driving without a license, but I was too tired to argue. I hadn't slept since being awakened by the telephone installer and I assumed that Duff had had at least some sleep in the morning, despite what Franny had said.

While I was hesitating, he picked up the car keys. He gave me a kiss—and tried to kiss Franny, but she backed away—and went out the back door. I telephoned Jack and told him Duff was on his way and shortly afterward Franny and I went to bed.

I slept soundly for several hours and then awakened suddenly in a state of unexplainable dread. It was two by my travel clock. I got out of bed and went to the window to see if the car was in the yard. It was parked near the house, and, feeling relieved, I was about to go back to bed when the full moon came out from behind a cloud and I could see clearly all the way to the barn. There were two people standing near the barn door.

I put on my robe, went to the kitchen and opened the back door. "Duff?" I called.

One of the two seemed to be Duff, the other could have been a woman. They were standing close together facing each other. The one I took to be Duff was taller and leaning toward the other as though listening. The second person was stockier, heavier. Could it be Mrs. Reddy?

Now the moon was clouded again and I could barely see the barn. I was frightened, but I told myself that this was the country. Nothing bad could happen in the country. I walked toward the barn, continuing to call Duff, but when I reached it the people were gone. I couldn't make myself open the door and look inside. Instead I ran back to the kitchen, slammed and bolted the door and stood there trembling for several minutes.

When I could manage to move again I went upstairs, thankful for the light in the upstairs hallway. We had been leaving it on at night since Jack's accident. Franny's door was closed, but Duff's was open. He was in bed.

"What's wrong, Mom?" he asked drowsily when I entered the room.

"When did you come in?" I demanded.

"Hours ago. I didn't want to wake you."

I pulled back his blanket. He was wearing pajamas.

"All right, go back to sleep," I said.

"You didn't ask me about Dad," he said in a whining tone.

"How was Dad?"

"Fine. Eager to get out of the hospital naturally. He also said he'd like us to get Stephanie Weber to nurse him here."

"We won't talk about that now."

He grinned. "Why did you look to see if I was wearing pajamas. You know I don't go to bed with my day clothes on."

"You used to sometimes when you were a little boy," I said. "Good night, Duff."

I went back downstairs. Could I have been wrong about his being in the yard? Of course he could have come in the front door while I was in the kitchen. (I checked and the front door wasn't locked.) But then who were the people? And if one was Mrs. Reddy, what was she doing in our yard at two in the morning?

At breakfast, Duff was chipper and much more talkative than he had ever been at similar times at home. I was waiting for him to mention Stephanie Weber again, but he didn't. Instead Jack brought up her name when he telephoned us. He said that Dr. Fowler had told him he could leave the hospital at the end of the week.

"Couldn't we possibly go home, Jack?"

"When I get the cast off. That's supposed to be in four or five weeks."

"Any good orthopedic man in New York can take off a cast."

"I'd rather have Dr. Vincent do it, since he put it on."

I gave in. It seemed selfish to do otherwise. If a month on the farm was what he wanted, surely the rest of us could put up with it. Duff seemed quite willing, even eager to go along with his father's wishes, but Franny made no comment on the decision.

I phoned Mrs. Reddy, who was overjoyed. No, Stephanie wasn't busy and, yes, she'd be glad to take care of Mr. Caine. There was no suggestion of consulting Stephanie, although I assumed the matter had been discussed with her earlier. I didn't have the courage to ask if Mrs. Reddy had been in our yard before dawn that morning.

At the end of the week Jack came back as he had left, by ambulance, and there was quite a welcoming party to greet him. In addition to the three of us and Stephanie, looking very professional in her starched uniform, Mrs. Reddy and her daughter and son-in-law were also in attendance. Jack was carried to his bedroom by the ambulance men and escorted by the rest of us, Franny bringing his crutches and Duff pushing the wheelchair.

I thought we might have Mrs. Reddy, Rose and Emil with us

for the rest of the day, encouraging Stephanie in her work, but after a short interval of congratulating us on securing Stephanie's services and assuring us that Jack was going to receive care such as he could get nowhere else in the county, they left us.

And I must admit that Stephanie did take good care of Jack. I gave her the room adjoining his, while I moved in with Franny upstairs, and from then on she seemed to spend all her days and half her nights attending him. When she wasn't bathing or massaging him or pushing him around in the wheelchair, she was reading to him from a pile of Perry Mason paperbacks she had brought with her.

Jack loved it. He never had as much attention from me, more's the pity, I suppose. And Duff and Franny seemed to like Stephanie too, not that she ever had much free time to spend with them. In fact, I was rather surprised at Duff's interest in her, not only because of her lumpish appearance, but because she didn't offer him any intellectual challenge. Her mealtime conversations were limited to monosyllabic answers to questions and occasional pointless stories of other nursing experiences she had had.

Then after two weeks or so of Stephanie, we received a phone call from the Scarsdale real estate agent. Jack had written him about prolonging our stay in Ohio, and now the agent wanted to make another offer. He had a client, an oil company executive, who was willing to pay a thousand dollars a month rent for our furnished home on a six-month lease with an option to buy for ninety-five thousand if we decided then to sell.

"No," I said.

"What do we have to lose?" Jack said. "We can sell or not, as we choose, in six months, and meanwhile we're getting a thousand a month for staying here."

"I still don't like it. The school year is coming on."

"Stephanie says there are good schools in Cainesville."

"Stephanie!"

Jack laughed. "See, I knew you were jealous. Cheer up, Maggie. I'll have the cast off and Stephanie will be gone in a couple more weeks. And do you realize how little we're paying that girl and what the same kind of nursing care would cost us at home?"

It was true, I had to admit. And I also knew that, in our present situation, it would have been foolish to pass up what seemed to be found money, considering that it also seemed Jack was never going to earn any money again.

Duff was all for calling the agent back immediately and accepting the offer. Franny still didn't seem to care one way or another.

"This place is fascinating," Duff said. "I'm learning a lot about the family and the area, but I'll need at least six months to read all the material upstairs."

"Why don't you all drive over to Cainesville and look at the schools," Jack said. "That won't cost anything."

So Duff, Franny and I went to Cainesville and visited the elementary school and the high school, summer classes being in session at both places. The elementary school seemed adequate, but I was less impressed by the high school. For one thing, the science facilities were minimal. However Duff reminded me that he had completed all his obligatory lab work anyway and the chemistry and physics textbooks used at Cainesville High were very similar to those used at Scarsdale. He also made the point that six months would include only one semester and that at the end of that time he and Franny could go back to their old schools if we so decided.

Back at the farm, I phoned Dr. Raphael in New York and asked what he thought of Jack's staying for six months in this out-of-the-way place. He said that off the top of his head he thought it would be great for Jack to be anywhere away from stress and pollution. Then he agreed to check on the cardiology situation at Ashland Hospital and call me back, which he did within half an hour. It turned out that the man in charge at Ashland had excellent credentials and was a friend of a friend of Dr. Raphael's.

Therefore it was decided. Jack called the real estate man and accepted the offer; Duff drove to the post office and mailed the keys; and I went to bed with a headache.

The next day I didn't feel as bad about it. For one thing, it was going to be necessary for someone to go home and pick up our car and the additional clothes we'd need. That someone logically was I, which meant a few days' respite from the rural life. That it also meant being away from my injured husband, I remembered guiltily a moment later.

Franny decided she wanted to come with me. I didn't like taking her away from Jack, and, in fact, I was a bit surprised she was so willing to leave him, since she was so fond of him. Duff, on the other hand, declared that he would rather stay and help Stephanie look after his father.

So Franny and I went in the rented car to Cleveland Airport, flew back to New York and completed a good bit of our packing that same night. The next day we visited the real estate office, where I signed the lease with our tenant, a Mr. Harold Shaffer, who was fiftyish, well dressed and had no small children to scratch our furniture or write on our walls.

Then we went to the two schools and made arrangements for the transfer of credits. An assistant principal at Franny's school said that she thought temporary new surroundings would be good for Franny, whom she described as an imaginative child who could become quickly bored with routine.

And of course the people at Duff's school only confirmed what I already knew. "There's very little more he can be taught in a high school classroom, either here or in Cainesville," said his former physics teacher. "If he has access to good books, Duff will do well no matter where he is."

He had access to plenty of books without doubt and some of them may have been good in the sense of being factual and informative, but they didn't serve Duff very well. On the other hand, I suppose it wasn't the books that caused what happened. They may have explained certain things to Duff, but the impetus to search for knowledge came from somewhere else.

Anyway the next day we loaded the Oldsmobile, took a farewell tour through the house and started back for the farm. Somewhere around Harrisburg on the Pennsylvania Turnpike, Franny told me what happened the night she and Duff drove home from the hospital.

Chapter Five

For the past two days Franny had been perky enough, having shed her gloom as soon as we left the farm. However, she didn't say at any time that she didn't want to go back there. I'm sure it would have influenced me if she had mentioned anything like that before I signed the rental papers, but she didn't suggest it even now. She only became more pensive and morose as the miles passed. Finally I asked her what was wrong.

She didn't answer that, but instead asked if she had to continue sleeping upstairs at the farm. I replied that it might be difficult to make other arrangements right now, since her father was crippled and Stephanie was with us, but that I would see what could be done.

"Why don't you want to sleep upstairs anymore? Is it because it's a strange house?"

"No."

"Maybe you've been having bad dreams like Duff had the other night."

"No, I haven't had any dreams."

"What is it then?"

She paused and sighed. "I don't like Duff anymore."

"You don't like your own brother?"

"No. Also sometimes I'm afraid of him."

"But why?"

She paused again for a long while as I tried to watch her and the road at the same time. Then she said, "He's mean."

"Mean?" I suppose I smiled. I assumed they'd had a disagreement over some trivial matter and Duff had put her down. "What did he say to you?"

"It wasn't what he said. He doesn't say much at all to me lately. It was what he did."

"Well?"

"He hit me."

"Oh, Franny." I couldn't believe a blow from Duff would ever be anything more than playful.

"Also, he tried to take my clothes off."

I almost went onto the shoulder of the road, but then I recovered control quickly. A sign said a service area was a mile away.

"Don't say any more," I told her. "We'll stop and have something to eat."

I pulled into the service area and we went into the Howard Johnson's. Franny had her usual away-from-home lunch—hamburger, french fries and ice cream. Then she ate my hamburger and fries and, on the way out, selected a candy bar.

Back in the car again, I said, "Okay, tell me."

She unwrapped her candy bar. "Well maybe he *was* only joking. That's what he told me afterwards anyway."

"What did he do exactly?" I was trying, not too successfully, to keep my voice down.

"Well it was that night after we all went to the hospital with Dad. On the way home Duff stopped the car suddenly, which scared me right off because the road was so dark and deserted looking. Then he put his arm around me and kissed me—which was all right, I suppose, but it did seem sort of ridiculous for my own brother to be doing it. After that he pulled my sweater off and pulled down my underwear. Then I cried, mainly because I was cold, I think. Then he slapped me."

"Then what?"

"Don't scream, Mama."

"What!"

"Well, I suppose I ought to include the fact that I bit him. I grabbed his finger and bit it and that's when he slapped me. Then I put my sweater back on and we drove home. You may have noticed that Duff had a Band-Aid on his finger the next couple of days."

"No, I didn't notice."

"Maybe he took it off when you were around. Anyway, I was going to tell you before, but he kept insisting he'd only been joking."

"Well, I'm sure he was joking."

She shook her head doubtfully. "It sure didn't seem that way at the time. People don't usually hit you that hard when they're joking, at least that's been my experience."

"It wasn't a very nice joke, that's certain. I'll speak to Duff about it as soon as we get back."

"Oh, Mama, don't make me a squealer." She finished the candy bar and licked her fingers. "I'm sure he won't try the same joke again, now that I'd be expecting it."

"Do two things for me," I said. "Don't say anything to your father about this. We don't want to worry him with the problems of you kids. And don't go anywhere alone with Duff for a while—just in case he might try the joke again."

"Okay," she said. She seemed more cheerful now that she had unburdened herself. "Actually Duff has gotten so weird lately that I don't even like to be near him. Sometimes he acts as though he doesn't know where he is—the way he goes around mumbling to himself. Have you noticed?"

I hadn't. I was heartsick as I drove back on to the turnpike. I just didn't know what to do, what to say to Duff, or even Jack. It was obvious that I had to get Duff to a psychiatrist as quickly as possible. But was there a psychiatrist in Cainesville or Ashland? There were certainly competent men around Scarsdale, but our house was gone, signed away for six months. Would Mr. Shaffer reconsider? Should we tell him that he had to reconsider because our son had molested his sister—

"Mama, watch that truck!"

We got back to the farm somehow. It was shortly after eight in the evening when I pulled in the drive. Duff came rushing out to greet us and began asking rapid and half incoherent questions about the trip and our states of health. Did we have a good time? Were we tired? Was the weather good? Then he looked directly at me and he knew that I knew.

"How's Dad?" Franny asked him. She seemed willing to be his friend again.

"Okay." He looked away and began unloading the luggage.

I went into the house and found Jack sitting in the wheelchair in his bedroom. There was a paperback book on his lap and he picked it up and opened it as I entered.

"Hi," he said, not very enthusiastically.

"Hi," I said. "Reading your own thrillers now? Where's Stephanie?"

"Taking a walk, I guess."

"How can you manage to get along without her?" No reaction. "Well, we did what we set out to do. We are now homeless for six months, except for this place. That's what you wanted, isn't it?"

"I guess so."

"You guess so!"

"Well, maybe this isn't the best place for us . . ."

"What's wrong? Is it Duff? Something Duff did?"

He stared at me. "Why do you ask that?"

"No reason. Tell me what happened."

He closed the book, which was upside down anyway. "There was some trouble with Stephanie."

"And Duff?"

He nodded. "Don't get excited, Maggie. Stephanie's not going to say anything."

"He attacked her!"

"Not so loud—Franny might hear. What I'm trying to tell you is Stephanie may have invited it. Anyway, it's all over now and Duff has promised it won't happen again."

"Tell me what happened!"

Jack paused and took a deep breath. "I don't see why you need the details. He was trying to—or possibly did—make love to her, that's all. It's really not surprising in a boy his age. He's almost seventeen and they say that's the time of peak sexual power. I remember when I was his age—"

"Where did it happen?"

"In the front room, yesterday afternoon. After lunch Stephanie went to the kitchen to do the dishes. Duff was helping her, I thought. I was half asleep here when I heard a noise from the front—moaning and then screaming. I wheeled myself in there. Duff had her on the floor, holding her down . . ."

"My God, she's twice his size!"

"Not quite that, but maybe a few pounds heavier. Anyway, Duff's a lot stronger than you think."

"He'd have to be. She's an amazon." She must have cooperated, I told myself. "What else?"

"What else could there be?"

"I can tell from looking at you that there's more to it."

"Maggie, I could understand it, if it was just a case of the family heir having a sly one with the hired help. No harm done and everybody happy. But Duff . . . well I think he was trying to hurt her. It seemed that way, anyway. And he *was* holding her down. She was trying hard to get loose and sobbing and yelling." Jack paused and shook his head. "The worst thing was when he saw me, Maggie . . . and he didn't stop. He turned his head and grinned at me . . . and kept right on with it . . ."

He began to weep.

"Don't say any more," I told him.

"Maggie, he didn't even look like Duff. His face was dark and twisted. I thought for a second it was someone else. I wheeled forward and kicked him with my good leg and he got up and raised his hand to hit me. Then his whole expression changed and he began to cry, the way I haven't heard him cry since he was five or six years old, and he ran out of the room. After a while Stephanie got up and fixed her clothes and she said, 'It's all right, Mr. Caine. It wasn't his fault.'"

"If she said it wasn't, it wasn't."

"Except he really was holding her down and really hurting her. It was really vicious, Maggie."

"I'm surprised she didn't leave immediately. I suppose it was good of her to stay until Franny and I got back."

"I talked to her about that last night. She's willing to stay on here. She doesn't want to go home. And Duff's sorry about the whole thing. He says he doesn't know what made him do it. Apparently it was a spur of the moment thing, an impulse he couldn't control. And, as I said, he's promised it won't happen again."

"If it was an uncontrollable impulse, what good is his promise? As long as Stephanie is around, she'll be a temptation for him."

"All right, you talk to her then. Send her away, if you feel you must, although I'd hate for her parents and her grandmother to know about it."

"They probably should be told anyway. What if he made her

pregnant? And the solution is not just to pack Stephanie off, but to get away from here ourselves. You'll have to get in touch with the people in Scarsdale and arrange to cancel the lease. I wish you had phoned me yesterday when the thing happened. It might have been easier then."

Jack shook his head. "Duff doesn't want to go back to Scarsdale, Maggie. He wants to stay here."

"What do we care what he wants? He's a sixteen-year-old child. He'll do what we think best for him."

"You talk with him then."

"I intend to do just that."

I was angry now, as well as horrified at what had happened. I knew Jack was incapacitated, but I felt he was acting spinelessly. In my opinion, he not only should have given the girl notice, but also ordered Duff to start packing immediately for the return to Scarsdale.

I went back out to the car where Duff was unloading the last of the luggage. Franny had apparently gone up to her room. Duff tried to avoid my gaze.

"Your father told me what happened yesterday," I said without preamble.

"I figured he would."

"Under the circumstances, maybe you'd better put all our belongings back in the car. We're going home."

"Tonight?"

That was ridiculous and we both knew it. It was almost dark.

"The first thing in the morning then."

"Is Dad able to travel in the car?"

He had me again.

"Dad and Franny can fly back and you and I will drive."

"Maybe I could drive back alone and you three could go by plane," he said guilelessly.

"No thanks."

"But who will look after Dad between the airport and home? Franny's a little kid."

"I'm surprised you remembered that."

He blushed then and his lip trembled. He ran to me and clutched me.

"Oh, Mama, I'm so sorry," he sobbed. "It started as a joke both times and that's all it ever was with Franny, but I guess Stephanie thought I was serious . . ."

I hugged him. What else could I do? He was my little boy. It was going to become increasingly hard for me to remember that.

"There's no point in crying over what happened, Duff," I said. "We'll just make sure it doesn't happen again. We'll take you to a doctor."

"You mean a shrink? What for—I'm not crazy." He pulled away from me and gripped my arms. "I don't need a psychiatrist, Mother. All I need is your trust in me. Give me a chance to prove myself."

"Why don't you want to go back to Scarsdale, Duff?"

"I do eventually, of course. But I don't want to go now, having failed you. Also, I'm doing some research here that I'd like to finish."

"What kind of research?"

"On the Caine family. There's a lot of fascinating material here on the family and the region. Lots about the Civil War too. I'm thinking of switching my college major from one of the sciences to history or sociology. What do you think, Mother?"

"I think there's plenty of time to decide that."

"How about it, Mama? Must we go back tomorrow?"

I hesitated. "I'll talk some more with your father. However, you've got to understand that, whatever we decide, it won't be in the nature of punishment, but rather what's best for you. Also, there are others to be considered. Franny apparently wasn't seriously harmed, thankfully, but what about Stephanie?"

"She wasn't a virgin, Mama."

I slapped him—hard. He began to weep again.

"Never mind what she was. You've violated her. You've taken something away from her—her dignity, if nothing else."

"But, Mama, she wanted me to do it."

"That's not what your father says. Also it's a sin."

"I'm not sure I believe in things like that."

I knew he didn't and it was my fault. I hadn't attempted to provide my children with any religious education, and neither had Jack. For a while we saw to it that Duff said the Lord's Prayer before going to bed at night, but by the time he was six we had begun to neglect that and we never started it with Franny. They both had vague notions about the origins of Christmas and Easter, and that, I assumed, was about the extent of their religious knowledge. On the other hand, we thought we had instilled in them the elements of morality. They supposedly knew the difference between right and wrong. Still, I felt guilty about not doing more.

"I know I'm to blame, Duff," I said. "You were never properly guided, I guess. We'll try to do something about it when we get home."

"As a matter of fact, I know about the Ten Commandments and Judeo-Christian ethics and all that. We had History of the Middle East last year in school."

"I'm afraid more than that is needed."

While he carried the remaining bags to the bedrooms, I went to the kitchen and made sandwiches for Franny and me. It seemed that Stephanie had fixed dinner as usual for Jack and Duff.

Later Franny went to Jack's bedroom to sit with him a while, and I did the washing up. It was almost dark and I was turning on the lights when Stephanie rapped at the back door and came in. She seemed agitated, even more so when she saw me. I hadn't liked her much, but I felt sorry for her now.

"Did you have a nice walk, Stephanie?" I said.

"It was all right," she said. Her head was jerking, as though she felt compelled to examine every corner of the room.

"Would you like some coffee? Franny doesn't drink it, and I made too much for myself."

"All right." She was trembling, although it was a warm night and she was wearing a sweater.

I poured her coffee. "Where did you go on your walk?"

"Nowhere in particular. Up the road a bit."

"I've been walking quite a lot myself since we came here. Sometimes I take that path down to the woods."

"At night?"

"At twilight sometimes. It's nice then when the birds are going to sleep."

"You shouldn't walk down there at night."

"I suppose it isn't too safe. It would be easy to trip over something and break a leg. Then you'd have two cripples on your hands." I sat down across from her. "I know what happened yesterday, Stephanie, and I'm sorry."

"You shouldn't blame Duff too much."

"We do blame him, and it seems we must blame you too, if you're implying that you encouraged him."

She sipped her coffee and thought for a while. "You don't understand, Mrs. Caine. It's not a question of what I did or what Duff did. It was out of my hands, and his too."

"You're right, I don't understand."

She spread her hands. "It's this house," she said.

"What's wrong with this house?"

"There are bad things in it."

"Oh come on, Stephanie," I said irritably. "You can't get off that easily, and neither can Duff. This place isn't haunted."

She shook her head hopelessly. "This house can cause people to do strange things."

"Did strange things happen when your grandmother was living here?"

She shook her head again and stared at the table.

"There is one thing I should ask you." I hesitated.

"I take the Pill," she said. "I have a boyfriend, although I don't see him very often. He's married."

"Oh, I'm sorry."

"No need to be. I don't want him as a husband." She paused. "I would like a home of my own though."

"Why don't you rent an apartment in Cainesville or Ashland?"

"My folks wouldn't like it. Gran and Ma like me to be at home in between jobs, not that I get that many patients lately. Mr. Caine is the first one in a long time."

"Why? There seemed to be plenty of people in that hospital who would need home care."

"Some folks don't like my family. They think my grandmother is odd. My mother too, though not as much as Gran."

"Odd in what way?"

"They're sort of ... spiritualists, I guess you could call them."

"And people disapprove of that?"

"Around here, some people. Anyway I don't go in for it—talking to the dead and all that—but I guess Gran and Ma get a kick out of it."

"What about your father?"

"He always goes along with whatever they say."

Suddenly I remembered something. "Has your grandmother been back to this place recently, Stephanie?"

"I don't think so. Why?" It seemed to me she grew paler.

"I saw two people out by the barn one night before you came. I thought one of them was your grandmother and the other one was Duff, but it turned out I was wrong about him."

"How do you know?"

"I checked upstairs and he was in bed."

"That doesn't mean—" She closed her eyes and bit her lower lip. "You'd better go away from here, Mrs. Caine. What happened with me could happen with someone else."

"He's not an animal," I said angrily. "He never did anything like this before we came here."

"That's what I'm telling you. It's this place."

"That's ridiculous."

"All right, Mrs. Caine." She went to the sink and rinsed her cup and saucer. "I'll get Mr. Caine ready for bed."

"Wait, Stephanie. You'll have to tell me more. What's in this house that's affecting Duff?"

She hesitated. "Evil things," she said finally.

"What are they?"

She shook her head. "I don't know."

"Why would they have an effect only on Duff's actions? Why not on Franny's too, or on mine or my husband's?"

"Maybe they will."

"But people have lived in this house for years. Has anything like this ever happened before?"

She hesitated again. "I don't know."

"I'm sure it hasn't. My husband's aunt lived here all her life —a good deal of the time under the care of your grandmother

—and Aunt Hannah was certainly never affected by the house or whatever you say is in it."

"No, I guess she wasn't."

"Why are you so sure that Duff will be affected then?"

"He's already been affected, hasn't he?"

"But that was the result of perfectly natural causes—his age, your presence . . ." I was trying not to think of the episode with Franny. But even that, I told myself, could have happened to a lot of sixteen-year-old boys with younger sisters.

"All right, Mrs. Caine."

"Stephanie, I think you're sincere in what you're saying, but I also think you're wrong. We do intend to leave here very soon, but we won't be driven away by such nonsense."

"I'm glad you're going, whatever your reasons."

"On the other hand, you've stimulated my curiosity. I'd like to find out more about these evil things. Could your grandmother tell me any more about them?"

"No, I'm sure she couldn't." Her voice was shrill now.

"But she lived here for a long time."

"Please don't go to my grandmother, Mrs. Caine. She'll know I told you."

"Why shouldn't she know?"

"Well, she wants you to stay here. She and my mother want this house occupied. They'd be angry if I frightened you away."

"But I told you we're not going to be frightened away. And you're a big girl, Stephanie, why should you be afraid of them? Of course, I can appreciate your not wanting trouble at home."

"That's it. I don't want trouble."

She waited another moment, as though she wanted to say more, then turned and went out. I stayed in the kitchen for a while, wondering if she was slightly unbalanced. Then I heard the sound of Duff's flute. He was playing a Haydn sonata.

I went upstairs. The door to the bedroom I shared with Franny was partly open and she was in bed.

"It's nice, isn't it?" she said smiling. "Duff's playing."

"Yes," I said, "it's very nice."

His door was open too. He was sitting cross-legged on the

bed, with the score propped on a pillow in front of him. He lowered his flute now and looked at me questioningly.

"It's nothing," I said. I put my arm around him and kissed him. He began to play again as I went downstairs. It was the last time I heard him play his flute until the night he died.

Book Two

Chapter Six

The next morning Jack telephoned the Scarsdale real estate agent and we learned that the tenant was already living in our house. He and his wife had moved in the previous afternoon, and the agent thought it was going to be difficult, if not impossible, to dislodge them. What reason could we offer for wanting to cancel the lease? How had our situation changed overnight? He suggested we call the people directly and explain our problem.

I made the call. Mrs. Shaffer answered and began telling me how much she and Harold were enjoying our house. I said we'd been having second thoughts about renting it, and she replied sweetly that it was too bad but she and Harold loved the place too much to give it up now. She did agree to discuss the matter with him when he returned from Dallas in a week or ten days.

"We're stuck," Jack said. "We've signed the lease and accepted their check. Of course, maybe until we cash the check—"

I had deposited it. I had stopped at our bank in Scarsdale on the way out of town in the morning.

"All right, we're stuck, but only until her husband comes back. Then we'll have to persuade them to find another place. We won't charge them for the time they've been in our house. In fact we might pay them something for the inconvenience."

"From what I was told about Shaffer, I don't think a few bucks will sway him."

"Something will—your health or something. We'll think of a good reason."

Duff had come into the room. "Why don't you tell the man

the truth?" he said. "Tell him your son has been caught up in the evils of country life and you have to get him back to innocent suburbia."

"Don't be a wise guy," Jack told him.

"Isn't it the truth? Isn't that why you want to go back?"

"We intend to go back because we'll all be happier at home," I said.

"I'm happy here," Duff said.

"We know what's best for you," I informed him.

"Well I'm not going back."

He stood there grinning defiantly. His face seemed dirty and I noticed that his beard was beginning to grow. Although he had been wearing his hair long for some time, it now seemed lank and greasy. To me his whole appearance was one of deliberate sloppiness, in spite of the fact that his clothes were what he usually wore—jeans, a sweatshirt and sneakers.

"Go to your room, Duff," his father told him quietly.

He stared at Jack for a moment, still grinning, then turned and obeyed. Or at least he went upstairs.

"That's something different," Jack said ruefully. "That's never happened before."

It was almost incredible conduct. Duff had never defied us. "It's this place," I said. I didn't really believe that—intending the remark only as comfort for Jack—but then I remembered what Stephanie had said. Coincidentally, or maybe not, she came in then, bringing him some vitamin tablets, and I wondered if she had heard the conversation with Duff. She had certainly heard my remark to Jack, because she glanced at me briefly, then blushed and looked away.

I wish now I had followed her out of the room and insisted that she tell me more of what she had talked about the night before. At that time, if I had been aware of what I was facing, I think I still might have been able to manage Duff. If I had known then what I know now, I would have cajoled him, bribed him, drugged and bound him, if necessary, in order to get him away from the Caine farm.

For the next couple of weeks however, we were in a period of relative calm. There were no more episodes of defiance from

Duff and indeed his whole manner seemed to change again. He was the mannerly, quiet and neat-appearing boy he had been of old. And his relationship with Franny became what it had always been, not exactly idyllic, but a normal brother-sister thing in which he put her down occasionally, but was still loving and protective toward her.

With Stephanie he was respectful but subdued. They had little to say to each other, but they didn't appear to be trying to avoid each other either. Duff didn't seem to be embarrassed by her presence and she didn't seem to be afraid of him. Dr. Fowler came to see Jack every few days. ("Try to get service like that in Scarsdale," said Jack.) The cast was off now and he was getting around very well on crutches.

I then suggested to Stephanie that we could get along without her help. She reacted by beginning to weep.

"Please don't make me go home," she sobbed.

"No one is making you go anywhere," I said. "As I recall, you wanted us to leave a while ago. What if we had gone back East immediately, as it seems to me you suggested we do?"

"I thought maybe you'd take me along."

"Oh, Stephanie," I said disgustedly, "go get yourself another job."

"I can't. They won't let me."

"Your parents? How can they prevent you? You're not a child."

"That doesn't matter."

"Let me get this straight. Do they want you to stay here, or is it just that you want to stay?"

She hesitated. "They'd like me to stay here with you and keep you living in the house. I'd like to be with you somewhere else."

"Why are you so fond of us?"

"You're different from the people I'm used to. At dinner you talk about things—books and music, things like that. At home we never talk at dinner."

I didn't think our table talk was all that cultivated, but I let it pass. "You can stay for another week or so, Stephanie," I said, "then we'll examine the problem again."

"Oh, thank you, Mrs. Caine." She clutched my hand. "And

will you think about my going back East with you too? Maybe just to travel with you, if nothing else."

I agreed to consider it, but I had no intention of taking her along. She was beginning to seem seriously neurotic to me, and I didn't want to be responsible for her. At that time, my determination to leave hadn't diminished in the least, even though I wasn't making any headway with the Scarsdale tenants. Mr. Shaffer was just as adamant as his wife about giving up the lease.

Compounding the problem was the fact that Jack was settling in on the farm. He had apparently put the Duff-Stephanie episode out of his mind and was writing a book. It was to be a novel, about the advertising business presumably. We never discussed it, and I haven't looked at the four or five filled yellow legal pads he left.

I know now I should have called the real estate man and insisted that he find us another place, no matter what the cost. If nothing was available in Scarsdale, then we should have gone somewhere else, maybe to my sister's in Albany. She has a big house and no children, and while I can't say she would have been eager to take us in—we have never really gotten along—she would have accepted the situation if I had presented it as an emergency.

Then it was mid-August and the school year was almost upon us. Something would have to be done soon. I assumed that Duff's and Franny's records had already been transferred to Cainesville, and reversing the process might take some time.

I decided to have another talk with Duff, hoping to get his cooperation, but at the same time resolved that we were not going to be on the farm when school started, no matter what he wanted. He was, as usual, reading from the books and newspapers in the upstairs storeroom on the afternoon I went up to see him. He hadn't been out of the house for several days, as far as I knew.

"You look ill," I told him when he finally noticed me. He was sitting cross-legged on the floor reading a book. His face was flushed and he was trembling.

"Maybe I have a little cold," he said.

I put my hand on his forehead. As I did so, he closed the book and casually put it on a stack of other books an arm's length away. All the books were old with worn leather bindings.

"You don't seem to have a fever," I said. "You should be outside, though, on this beautiful day, and not cooped up here in this stuffy room. What was that book you were reading?"

"Just an old history book."

"It's in Latin, isn't it? I didn't know you could read Latin." I picked up another book from the floor. "Do you read Greek too? You've never studied it in school, have you?"

"No, but I've picked up a smattering of both languages on my own."

He had never mentioned it, and I didn't remember ever seeing any books in Latin or Greek around the house in Scarsdale.

"I used to be able to read a little Latin," I said. "We all had to study it for a couple of years at Sacré Coeur Academy. That was before the Church became liberated and threw out the Latin rites."

"Do you know the Mass in Latin?" he asked.

"I used to."

"You must say some of the prayers for me sometime. I'm very interested in such things. There's a beautiful Catholic church in Cainesville, Saint Mary's. I've been there several times. The pastor, Father Fogarty, is a very interesting man."

"Duff, school is going to be starting soon."

He took my hand. "Mother," he said earnestly, "I'd like to go to school here for at least one semester. I really would."

"Impossible, Duff."

"Mother, I'd like to write a book about the Caine family. As long as Dad is writing a book, why couldn't I do it too? There's so much fascinating material here. Let me show you." He rummaged in a pile and pulled out a tattered book without a cover. "Here's a history of Ashland County. The county was created in 1846, but the town of Ashland was laid out much earlier—in 1815. Cainesville was settled even before that. Hosiah Caine went there from Connecticut in 1795, and then a year or two later he moved out here."

"Duff . . ."

"His oldest son, Enoch, was killed and scalped by Delaware Indians in 1806. It must have been awful for his mother, mustn't it?"

"Yes, awful."

"Of course she had a number of other children, including the one who became General Caine. He's said to have killed quite a few Indians himself, when he was younger than I am now." Duff took a large scrapbook from a stack of similar ones. "Here are some newspaper clippings about him. Aunt Hannah made some notes in the margins."

He selected a page for me to read and pushed the book over. The clipping was from the *Ashland Times* of February 15, 1883. The heading was ASHLAND COUNTY RESIDENT HONORED, and the two-paragraph story stated that Brigadier General Duffin H. Caine had been proposed for membership in the Ohio Commandery of the Loyal Legion, an organization of former Union officers who had served with distinction during the war. Next to the clipping was a faded line written in a spidery hand. "He was a great man." The verb was underlined several times.

"Why did she have to be so emphatic about it?" I asked. "Did somebody suggest he wasn't a great man?"

"Well, you know, Dad told us about how some of his neighbors didn't like him." Duff turned the pages and showed me a clipping from May, 1862. I read part of it.

Colonel Caine took command of the Ohio Brigade on the second day at Shiloh after General Wilkinson was killed. Taking a position on the right flank of General Grant's Army, he led his cavalrymen in charge after charge against Confederate General Wallace's Division . . .

"He was made a general himself after that, and fought in several more battles before he was captured," Duff said. "And even though he was captured in the western area of fighting, he was taken to an eastern prison—Libby Prison in Richmond—for greater security."

"He must have been considered an important prisoner."

"He was. He was one of the greatest cavalry leaders in the

war, maybe the very greatest on the Union side. He was never recognized as such though by his contemporaries."

"Why?"

"Oh, politics, I suppose. Maybe he wasn't enough of a self-promoter." Duff took the scrapbook and put it back on the stack. "Anyway, you can see there's a lot of valuable material here."

"It's transportable, isn't it? We could rent a trailer and take all those books back East with us."

"But it's not only these books, Mother. It's the books in the libraries in Ashland and Cainesville and all the microfilms of newspapers I need to read. Mother, couldn't we please stay here for just one semester?"

"That gets us into January. That would be half the winter."

"It's not so long. The time will pass before you know it. And if we go now, I'll always think it was because you didn't have any faith in me. Also, it occurred to me that maybe you're afraid this place has had a bad effect on me, and I'd like to prove to you that it isn't true."

"Did Stephanie tell you that?"

"Stephanie? No, I don't talk much to her anymore, Mama. I realize now that what happened between me and her was just a part of growing up. I know myself a lot better now and I'm positive that nothing like that will ever happen again. Mama, won't you please agree to stay for just a few more months?"

I hesitated. "I'll think about it," I said finally. "I'll talk to your father." We both knew that didn't mean anything. If Duff could sway me, the battle was won. Furthermore Jack no longer wanted to leave either, if he ever did.

"All right, Mama," Duff said solemnly. "I know you'll do what's best for me."

I held his hand for a moment and was struck by how old and tired-looking he seemed. I thought then that maybe it was the light that made his face so long and gaunt and caused the shadows under his eyes.

Well, I went downstairs, God help me, and told Jack I had decided that we ought to stay at the farm for one school semester. I said that by the end of that time the real estate man ought to be able to find the Shaffers another place comparable to our own. Jack nodded agreement and hardly looked up from his writing.

Chapter Seven

Registration for the Cainesville schools took place during the first week of September. After I had seen Franny through the enrollment procedure at her school, I went on to the high school with Duff.

There was no real need for me to do it, but I tagged along anyway for his interview with his counselor, a Mr. Harvey Willis. Duff had decided he wanted to study as much American history as possible, and luckily there were three senior courses available, including one taught by a man who was supposed to be particularly well informed about events in Ashland County.

"Has your son been held back in school because of illness?" Mr. Willis asked when Duff had gone off to the gym for his physical examination.

"Not at all," I replied. "You can see on his transcript that he won't be seventeen for another two months."

"By George, that's right." Mr. Willis chuckled. "He looks much older. When he walked in here, I thought he was in his mid-twenties at least."

"And still in high school?"

"Oh, we get fellows like that once in a while. Farm boys mostly, who might take seven or eight years to get through. Used to be more of them than there are now. By golly, not yet seventeen . . ."

"We have a birth certificate at home," I said irritably.

"Oh, no need for that." He still shook his head. "I've never misjudged a boy's age that much before."

Half angry and half amused, I dawdled in the school library before going to the gym to meet Duff. He was with a group of boys taking turns on the parallel bars, while a sweat-shirted instructor was conferring with an elderly man wearing a white coat and stethoscope. I waved to Duff and the doctor came over to me.

"Is that your son?" he asked. "What do you feed him? He looks like an invalid, but he has more stamina than any other two boys here."

"He's always been good at gym activities," I said.

"For his size, he's the strongest boy I've ever seen."

It was a surprising evaluation. Duff had always been fairly well coordinated, but I had never thought of him as being exceptionally strong. Rating him that highly, it seemed to me, wasn't saying much for the local talent.

The next day Duff and Franny started school. Duff was late in coming down for breakfast—something that had never happened at home—and as a result he missed the bus. We permitted him to drive the car to Cainesville, and that set a pattern. He was late again the next day and the day following, and by the next week he had persuaded us to let him take the test for a license, which he passed easily. A boy can drive legally at sixteen in Ohio.

Then on the Tuesday of the third week of school, we had a call from the principal of Cainesville High. He would like to meet with the parents of Duffin Caine as soon as possible. The secretary couldn't (or wouldn't) tell me what Mr. Wheeler wanted.

That evening Duff claimed to know nothing about it.

"Except maybe it's because I had an argument with a couple of fellows this morning."

"An argument about what?"

"Oh, one guy called me a 'dude' and I called him a 'hick.' It was nothing. It was really stupid."

"What happened after the name calling?"

"Nothing. Oh, I shoved the creep, but that's all. I suppose Wheeler is blaming me because I'm a stranger in the school. If I were you, I'd ignore the call."

"I can't ignore it. I promised to see Mr. Wheeler."

"You'll make it harder for me, Mom. The kids will say I need my mother to stick up for me."

"I'm sorry, Duff. You'll just have to explain that it wasn't your decision."

The next morning he gave me more arguments. It was probably a mistake—the secretary had summoned the wrong parents. Mr. Wheeler was noted for summoning parents and then forgetting why he wanted to see them. This was only a device for frightening new students, and Mr. Wheeler really wouldn't expect me to show up. Then the car wouldn't start—for Duff. When I got behind the wheel, it started instantly.

Oddly enough, on that morning he seemed more his old self than he had in weeks. He looked younger and more frail than he had even the previous evening, anything but a boy who could cause trouble in school.

We dropped Franny off and then went on to the high school and were ushered into Mr. Wheeler's office. After he had greeted us and we were seated, there was silence for several moments while Mr. Wheeler, with a puzzled expression, kept switching his gaze from us to a sheet of paper he held in his hand.

"You *are* Duffin Caine?" he asked after a while.

"Yes, sir," Duff said politely. He took off his glasses and polished them with his handkerchief.

"And do you know what is stated in this report submitted to me by your counselor, Mr. Willis?"

"I have a general idea, sir."

"It states that you assaulted another student, Gerald McCabe. You seemingly hit him hard enough to cause him to lose consciousness for several minutes Do you admit this?"

"I didn't intend to hurt him, sir."

"He was taken to Ashland Hospital, where it was determined he had suffered a slight concussion. He was kept in the hospital overnight for observation."

"He's going to be all right, isn't he?" Duff was truly anxious now.

"Apparently so, but his injury could have been much more serious—not that this isn't serious enough." Wheeler stared at Duff again. "Did you hit Jerry McCabe with some object in your hand?"

"No, sir. I didn't even really think I hit him that hard."

Wheeler turned to me. "Jerry McCabe is a tackle on our football team. He stands six-four and weighs about two hundred fifty."

"Then what you say happened is impossible," I said. "Duff weighs a hundred pounds less than that."

"It happened all right. There were plenty of witnesses." Wheeler paused for a moment. "I'm inclined to think it was just a lucky blow—or, from Jerry's point of view, an unlucky one. Also there's some evidence that he started the trouble with a remark he made."

"That doesn't excuse Duff's lack of control," I said.

"I agree," said Wheeler. "Duff, we don't like violence of that sort at Cainesville High."

"Duff has never done anything like this before," I said, "and I'm sure he never will again."

"Duff?"

"No, sir," Duff said. "I'll never do anything like that again while I'm here at Cainesville High."

"Good enough, son. Go along to your classes now." When Duff had gone, Mr. Wheeler turned to me with a half smile. "Frankly, Jerry McCabe has been a bit of a bully around here. It's time he was taken down a peg, although I'm not sure he deserved that much punishment. Anyway, I'm amazed that your son was able to do it."

"I am too," I said. I thought I detected a note of admiration in Mr. Wheeler's voice. He was a mousy little man who may have been dreaming for years of taking care of bullies like Jerry McCabe.

"I'd've done the same thing when I was Duff's age," Jack said when I got home. "I wouldn't take any guff from the jock types either."

I had my doubts about that. I had known my husband to take plenty of guff from waiters, clerks and cab drivers. If Duff had gumption, I decided, it came from my side of the family and not Jack's.

That same day there was another call from the secretary. Mr. Wheeler had forgotten to mention that if Duff was going to continue to be absent from classes because of the illness of his father, the school would need a letter to that effect. I was noncommittal, saying only that I would get in touch with Mr. Wheeler again.

But Duff wasn't at all evasive about it that evening. He explained that he had been busy with his research on the Caine family, working with material in the Cainesville Public Library. He hadn't told the truth to his teachers because he wanted to keep the work a secret until he was further along. If professional historians got wind of what he was doing, one of them might try to steal the idea.

We weren't satisfied, but we accepted it after he promised not to cut classes again. I suppose the fact that he already had enough credits to graduate caused us to treat the matter rather lightly. Also, I'm afraid that both Jack and I were inclined to think of Cainesville High as an inferior place, not really up to the intellectual capacities of our son.

A few days later we received another call about Duff's activities. This time it was from the Ashland County sheriff's office. Our car had been wrecked and Duff was in jail, charged with several offenses, including reckless driving and assaulting policemen. He was unhurt and could be released on payment of five hundred dollars bond—an outrageously small sum, the deputy intimated, but the limit, considering that Duff was a minor.

Stephanie was in the room when the call came, and she suggested that her father would be willing to drive me to Ashland, if he was available. I accepted, since I had no other choice. Mr. Weber was at home and he agreed to leave immediately to pick me up.

However, it was Stephanie's mother and her grandmother who arrived in their station wagon. Stephanie was at the front door and she turned to me in a panic.

"Don't go with them!" she pleaded.

"But why? You called them," I said.

"I called my father. I didn't think the two of them would come."

"Well, I'm glad they did. I would've felt guilty, imposing on your father's workday." Rose Weber was at the door. I picked up my purse and started out.

"Don't say anything to them about what I told you," Stephanie whispered.

"Oh, really, Stephanie," I said and closed the door.

Mrs. Reddy and her daughter were most cordial and sympathetic on the journey to Ashland. Mrs. Reddy said that she was sure the charges against Duff had been exaggerated by the deputy who called and that very likely Duff would be let off with a reprimand. She said, and Rose Weber agreed, that Duff was only "letting off a little steam," "sowing a few wild oats," and that his conduct showed that he was a real boy and not the wishy-washy sissy type they had first taken him to be.

"Do you have a lawyer?" Mrs. Reddy wanted to know.

"Is that necessary?"

"If Duff has to appear in court, you ought to have someone, just to be on the safe side. I know the best man in the county, Oliver Matson. He won't charge you much either."

At the Ashland County Jail, we found that Duff would indeed have to appear in Juvenile Court and that he would be notified shortly of the scheduled time.

"What happened?" I asked the deputy sheriff at the booking desk.

"Why don't you wait and ask Duff?" said Mrs. Reddy at my elbow.

"I'd like to hear the official version."

The deputy leafed through some papers and selected one. "Your son, driving a nineteen seventy-four Oldsmobile station wagon, was clocked by radar at a speed of ninety-three miles an hour on Route Ninety-Six. He was pursued by state highway Patrolmen Higgins and O'Donnell. In attempting to escape from the state patrol car, your son sideswiped a nineteen sixty-seven Dodge sedan, driven by Arthur Henderson, of Rowsburg, Ohio. Mr. Henderson suffered multiple facial cuts and possible head injuries and his car was badly damaged. The Oldsmobile was overturned, but your son managed to get out unaided, and after abusing the officers verbally, he assaulted both of them." The deputy put down the report. "If you want a more complete description, I suggest you talk with one of the arresting officers who came in aid of Patrolmen Higgins and O'Donnell."

I said I thought I wouldn't bother them just then. My check was unacceptable for the bond, but luckily I had enough traveler's checks. After studying them suspiciously for a moment, the desk man sent another deputy to fetch Duff.

"They're taking it out on Duff because he isn't a local boy," Mrs. Reddy whispered.

"We've had some behavior problems with him recently. This isn't the first incident." I hesitated. Should I tell them what had happened with Stephanie?

"You're probably just paying more attention to him lately, that's all," said Mrs. Reddy. "Probably back East he was on his own a lot and you didn't know what he was up to."

"I'm sure my husband and I have tried to be responsible parents," I said angrily.

"Oh, I didn't mean you let the boy run loose. I just meant that with all his chums back there and lots of things to do, you probably didn't see as much of him."

"Maybe we ought to introduce Duff to some nice boys and girls around here, Ma," Rose Weber put in.

"I'm sure he could make plenty of friends at the high school, if he wanted to," I said. "Lately he doesn't even seem to want to go to school."

"Cainesville High is probably not as much of a challenge for him as his old school," said Mrs. Reddy.

"Let me ask you something," I said. "Do you think living in the Caine farmhouse could have anything to do with Duff's behavior?"

The two of them stared at me with puzzled expressions.

"Whatever gave you that idea?" Mrs. Reddy asked.

"Stephanie mentioned it. She thought there might be something about the house that was causing Duff to act differently."

"Our Stephanie said that? She must be losing her mind," said Mrs. Reddy.

"Steph probably meant the total environment, the isolation, Ma. I can see that. Duff feels strange here. It'll take him a while to get used to it," Rose said.

"She didn't mean the environment, she meant the house itself—or rather something in the house. She was quite definite about it, although she wasn't very explicit."

"I can see why," said Mrs. Reddy. "It would be pretty hard to be explicit about something like that."

"Then you don't believe it? You don't think the house is—?"

"Haunted?"

"Stephanie didn't use that word. In fact she didn't seem to be talking about ordinary ghosts."

Rose Weber laughed. "I should think all ghosts would be extraordinary."

"Are they to you? I would have thought they might be commonplace to a spiritualist."

"Is that what Stephanie said about us, that we're spiritualists?" asked Mrs. Reddy.

"Well, I suppose we are in a way, Ma," said Rose. "We believe in an afterlife, don't we? And we believe that sometimes it's possible to communicate with the departed."

"That's right," said Mrs. Reddy. "See, we have a little study group that meets now and then to discuss those things. That's what Stephanie was thinking of. But we don't have séances and things like that."

"Oh, my, no," said her daughter.

Duff was led in then by the deputy sheriff. Astonishingly, he didn't look like someone who had been in an auto wreck, let alone a fight with the police. As on the day I had gone with him to the high school, he seemed his old self. His shirt, sweater and jeans were clean. His face was unmarked and his hair was neatly combed. In fact, he seemed more presentable than he had when he went off that morning.

"Hello, Mother," he said brightly. His smile faded when he saw Mrs. Reddy and Mrs. Weber, but he greeted them politely.

"We've got a good lawyer for you, Duff, so you don't have to worry about anything," Mrs. Reddy told him. "Let's go talk to Mr. Matson."

"I'd rather do it another time," I said, but I let her lead us out to the street.

Rose drove us to the garage to which the Olds had been towed. It was a mass of junk—unrepairable, in the view of the insurance agent who joined us at the garage. The agent also implied that his company might be canceling our policy.

Since we needed another car immediately, I rented a Plymouth from a Hertz agency. Then I managed to convince Mrs. Reddy that I really couldn't talk with her lawyer before consulting my husband. I thanked her and her daughter—I really was grateful for their help—and Duff and I got in the Plymouth. I was waiting for it, but he didn't suggest that he would like to drive.

Mrs. Reddy leaned in the window on his side. "Come see us the next time you feel like running around the countryside," she said.

"Duff won't be driving anywhere for a while, since the police have taken his license," I said.

"He can walk to our house. It's not that far from yours. And we can tell him things about the history of this area and the Caine family. That's what you're interested in, isn't it?" She paused and then said, "Duff." It was as though she had forgotten his name momentarily.

"Any explanations?" I asked him when we were on our way.

"No, Mother," he said.

"Then do you mind if I ask some questions? Why were you driving the car instead of being in school?"

"Oh, I had an early study period and it was such a nice day . . ."

"Route Ninety-Six is on the other side of Ashland. You couldn't possibly have gotten all the way over there and back to school during one study period—even at ninety miles an hour."

He shrugged. "I can't explain it. I just found myself driving farther and farther."

"And did you just find yourself attacking the policemen?" It was incredible that my Duff had done that.

"One of them grabbed my arm and twisted it, and the other kept poking his finger in my chest." He paused. "At least I think that's why I reacted as I did."

"You don't know? That's hardly an acceptable excuse, Duff."

"I'm sorry, Mother, but it's the only one I have." He really sounded forlorn now.

"Can we expect a continuation of this sort of thing?"

"No . . . I don't know."

"Is anything wrong? Anything we don't know about?"

He didn't answer for a long time. Then he said, "Nothing you would want to know about."

His voice sounded different, guttural. I glanced at him. He was grinning. There was a stubble of rough dark beard on his cheeks and chin, where only moments before there had been —I thought—light down. Also, he had removed his glasses, and that, I decided, gave him a different look.

"Try me and see," I said.

"Maybe I will—sometime."

There was no conversation for a minute or two. I turned on to the road that led to the farm and then I said something about his being popular with Mrs. Reddy and Mrs. Weber.

"Oh, yes, very popular," he said. The same guttural voice, but coldly cynical now, and also his breath had become foul.

I lowered my window. "What did they give you to eat in jail?" I asked.

He didn't answer. Now the stench was overpowering. I turned to him again and then I screamed. It wasn't Duff sitting beside me but a stranger—a man of forty or so, with glaring bloodshot eyes and a short, thick beard. He was grinning, as Duff had been before, only now, instead of Duff's well-cared-for teeth, I saw broken and jagged yellow ones.

Chapter Eight

I fainted. When I regained consciousness, the two right wheels of the car were in a ditch. Duff—the real Duff—was slapping my cheeks frantically.

"Are you all right, Mother?" he kept asking.

My ribs and my chin were sore. I wasn't wearing the seat belt, and I had been slammed against the steering wheel. I didn't remember Duff fastening his seat belt either, but he seemed unhurt.

"I think I'm okay." I took a couple of deep breaths, despite the pain in my ribs.

"What happened? You just suddenly went off the road for no reason."

I didn't know what to say, or what to think. Had there been someone else there? Was I losing my mind?

"I thought maybe you had a heart attack like Dad. Maybe the road is slippery here."

It was hard-packed gravel on that side of the farm and perfectly dry. Could it have been a sudden change of light distorting his features? No light could have caused changes like those I had seen.

"I'll have to say what you said. I don't know why I did it."

With Duff pushing, I managed to back the car a short distance to a place where I could get it back on the road.

"Only a scratched front fender," he said, getting back in the car. "I'm still the champ."

"Don't try to be cute. It's not at all funny." My voice was quavering and my hands were trembling on the wheel as I drove the mile or so to the farm, glancing sideways every few seconds to make sure it was still Duff beside me.

Jack and Stephanie were waiting for us at the door. Jack was anxious, but Stephanie seemed really worried.

"Which one had the accident? The mother looks worse than the son," Jack said.

"I wasn't used to the car and I went off the road," I said. "I don't think we're liable for damage to a rented car, are we? It's about the only thing that's happened today that we aren't liable for."

I called Franny's school and asked that she be told to take the bus home. Then I took two of Jack's Libriums and lay down on his bed. When Stephanie knocked at the door and asked if she should start preparations for dinner, I told her to go ahead. It was the last time I spoke with Stephanie.

I fell asleep and apparently slept for hours without having any of the nightmares I expected. When I awoke it was dark. I went out to the living room and found Jack sitting under the old fringed Art Deco floor lamp, writing on his yellow pad.

"Feel better?" he asked. He didn't sound awfully concerned.

"Somewhat. Where's everyone else?"

"Franny went to bed bewailing our lack of a television set. Duff went out."

"Not in that rented car, for God's sake, Jack!"

"No, no. I wouldn't allow that. Some kids came by on motorcycles and picked him up."

"And you let him go? You and your goddamn book!"

"Maggie, I saw no reason to keep him in the house on a warm September night. He said he didn't have any homework."

"Naturally, since he wasn't in school today. Were they the same motorcyclists we saw that day we arrived—the ones in the supermarket parking lot?"

"I don't remember seeing any motorcyclists that day."

"Oh, for God's sake, Jack! Where's Stephanie? Did she go with them?"

"I don't think so, but I haven't seen her since dinner." It was obvious he couldn't wait to get back to his writing.

I wanted to ask Stephanie (hoping I could trust her not to repeat it) if what I had seen in the car could be related to what she had described as the evil in the house. Also, for some reason I felt I ought to warn her that I had talked to her mother and her grandmother about her. As it turned out, it was too late for any warning. Maybe it wouldn't have done any good anyway.

Upstairs, the door to the bedroom I shared with Franny was closed and her portable radio was blaring rock music. I went into Duff's room and turned on the light. The bed was made and his brush and comb and some paperback books were arranged neatly on the dresser. I had been expecting to find disorder, reflecting the changes in him, but this room looked the way his always did at home.

Then I went into the storeroom. Again, the piles of books and scrapbooks had been neatly arranged. On top of the nearest pile was Duff's loose-leaf notebook, containing a few filled pages in his handwriting. The first few lines were in his customary scrawl—I had helped him with enough homework to be able to decipher it—but, after that, the letters were larger and better formed.

Something else occurred to me later. Considering where the notebook had been left and the legibility of the writing, it was quite possibly intended that I read it.

July 25, 1976. I have decided to keep this journal because I think it is important that what is happening be recorded. I want my parents and my sister to know how I feel now and how I felt in the past about them. I do love them, just as much now as I did at home, but I'm beginning to be afraid of them. I'm afraid they might try to prevent me from becoming what it is intended I become. What is that? I don't know yet, but I have a feeling I will become a person of great power.

July 25, 1976. Evening. I got out of bed to write something, but now I don't know what to write. I am very confused.

July 26. Early morning. I am Duffin Caine. I am Duffin Caine. I was born November 10, 1959. I *am* Duffin Caine.

July 26. After breakfast. I am not quite sure when the change began, but I think I began to feel different from the first moment I entered this house. I had a sense of belonging here, of having been here before. When I first came upstairs, the feeling was very strong. I seemed to remember all the rooms and even some of the furnishings. For instance, before I entered my room, I knew there would be a window directly opposite the door and that through the window I could see the front of the barn. I also expected to see a shelf in the corner with an oil lamp on it. The lamp would be sitting on a cracked blue plate. There was a shelf in the corner but no lamp or plate on it. However, today I discovered the very lamp and plate I had anticipated on the floor in the storeroom.

July 27. This is all mixed up. I meant to say something in the last note about Dad's accident, but then I remembered what happened with Franny and I didn't want to talk about that. However, now I feel I should say that I didn't intend for any of it to happen. I, Duff Caine, I mean. Someone screamed upstairs, but it wasn't Duff, I don't think. I mean I could hear the screaming— could even see the man screaming and grinning as he screamed —and I know that screaming was what caused Dad to fall. Likewise, I could see someone—it wasn't quite the man yet, but more like Duff—trying to undress Franny. But Duff didn't want to do it. He really didn't, Mother.

July 28. Sometimes he doesn't like to come in the house. He calls to me to meet him outside. At first, I was afraid of him, but I'm not afraid anymore.

July 29. Now I don't see him anymore. He comes and then he is Duff.

The last penciled entry ended a page. It was almost two months since the date of that entry. Had he given up keeping the journal—or had he been told to give it up by whoever was in control of him?

And was the man I had seen in the car the man Duff was referring to in his notes? Could he have been hiding in the back, crouched down behind the seats, ready to suddenly switch places with Duff? But how could it have been done without my seeing it—unless my attention had been diverted the way a magician does it, or unless I had been hypnotized? Hypnotized by whom? Duff? But if Duff had done it, perhaps there had been no other person. Maybe Duff had merely caused me to think he was someone else.

Ridiculous. My sixteen-year-old son a hypnotist? He had written that he was meeting the man outside the house, hadn't he? Maybe it was that man, and not Mrs. Reddy, that I had seen with him the night after Jack's accident.

I went back downstairs, put on my glasses and picked up my sewing basket. Jack was still scribbling on his yellow pad. I sat on the settee near him and began mending a torn blouse.

After a while, he got up, picked up his crutches and said he was going to bed. I said I thought I would wait for Duff and Stephanie to come in. I was trying to seem calm about it, but I didn't feel that way. I was frightened and I grew more so as time went by and neither of them returned.

I kept listening for the sound of motorcycles on the road, but it never came. I repaired the first blouse and then another and then a number of torn shirts, socks and sweaters that had been collecting in my basket since before we left the East. The work wasn't my best, but it kept my hands from trembling.

After a while I dozed off, but I was sure it was for just a few minutes. I did have a terrible dream, although I couldn't remember the details of it later. My glasses had slipped off and I looked for them behind the settee, but there wasn't enough light to search properly. Then I went out to the kitchen to check the time on Aunt Hannah's old wall clock. It was three o'clock.

Where was Duff? Where was Stephanie? I went to her room next to the kitchen, but she wasn't there. Were she and Duff together somewhere?

I went upstairs and opened his door. He was in bed asleep, or pretending to be. I stood by his bed and watched him for a long time. Just as I was about to turn away, I saw his lips move, although his eyes remained closed.

He said very distinctly, not in Duff's voice but rather the voice of the man in the car, "People in this house are going to die."

"Who, Duff?" I whispered.

"Maybe John . . . maybe others."

"When, Duff?"

He didn't say any more. I put my hand on his forehead and he stirred a bit, but he still didn't open his eyes.

"Duff, why did you say that?"

There was still no answer. I waited a minute or two longer and then went to my bedroom. I guess I was sobbing because Franny awakened.

"Mother, is something wrong?" she asked.

"No, I'm just overly tired, that's all." I undressed and got into bed with her. "Did you hear Duff come in tonight?"

"Yes, a long time ago," she said.

"How long?"

"Hours. He was walking funny, sort of dragging his leg, you know? He was putting both feet on each step as he came up. I thought of getting up and asking him if something was wrong, but he's been acting so weird lately I thought I'd better leave him alone."

"How did you know it was Duff and not someone else?"

"Who else could it have been? You or Stephanie wouldn't have made such a racket, and Dad doesn't come upstairs. Also the person went into Duff's room, so it had to be Duff."

After a while I said, "Franny, there's a key to the door of this room, isn't there?"

"Yes, it's on the dresser."

"All right, from now on, the last one of us to come to bed will lock the door."

She sat up. "But why, Mama?"

"There are prowlers in this area. Someone told me today."

"But if we just lock our outside doors—"

"We'll do that too, but in addition I think it's a good idea to lock the bedroom door."

"Daddy too, and Stephanie?"

"We can suggest that they do it."

"And what about Duff? You'll have a hard time convincing him to lock his door."

"We can tell him we're doing it. Maybe that will cause him to follow suit."

There was silence for a moment and then Franny asked, "Mama, should I get out of bed and and lock the door now?"

"No, we'll let it go for tonight."

He's asleep now, I thought, and likely to stay that way until daylight. But who was it asleep in that bed? Was it Duff speaking like the man or—a really wild thought—the man looking like Duff?

I stayed awake until daylight and then (moments later, it seemed) the alarm went off. While Franny was getting ready for school, I went to Duff's door and knocked. He answered in his normal voice, saying that he was getting up and would be down for breakfast shortly.

But he didn't join us for breakfast. Stephanie didn't either, which was strange because she was usually up and around before any of the rest of us. Her bedroom door was still closed, however, so I assumed she had come in after three o'clock when I checked the room.

After a few minutes of waiting for Duff, I went upstairs to look for him. He wasn't in his room and he wasn't in the store-room either. I assumed he had gone downstairs and out the front door, without any of us seeing him from the dining room. It was unpardonable behavior to leave the house without saying anything to us, but, to tell the truth, I wasn't anxious to confront him that morning anyway.

Franny finished her breakfast and went out to the road to wait for the school bus. Jack was reading a magazine in lieu of the morning newspaper that usually arrived in the mail about noon. After another short while I went to Stephanie's door again, knocked and, receiving no answer, opened the door. She wasn't in her room and her bed seemingly hadn't been slept in.

"Stephanie isn't in her room," I told Jack.

He didn't look up from his magazine. "She's probably left us. That's what you wanted, isn't it?"

"Don't make it sound like a vendetta. And I don't think she'd leave us without saying good-bye—or taking any of her things."

I had seen a couple of her dresses in the closet when I looked in from the doorway. I went back now and inspected the room. As far as I could tell, she had taken nothing with her other than the nurse's uniform she had been wearing.

"Maybe she went home for the night," Jack suggested.

It didn't seem likely to me, considering her feeling about her mother and grandmother, but I decided to call them anyway.

Mrs. Reddy answered. "No, Stephanie isn't here," she said. Then there was silence. She didn't ask why I was calling or why Stephanie wasn't at our house.

"She went out and didn't come back last night," I finally said. "We're concerned about her."

"Oh, you mustn't worry," Mrs. Reddy said breezily. "She'll turn up. You don't really need her anymore anyway, do you? I'll get you someone else if you do. There's a very well qualified girl in Cainesville who trained at the hospital with Stephanie."

"I guess we can get along without anyone now. Where do you think Stephanie has gone?"

"She probably got on a bus and went to Cleveland. She has friends there. Or maybe she went to Columbus."

"But she didn't take her bag or any extra clothes, as far as I can tell."

"That wouldn't matter. Probably she just decided to go on the spur of the moment. She does those things."

"Without even telling us?"

"Ashamed to tell you, very likely she was. And she ought to

be. I'll give her a good talking to when I see her." She promised to call us if she heard from Stephanie.

"What should we do now?" I asked Jack.

"Nothing."

"Should we call the police?"

"Don't be ridiculous. That's up to her parents."

"But they don't seem to be concerned about her."

"Then why should we be?"

I went back to Stephanie's room and had another look around. In a dresser drawer I found her purse with forty or fifty dollars in it, her driver's license and a couple of Ashland department store credit cards. She surely wouldn't have gone on a trip without taking those things.

Shouldn't I call the Cainesville police or the sheriff's office, despite what Jack had said? Then something else occurred to me. A member of our family was already in trouble with the police. Wouldn't their first impulse be to question Duff about Stephanie's disappearance?

My first impulse was the same, I don't deny that. I wondered if Duff was involved as soon as I realized Stephanie was missing. He had assaulted her once. Could he have done something worse to her this time?

I went back to Jack. "Do you realize Duff isn't here either?"

"So he's gone to school."

"He didn't come down for breakfast, did he? And he didn't take the bus. I saw Franny get on the bus alone. And the Hertz car is in the yard."

"Maybe one of his friends picked him up."

I walked away in disgust, still more worried about Stephanie than Duff, although I kept telling myself she hadn't been gone all that long. She could've gone to a motel with the married boyfriend she had told me about. She wouldn't have needed her purse or any extra clothes to do that.

Somewhat relieved by that thought, I went out to the kitchen to get a cup of coffee. I should explain now that the Caine kitchen is an extraordinarily large one, typical, I suppose, of nineteenth century farmhouses, with plenty of work and storage room. It's a gloomy place, even with the electric lights on, and it's particularly gloomy in the morning, since there is just one small window overlooking the yard.

I mention these things to indicate that it wouldn't be difficult for a person to remain unobserved in the room, even if he wasn't intending to hide. Thus it happened that I was standing by the electric stove for a good five minutes, waiting for the water to boil for my instant coffee, before I became aware of someone else in the room.

The first time I turned to look, I didn't see anyone, but I still had the feeling that someone was watching me. I turned again and saw him.

He was tilted back in one of the old wooden kitchen chairs, his feet on the open door of the wood stove. He was the man I had seen in the car, and he was grinning at me as before.

This time I noticed that he was wearing clothes like Duff's, a sweatshirt and jeans, but the shirt was too small for his bulging shoulders, and the jeans were open at the top, revealing an expanse of hairy belly.

I couldn't scream. "Who are you?" was all I could manage.

"You know who I am." It was that same guttural voice. "I am Duffin Caine."

I shook my head. "You're not my son."

"I am Duffin Caine." He lowered his feet and stood up. He was taller than he had seemed sitting, and even broader in the chest. He came limping toward me and then I managed to scream.

I ran out of the kitchen and through the dining room. Jack was still in the front room, struggling to his feet and trying to get his crutches under his arms. I yelled something about a man in the kitchen.

"What man?" He swung past me into the dining room.

"Don't go out there, Jack!"

I expected to hear shouts, blows, the sound of Jack falling, but there was nothing. In a moment Jack reappeared.

"There's no one in the kitchen but Duff," he said.

Chapter Nine

"Calm down, Maggie. Get a grip on yourself."

Jack stood aside and Duff came out of the kitchen. He was dressed in his usual sweatshirt and jeans.

"Mama, what happened?" He seemed genuinely concerned.

I went past both of them out to the kitchen. It was indeed empty.

I turned back to Duff. "When did you come in here?"

"There's no need to shout, Mother. Ten or fifteen minutes ago."

He was lying, I was certain.

"You came in the back way?"

"No, Mother. I haven't been outside today. I came downstairs and went right into the kitchen."

He was lying. He hadn't been upstairs when I went looking for him. He must have come in the back door and the man must have gone out at the same instant I ran to the front of the house.

"What about school?" Jack asked him.

"I don't feel well," Duff said. "I thought I'd stay home today and work on my history of the Caine family."

"You might have asked our permission," Jack said. He went to the back door and tried it. It was locked. "No one could've gotten out this way without Duff seeing him and then locking the door afterward."

Did he think that was impossible? "Where were you when I looked in your room a few minutes ago?" I asked Duff.

"In the storeroom, probably."

"You weren't there either."

"Then in the bathroom."

I hadn't gone into the bathroom. The door had been partly open, so I had assumed he wasn't there.

"You sounded perfectly well when I talked with you early this morning," I said.

71

"I was all right then, but now I feel lightheaded and nause-ated."

"Maybe he's getting flu or something," Jack suggested. Duff did look ill at the moment, but I was convinced it was a sham.

"Do you deny there was someone else in the kitchen?" I asked.

"No, Mother," he said quietly. "I don't deny it. I can only say I didn't see anyone here except you."

"And where were you when you saw me?"

"Sitting in that chair." He pointed to the one in front of the wood stove.

"And you remained in that chair all the while I was here?"

"Yes. I was sleepy and I think I dozed off for a minute, but then I got up and walked toward you. I felt very sick and I wanted to tell you, but you screamed and ran out—"

"Liar, liar!"

Jack dropped his crutches and grabbed me from behind as Duff backed off.

"Get out of here," Jack told him. "Go up to your room and lie down. If you're sick, we'll get a doctor for you."

"I don't think it's all that serious," Duff said.

"I don't think it is either," I said—or screamed, I suppose would be more accurate.

As he went up the stairs, I noticed that his sweatshirt was ripped along the shoulder seams. Moreover there were slits in the sides of both of his sneakers.

"How long have your shoes been torn like that?"

He stopped and looked, lifting one foot and then the other. He seemed genuinely puzzled. "This is the first I've noticed it."

"Don't wear those shoes to school, for God's sake," Jack said. "People will think we're on welfare."

"Where are your glasses?" I shouted.

"Upstairs, Mother, for pity's sake." He gave me a look that seemed to combine fear and incomprehension and continued up the stairs.

"Well now," Jack said, "what is it with you, old lady? Are you drinking in the mornings now or what?"

I didn't want to discuss it with him. I went into the living room, but he followed me.

"Do you think you might be going through menopause?"

"Shut up, Jack!"

"Do you really still think you saw a stranger in the kitchen?"

"What's the use in talking about it. You don't believe me. You'd rather believe Duff."

"But why would he lie about something like that?"

That I couldn't answer. It could hardly be because he wanted to keep the man's existence a secret or he wouldn't have written about him in his notebook and then left the book where I could find it. On the other hand, perhaps I was the only one in the family who was supposed to know about the man. Perhaps the man and Duff were conspiring to drive me crazy. But why?

"Look, Maggie, I'm sure you're all right mentally," Jack said. "I don't doubt you thought you saw someone, but it was probably only a trick of the light."

I didn't tell him that I had used that rationalization the first time I'd seen the man. But that explanation was impossible to even consider now because the man had walked toward me into the light, so close I could have touched him.

"Forget it, Maggie, that's my advice. It won't happen again."

"How do you know?"

"I just know." He picked up his writing pad. "Please, Maggie, don't stand there staring at me. Why don't you get out of the house for a while. Take a drive to Cainesville or somewhere."

Angrily I got my purse and the car keys. In truth I didn't want to stay in the house, but I resented being asked to leave it. For some reason I wasn't afraid of the man's appearing in the car again since Duff wasn't with me. The obvious extensions of that thought didn't occur to me until later.

I drove to Cainesville, not because Jack suggested it, but because there didn't seem to be anywhere else to go. I didn't want to drive toward Ashland, and of necessity pass the place where I had seen the man and gone into the ditch.

As I got into the outskirts of town I decided maybe I could kill some time at the public library. I could take a book and retire into a corner and maybe even come up with a constructive idea for dealing with the situation. At least maybe an hour of quiet would settle my nerves.

The Cainesville library is on Whittier Street, just off Main. All the parking spaces in front of the building were filled, so I drove farther down Whittier. The first open space was in front of Saint Mary's Catholic Church.

I remembered that Duff had mentioned a Father Fogarty, and I wondered if he had talked with the priest and possibly told him about his problems. The rectory was next door to the church and I decided it wouldn't do any harm to try and find out.

As I walked to the door, I didn't intend to ask for any help or guidance for myself. It wasn't that I would have been ashamed to do it—under the circumstances I would have gone anywhere for help—but I had been away from religion for a long time and I really didn't believe I could be comforted by it or by any of its practitioners.

Father Fogarty was in—maybe.

"I'll have to see if he is in," said a stout, white-haired woman with a German accent who let me advance as far as a small vestibule. "He isn't too well, you know, and he don't like to be bothered by strangers. You're not here about the miracle, are you?"

No, I had never even heard of their miracle.

"Father John was pestered quite a lot about that miracle, even by reporters from Cleveland and Columbus. He don't like to talk about it now, though I think that's partly Father Jackson's fault. Father Jackson don't believe in the miracle at all. You're not selling something—church candles or something like that, are you?"

I assured her I wasn't.

"'Cause we don't need anything. And Father John will be madder than blazes if it turns out he's in and you're really a peddler."

"I'm honestly not selling anything. I just want to ask your Father Fogarty a couple of questions."

She stared at me for another moment, then sighed and led me into a small office just beyond the vestibule.

"Wait here," she said. "I'll see if he's in, but don't be too disappointed if he isn't."

After about five minutes I heard the shuffling of slippered feet and an old priest came into the office. He had a day or two's stubble of beard and he was wearing a half-unbuttoned cassock on which was a plentiful supply of ashes from the cigar he was smoking, and probably several previous cigars. He looked eighty or more but his eyes were bright.

"What's your name?" he demanded.

I told him.

"Caine," he said, still watching me. "That's a well-known name here. This town was founded by Caines."

"My husband's ancestors."

"Indeed. But you're not from around here."

"No, we're from Scarsdale, New York, but we're living temporarily in my husband's family home."

"Are you now. Are you a Catholic?"

"I used to be."

"Hah." He relit his cigar stub with a hand that was shaking so much I thought he would burn his lip. "If you want to go to confession, you'll have to see Father Jackson. I'm too tired to be cooped up for a half hour or so in the box."

"I don't want to go to confession."

"Hah. It's that way, is it? Well I've run across your sort before. You've come here to defy the Lord and His Mother. You'll want me to show you the shrine now so you can mock the Mother of God. It would take nothing less than another appearance by her, and even then you wouldn't believe it."

"When did she appear the last time?" I inquired.

"You know. It's why you're here."

"Truly it's not, Father. And if that's the miracle your receptionist referred to, I told her I didn't know anything about it."

"She's not a receptionist, she's a housekeeper. We're not fancy enough to have a receptionist. And we're not sure yet whether it was a miracle or not, so I'll thank you not to be spreading it around that Father Fogarty said it was."

"What did happen then?"

"I thought it wasn't that you came about."

"Forget it," I said irritably. "I'm not that interested." I moved toward the door, but he held up his hand.

"Hold your temper. Sit down." He indicated a chair, then

shuffled around to the swivel chair behind the desk and lowered himself into it with some difficulty. "I just have to be careful. I can't have every Tom, Dick and Harry coming in here pestering me. I'm too old for it."

"That seems an odd way of operating a religious institution," I said.

"You wouldn't think it so odd if you were in my shoes and could see some of the nuts we get. And some of them pathetic too, I don't deny that. People wanting jobs, wanting husbands back and wives, wanting sons and daughters to come home and, more than anything else, wanting to be cured of every disease you ever heard of and a lot you haven't. We've had ambulances pull up to the door and people carried into this rectory on stretchers because they couldn't get into the church."

"Why couldn't they get into the church?"

"Because it's kept locked most of the time now, except for Masses and other devotions. For one thing some of them were spending the night there. Others were crawling from the curb up the steps of the church and down the aisle to the shrine on their hands and knees. One old fella, so crippled with arthritis he couldn't straighten up, told me he had crawled back and forth three hundred and forty-nine times."

"Was he cured of his arthritis?"

"Not at all. He's probably worse off now than before."

"Have you had any cures as a result of people coming here?"

"None that I know of, unless you want to count the one who caused all the trouble. You see, we always had a nice quiet little shrine here where parishioners could come and offer their devotions to the Mother of God, and if they wanted anything, they could ask for it, but nobody ever pretended he had any more advantage praying here than he had at home on his knees beside his own bed. Then this Eyetalian woman, this Mrs. Scaravelli, came along and ruined everything. She was cured of cancer, or so it's claimed."

"Is that bad?"

"It is when people start thinking that's what the shrine is for." He regarded me balefully. "This shrine was founded as a place where the faithful could pay honor to the Blessed Virgin. Petitioners were never discouraged, but we never gave out that it was worthwhile for them to come either."

"I don't understand you," I said. "I should think that any normal person, let alone a priest, would be happy when suffering was relieved."

He glared at me for another moment, then sighed. "I suppose I ought to be happy," he said gloomily, "and I would be if I was certain it was true—and also certain that it came about through the intercession of Mary."

"Who else's intercession, if the woman came here to pray?"

He didn't answer that, just glared again.

"And why do you doubt the cure? Is there any medical evidence that the woman had cancer?"

"Oh, yes, X rays. I've seen them myself. The thing was as big as a football. The doctors at Ashland Hospital didn't even want to operate on her."

"And has she been X-rayed since her visit here?"

"Yep, and the thing has disappeared. There's no doubt of that, it's gone. All the doctors have to admit it. They can't explain it, but they've signed statements for her, attesting to the before and after condition."

"Why did she want the statements?"

"To publicize this place."

"And you don't want it publicized?"

"I do not! That's why I've chased off the reporters and the television people. It would probably mean a lot of money for us in donations, but I don't want it."

"But why?"

"Never mind why. It's none of your concern. Now you've taken up a lot of my time already, without telling me why you came. You say you're not a petitioner."

"No, I just want some information. It's about my son. I think he may have talked with you."

"That's possible. I talk to lots of people, though nowadays mostly when I can't avoid it."

"We've been having difficulties with him. If he did talk with you, I'd like to know what he told you about himself. It might help his father and me in dealing with him."

"You could be asking me to break the seal of confession."

"No, no, it wouldn't have been in confession. Duff isn't a Catholic."

"So you're not raising your children in the faith, either?"

"Oh, really, Father . . ." I arose.

"Sit down." And when I didn't do so immediately, "Sit down, dammit!"

I obeyed.

After a while he said grudgingly, "I apologize. It's none of my business if you want to go to hell and take your family with you."

"You're right. It's none of your business."

"But, still, you're asking me to reveal the substance of a private conversation."

"Oh, forget it, Father. It's for the boy's own good, but if it goes against your conscience—"

"Sit down!" He paused. "You said your son's name is Duff?"

I nodded. "Short for Duffin."

"General Duffin Caine was a big man in these parts."

"So I'm told. He was Duff's great-great-grandfather."

"And you're living in Miss Hannah Caine's place?"

"That's right."

He relit his cigar. It wasn't more than an inch long now. "If I ever talked to your son, he didn't identify himself. Describe him."

"Well his hair is on the blond side. He's fairly tall, about six feet, but rather frail looking . . . sometimes . . ."

"What do you mean sometimes?"

"Just that sometimes lately he seems stronger. Also, he wears glasses."

"Sometimes?"

"Occasionally lately it seems he doesn't."

"I think I may have met your son, but he didn't tell me any of his problems."

"When was this?"

"One afternoon a couple of weeks ago. If he's the lad I'm thinking of, he was in the church. He was standing in front of the statue of Our Lady."

"I thought you said you kept the church locked."

"It was after that we started locking it."

"What was Duff doing? I can't believe he was praying."

"No." Father Fogarty took a final regretful puff and then squashed the soggy cigar stub in an ashtray. "He was urinating."

"Oh, my God, it couldn't have been Duff!"

"Well, he looked like the boy you've described when Father Jackson caught him outside. When I saw him in the church, he seemed heavier and older. I was at the main altar, reading my office, when I heard some women yelling over by the shrine. It's in a kind of apse, you see, off to the left. I rushed over there and saw him. He turned his head and grinned at me, but kept on doing what he was doing until he was finished. Then he rushed at me, almost knocking me over, and ran down the aisle. He would've gotten away, but I yelled and Father Jackson and a couple of men of the parish caught him outside."

"Did you question him?"

"Yes, but he denied doing what I had plainly seen him doing. He even continued to deny it after we marched him back into the church and showed him the puddle on the floor. He just kept saying that he hadn't done it, that it had been somebody else."

"Did you call the police?"

"No. Father Jackson wanted to, but I couldn't see that it would do any good. I thought that having the boy arrested would just mean more publicity for us. I knew he wasn't from around here and he promised not to come back again, so we let him go."

"But it couldn't have been my son. Why would he have mentioned you at all, if he did what you say? Wouldn't it have been more natural to avoid saying anything about you?"

Father Fogarty sighed and took another cigar from a box on the desk. "You'd better tell me all about your troubles with Duff," he said.

So I told him everything. When I began, I intended to hold back some of it and tell only about the attack on the boy at the high school, the car accident, and the attack on the police, but then I decided to include the rape of Stephanie (I didn't use that word but said something about making love brutally) and hesitated for only a moment before going on to tell of Duff's molesting Franny.

"What else?" asked Father Fogarty when I paused.

"Isn't that enough?"

"I get the impression there's more."

I definitely hadn't intended talking about what might be my own lunacy, although I had mentioned the seeming change, at times, in Duff's physical appearance. Now I told the priest about the man I had seen in the car and later in the kitchen. Then to bring the story completely up to date, I mentioned Stephanie's disappearance and my fear that Duff might have had something to do with it. I also said that Stephanie's mother and grandmother didn't seem at all worried about her.

"They're bad news, those people," said Father Fogarty. "The old one especially."

"Why?"

"She's a Satanist, a devil worshiper. She's been at it for a long time, long before that kind of thing became popular with the hippies and such. Some people say she's a witch, and her daughter too. I've had trouble with both of them. I tried to get your husband's Aunt Hannah away from Mrs. Reddy, did you know that?"

"No, I didn't."

"It's true. First I tried to get Miss Caine to pension off the old biddy—give her a couple of thousand and get her out of the house. I could've gotten a decent Christian woman to go in there and take care of your aunt, but she wouldn't have it. Then I wanted her to go into a nursing home, but she wouldn't agree to that either."

"My husband told me of your efforts to have Aunt Hannah buried in a cemetery here."

"Did he? Well, there's something else that went on between your aunt and me that I'll bet he didn't know. Your Aunt Hannah contributed most of the money for the building of our shrine. Forty thousand dollars she gave me, and that was thirty years ago when forty thousand was a lot more money than it is now. That's how I became acquainted with her and why at the end I wanted her to be buried in a Christian place."

"Why did she give you all that money? She wasn't a Catholic."

"No, and never wanted to be, as far as I know, and I never tried to push her into it. But she did believe in Christ and His Mother, and she wanted to make atonement for some of the evil committed by a member of her family."

"Who?"

"Her father, General Duffin Caine. He was a Satanist too."

That shocked me into silence for a moment, but then I said, "Father, do you think that means anything? Even if what you say is true, does being a Satanist mean any more than belonging to some local lodge or college fraternity?"

Father Fogarty didn't answer immediately but sat puffing his cigar. The room was so filled with smoke now that I found it difficult to breathe. Then he rose and shuffled to the door.

"Mrs. Guenther," he yelled. "Oh, Mrs. Guenther!"

The housekeeper answered him from somewhere in the back of the house.

"There's a book in the upstairs library, *Ashland County in the Civil War*. Fetch it for me. It's a big book with a red cloth cover. And ask Father Jackson to step down here."

He shuffled back to his seat. "Father Jackson would tell you 'no' if you asked him. No, except for the deplorable attitude of mind of the member, it doesn't mean any more than belonging to the Masons or the Elks, or, for that matter, the Knights of Columbus."

"But you think otherwise?"

"Yes, I think otherwise."

There was a lapse in the conversation then while I coughed and he puffed, ignoring my coughing. Then Mrs. Guenther came in, carrying a large book. She handed it to Father Fogarty and he blew the dust off it and began leafing its pages. Mrs. Guenther opened a window.

"Thank you," I said.

"It's for him," she said, jerking a thumb at her employer. "The doctor has warned him about smoking in a closed room."

She went out. Father Fogarty continued to browse through the book. Then he found what he evidently wanted, a full page reproduction of a photograph. He studied it for a moment, then turned the book around for me to see.

It was a photo of a seated man in a Union army uniform. Behind him was draped an American flag and what could have been a regimental flag. The reproduction wasn't a very good one, but the man's features were clearly visible. He had a short beard and a thin, hard-looking mouth. He wasn't grinning in the photo.

Chapter Ten

"You're upset by the picture," Father Fogarty observed.

I nodded.

"Do you know the man?"

"The caption says 'Brigadier General Duffin Caine.'"

"Yes, that's who it is. I found this book in a secondhand store several years ago, and I bought it because of the picture. I had been curious for a long time to know what he looked like. The *Ashland Times* thought they had a photo of him in their files, but when I asked them to look, they couldn't find it. It seems that General Caine didn't like to have his picture taken, and after the one occasion when he did permit it—for this book—he regretted it and went around buying up and destroying all the copies he could find. He evidently missed this copy somehow."

"Why didn't he want his photo published?" My teeth were chattering.

Father Fogarty got up again, went to a cabinet and took out a bottle of John Jameson's and two water tumblers. He poured me a good slug and himself a better. "Down it," he said. "There's nothing better for the nerves than Irish whiskey. Now, in answer to your question, maybe it was one of the rules of the religion he practiced. It's not unusual, you know. The ancient Hebrews didn't like graven images, nor did the old-time Mohammedans. Even today there are people in wild areas of the world who think that taking their photographs means taking their souls. However, there is also another possibility. Maybe our friend here just didn't want to be recognized as General Duffin Caine."

"But why?" The whiskey was helping some.

"Maybe he thought that he was going to be around for a long time and it seemed wiser that he not be associated with a man who lived so long ago."

"But how could he be around? General Caine died and was buried years ago."

"Nevertheless he seems to be still with us. Isn't he the man you saw in your kitchen, and before that in your automobile?"

"I'll agree that man resembled General Caine."

"I'll tell you something else. The man I saw doing his business in the church resembled the General too. The church was dark and I only caught a quick glimpse of his face when he came at me, but now that I study the photo I can see that it could've been the General."

"But you told me you caught a boy who had done it."

"And you told me that your son Duff was in your car and that he disappeared and you saw the man. And then you said the man was in your kitchen and after he vanished without a trace, your son Duff was there."

"What are you suggesting, Father?"

"What suggests itself to you, Mrs. Caine?"

At that moment another priest came into the room. He was young, not much over thirty, and slight, with thin shoulders under his too large cassock. He had a bad complexion, extending up to the line of his receding blond hair that seemed rather long in the back for a priest. He also seemed petulant, perhaps annoyed at being summoned.

"This is my assistant, Father Peter Jackson," said Father Fogarty. "Mrs. Caine, Father, of the famous—or should we say infamous—Caine family."

"I don't think one could describe Miss Hannah Caine as infamous," said Father Jackson after greeting me coldly.

"No, she was a good woman," Father Fogarty said. Father Jackson had been staring at the whiskey bottle. The old priest got up and put the bottle and the glasses away.

"It's a pity you couldn't have had your way after Aunt Hannah's death," I said. I was angry and sorry I had come. I didn't want to believe what he was seemingly trying to make me believe. I told myself there was nothing remarkable in the resemblance between the man I had seen and the photograph. In an old black-and-white photograph, any dark-bearded man might look like another.

"What do you mean, 'I couldn't have my way'?" Father Fogarty asked.

"Aunt Hannah was buried in the Caine graveyard against your wishes, wasn't she?"

"She was not. She was buried in Cainesville Cemetery, the Protestant one, but I blessed the grave, so it's just as snug a place for her as if she was resting in ours. The undertaker here, John Nichols, found a letter she had sent him twenty years ago requesting that she be buried in Cainesville instead of in the plot behind the farmhouse."

"But there's a new grave in the family yard."

"Well, it isn't Miss Hannah's, I'll guarantee you that. I saw her coffin being put into the ground right here in Cainesville." Father Fogarty paused. "Where approximately in the yard is this new grave, do you remember?"

"Near the fence on the far side, opposite the gate."

Father Fogarty nodded. "They've dug up the General again."

"What?" Father Jackson was astounded.

"That's why I sent for you, Father. I want you to listen to this lady's story. Maybe it will give you a better perspective on what's going on around here. Incidentally, let me put your mind at rest on a couple of matters, young lady. One, you're not crazy. Two, whomever or whatever you saw in your car and your kitchen, it wasn't the bones of General Caine, although it might have had something to do with them. I would guess there couldn't be much left of those, since he's been dead for more than eighty years. Now tell your story again please, for this young fella's benefit."

I told it again, although more briefly this time. Father Jackson didn't seem very impressed.

"It could be the result of suggestion, maybe even auto-suggestion," he said, shrugging.

"You think I wanted to see the man?" I asked angrily.

"It's not necessarily a question of wanting to. Hallucinations can be prompted by fears as well as desires."

"I don't think I want to discuss this anymore, Father Fogarty."
I rose again.

"Sit down, sit down," said the old priest impatiently. "Father
Jackson didn't say it was a hallucination."

"I don't know what else it could've been, unless the man was
really there," said Father Jackson.

"Be quiet," his pastor ordered. "No matter what it was, we
have to consider what caused it. Now I happen to believe that it's
quite possible for someone of the soundest mind to see something that other people can't see."

"Like visions of Mary," put in Father Jackson.

Father Fogarty turned on him. "Would you please have the
courtesy to let me finish what I have to say?" The young priest
threw up his hands and slouched in his chair. "Now then, I do
believe it's possible for such a person to have a celestial vision,
and that might include a vision of Mary. Also it needn't be
caused by any suggestion, auto or otherwise."

"What causes it then?" Father Jackson inquired.

"The holy will of God."

"You seem to be taking a different tack than you did the last
time we discussed Mrs. Scaravelli."

"I never denied that Mrs. Scaravelli might have had a genuine
vision," said the old man irritably. "Note that I said 'might.'"
He turned to me. "However, it so happens that Mrs. Scaravelli
is—or was—a friend of Mrs. Reddy's. And I've already told you
what Mrs. Reddy is."

"Are you sure of your facts?" asked Father Jackson. "You've
never actually had a conversation with Mrs. Reddy, have you, in
which she admitted being what you think she is."

Father Fogarty struggled to his feet, clenching his fists. "I've
never had a conversation with the Lord Jesus Christ either," he
roared, "but that doesn't mean I don't know He exists! I've never
met the Queen of England either, or the President of the United
States—"

"All right, all right, never mind." Father Jackson slumped further in his chair and closed his eyes.

Trembling, Father Fogarty turned back to me. "Now since
we know what Mrs. Reddy is, we can assume that her asso-

ciate Mrs. Scaravelli is, or was, the same thing. And now you know why I've been reluctant to have Mrs. Scaravelli's story publicized. There seems to be no doubt that she was cured of cancer, so it's quite possible that she had an authentic vision too. The point is, what caused these things to happen? Also, what caused you to see the General on two occasions, Mrs. Caine?"

"This is where I came in," said Father Jackson, rising.

"Sit down! I want you to investigate this case."

"Oh, for pity's sake, Father . . ."

"I'm not able to get around, so you'll have to do it. There may be some connection between Mrs. Caine's case and ours."

"That's ridiculous, Father."

"So you say. Check on it and find out."

"What do you want me to do—perform an exorcism on her son?"

"Over my dead body," I said.

"From what you've told me, it could come to that," said Father Fogarty. "However, there are many preliminaries before we could do anything like that."

"And there are other priests in the diocese more qualified to handle it," said Father Jackson. "Call the Bishop and have someone assigned."

"The bishop will want more evidence than we have now. We're not in the good graces of our Bishop Driscoll at the moment," Father Fogarty told me. "He blames me for encouraging the likes of Mrs. Scaravelli. He also thinks it was a mistake to build this shrine in the first place. But do you want to know why I did it? It was because of Mrs. Reddy and her kind. Like your Aunt Hannah, I wanted to do something to counteract the evil that was going on around here." He got up. "Well, I'll leave you in Father Jackson's hands, Mrs. Caine. By the way, the church is open now if you want to go in and say a prayer. You could be in danger too, you know. It's not only your son."

He made his creaky way to the door, then paused and said, more to himself than to either of us, "Maybe the whole thing was a mistake. Maybe he wanted it here so he could pervert it to his own purposes."

He went out and Father Jackson twirled his forefinger at the side of his head.

"What was he talking about? Who wanted what here?"

Father Jackson smiled for the first time, revealing a badly made partial denture. "The devil," he said. "Now he's thinking that the devil prompted him to build the shrine."

"And you don't believe in the existence of the devil?"

"Let's say I believe in the existence of evil. Hitler, Nero, Herod Atinpas, Joe Stalin maybe."

"But not a supernatural being?"

He smiled again. "Not a commander-in-chief with thousands of imps to do his bidding, no."

"Therefore you also don't believe in such things as demonic possession."

"No. I think there is nothing in the recorded history of such things that can't be explained by hysteria or some other mental aberration or, as I said before, by the power of suggestion. You seem an intelligent woman, Mrs. Caine. Do you believe in the possibility of possession by devils?"

"Of course not." He was buttering me up to get rid of me, I thought.

"Why did you come here then?"

"Because Duff said he had been here and I thought maybe Father Fogarty could help him. Help both of us."

"Well, maybe I can help you. I'll try."

"What can you do if you think it's all in my head?"

"I'm not sure all of it is in your head, and perhaps none of it is. What you saw may have a very simple physical explanation. For instance, maybe there's someone around here who looks like General Caine. Did you know that General Caine was said to be a great lecher, so there could be hundreds of his descendants in this area. And, as for your son, there's nothing very unusual in a boy's behavior changing suddenly. Probably the new environment had a lot to do with it. The fact that he's a stranger here and feels the need to prove himself, that sort of thing."

"You make me feel much better, Father."

"I'm glad. And you mustn't be concerned either by what Father Fogarty said about Mrs. Reddy and Mrs. Scaravelli. Both of them are harmless, although somewhat looney."

"I know Mrs. Reddy is a bit strange."

"So is the other one. She's a local charwoman who has no children and no relatives, as far as I know."

"Poor thing."

"If you're thinking she's exactly the sort of person to want to add a little excitement to her life by seeing visions, that thought has occurred to me too. And, as for her cancer cure, I'm not sure the local doctors are that reliable as authorities on cancer."

I went to the door. "Do you want me to call you if anything else happens?"

"Of course."

He didn't. He didn't want to become involved in the problems of a menopausal woman and her delinquent son, especially since they were out-of-towners and not even Catholics.

On my way to the car, I decided to have a look at the church. It was mostly curiosity, a desire to see the place where Duff—if it had been Duff—had committed the outrage.

It wasn't a very large church, possibly of a size to accommodate three or four hundred people. The furnishings and decorations were fairly plain—no pads on the kneelers, for example —and the wall paintings of the Stations of the Cross were small and amateurishly done. The altar furnishings were simple too— no statues or paintings behind the plain wooden altar, no carpet on the floor.

The shrine was in a small chapel which, in contrast to the rest of the church, was garishly decorated with woven tapestries depicting the life of Mary and a large seven- or eight-foot statue of Mary at the back. It was of marble, not very well carved, but impressive, considering its surroundings. I imagine it was imported, and probably represented the major portion of Aunt Hannah's contribution.

In front of the statue were a half dozen stands of vigil candles, all but a few of them lighted. There were no displays of discarded crutches, leg braces and wheelchairs, such as one sees at Lourdes and other Marian shrines. Evidently Mrs. Scaravelli's miracle was the first one to happen here, or else the first one a recipient wanted publicized.

There were eight to ten people kneeling at *prie-dieux* in the chapel, most of them elderly women. The one young woman present seemed especially fervent in her devotions. She was saying her rosary with her eyes fixed on the statue, and her gaze never wavered as I knelt at the *prie-dieu* next to her.

It was the first time I had knelt in a church in more than twenty years, although I had visited a few old ones during our vacation in Europe in 1974. At that time, I had no reason to pray. My life wasn't particularly happy, but there was nothing much I wanted either, other than relief from occasional boredom.

This time—and I was a bit ashamed of myself for it—I prayed. My doubts about my former religion hadn't been swept away, but I was afraid to take any chances. I prayed that what Father Fogarty had suggested not be true, but that if there were such things as devils, they be kept away from me and my family.

After a few minutes I decided I was being ridiculous. If there was such a being as the Mother of God, she could hardly be expected to respond to someone who had no faith in her. I got up from the *prie-dieu* abruptly, but then was instantly fearful that I would see the General again as a punishment for my lack of faith.

I left the chapel and started down the aisle toward the front door. Almost immediately there were footsteps behind me and I turned and saw the young woman who had been praying so devoutly. She beckoned to me as she hurried toward me. My first thought was that I had dropped something, although I had my purse and gloves.

She was younger than I had first thought, in her early twenties maybe, but thin, really emaciated-looking in a cheap print dress that was too large for her. Her dark eyes were bright, almost feverish as she took my arm.

"I have a message for you," she said.

"From whom? I don't think I know you."

"I don't know you either, but I was told to give you a message." We were outside the church now and she was still clutching my arm. "It's from Our Lady."

"I see." Gently I tried to disengage her fingers, but she held on all the harder.

"The message is: 'Don't worry about your son. Everything is going to be all right.'"

"Thank you very much." I couldn't get her fingers loose and I began to wonder if I should call for help.

"I come here every day and I get messages all the time for people."

"I see."

"I don't ask for anything for myself, that's the reason. I used to ask that I get a boyfriend, but I don't do that anymore. I know now I'm just supposed to come here and help other people. I've got something else for you."

She let go of my arm and reached into her shabby shoulder bag. After some fumbling, she produced what looked like an aspirin bottle. There was a liquid in it.

"This is holy water, blessed by Our Lady," she said handing it to me.

"I see." Although I was free now, I was curious. "How does she bless the water?"

"I bring several bottles down here every day and put them behind her statue. Then the next day I collect the old ones and put new ones."

"Well, thank you. What should I do with the water?"

"Sprinkle it around. It will keep him away."

"Keep who away?" I was frightened now.

"You know." She smiled knowingly. "I'm a friend of Mrs. Scaravelli's. I go to see her every day. I take holy water to her too. She doesn't like to come here much anymore because Father Fogarty doesn't like her."

"Did Mrs. Scaravelli tell you I would be here?"

"She thought you might be." The girl patted my arm. "You mustn't be afraid of Mrs. Scaravelli. Mrs. Scaravelli doesn't have anything to do with those people anymore."

"What people?"

"You know." She smiled and backed away.

"What people!"

She waved to me and reentered the church. I stood on the steps a moment longer, undecided about what to do with the aspirin bottle. Then I went to the car and put it on the shelf above the dashboard, thinking I would dispose of it when I got home.

There has to be a logical explanation for the girl's knowledge, I told myself. Her information about me—the fact that I have a son whom I'm worried about—had to have come from somewhere other than a supernatural source, and the most likely informant, it seemed to me, was Mrs. Reddy.

It seemed obvious that the girl was unbalanced, and if she was typical of the kind of people being attracted to the shrine now, I didn't blame Father Fogarty for being upset. Then another frightening thought came to me. I hadn't said anything to Mrs. Reddy about the man I had seen. How could she have known I wanted to keep someone away?

Because she was involved in the man's appearances obviously. It was the only logical answer. She had sent the man to me, or at least she knew about his coming. Maybe she wanted to frighten us away from the farm, in spite of the fact that she seemed to be trying to encourage us to stay. Maybe the property was more valuable than we thought and she wanted to be able to buy it cheaply. Maybe there was oil on the place, or natural gas. Hadn't I read somewhere about rich oil deposits in this part of Ohio? Or maybe it was mineral deposits.

Trying to comfort myself in this manner, I drove around the countryside for a while, wasting gas. I just didn't want to go home. I stopped at a hamburger stand somewhere and ate half a greasy sandwich, and then drove around some more. About four o'clock, I realized I couldn't keep putting it off, so I went back to the farm.

Duff was at home and presumably in his room, but Stephanie was still missing. Franny was home too, having just arrived on the bus.

"You might've picked me up if you were in Cainesville," she complained.

"I intended to, but I was detained longer than I expected."

"What were you doing?"

"Oh, lots of things. For one thing, I visited a church."

"A church!" Her incredulity made me ashamed for a moment of the way I had raised her. But then I thought, why should it bother me? She's a good girl and surely will remain so despite the fact that she's never had any religious training.

"Was it nice?" she asked.

"Very nice. I'll take you sometime."

Jack came into the room then and grinned when Franny told him where I had been. That infuriated me and I refused to answer any questions about it. I had planned to tell him about my talk with the priests, but now I was too angry to do it.

It was time to be starting dinner and I went into the kitchen with some trepidation, but the room was empty. I made sure of it, turning on the lights and inspecting the pantry and all the dark corners.

I was terrified of spending another night in the house, especially after what Father Fogarty had said about the activities of Mrs. Reddy and her daughter. I was also growing increasingly concerned about Stephanie, and I was trying to decide whether or not to phone the police when it became no longer necessary to make a decision. The doorbell rang and I went to the front door to find two sheriff's deputies calling on us.

Chapter Eleven

My first thought was that they had come to take Duff back to jail. However, they didn't ask about Duff, or at least not immediately. The older deputy's first question was about Stephanie, specifically had she been living with us. The tense of the verb didn't escape me.

"What's happened to her?"

My reaction didn't escape him either. "Were you expecting something to happen to her?"

"She's been missing since yesterday?"

"Since what time yesterday?"

"I don't know. Around dinnertime, I think."

"Did you notify the Ashland Sheriff or the Cainesville police?"

Jack came over on his crutches and intervened. "We notified her parents and they didn't seem alarmed, so we didn't do anything more about it. Now let's not play games. Something has happened to her or you wouldn't be here."

"She's dead. Her body was found a couple of hours ago in the woods on the Waterson place."

"Was she—?"

He stared at me for a moment before answering. "Did she die a natural death? No, Mrs. Caine, it was very unnatural. Among other things, she seems to have been strangled."

The room began to spin. The younger deputy helped me to the settee and asked if he could get me a glass of water.

"When did it happen?" I heard Jack ask.

"Between nine and ten last night, we think. Least the Watersons heard some yelling around that time and saw some lights. We don't have a coroner's report yet."

"Where is the Waterson place?" I managed to ask.

"Three or four farms down the road from you. About three quarters of a mile maybe."

"Toward her family's place?"

"That's right."

"Do they know?"

"Yes ma'am."

How did they take it? I wanted to ask, but didn't. It would serve no purpose and might just complicate matters.

How long had Stephanie been with us? the deputies wanted to know. Did she have any boyfriends? They knew about the married man she had told me about. He had been out of town for a week or more. Had we noticed anything strange in her behavior? Had she ever said she was afraid of anyone or anything? I said no to the last two questions—too quickly maybe, because both deputies studied me for a long moment.

"You seem to be getting around pretty well," said the older man to Jack. "Was the girl staying here because you still need nursing care?"

"She was going to leave in a few days," I said.

"To go where?"

"I don't know where."

The older deputy jotted the information in his notebook. Then he looked up. "You have a son," he said.

Here it comes, I thought. "A son and a daughter."

"Is he home?"

I looked at Jack. "He's upstairs," Jack said.

"We'd better talk with him."

"He's only sixteen," I said.

The older deputy smiled. "Sixteen-year-olds can get into plenty of trouble, Mrs. Caine. As a matter of fact, I understand your son is in some trouble now because of a traffic accident."

Franny had come downstairs and was staring wide-eyed at our visitors. I told her that something had happened to Stephanie and that the deputies wanted to talk with her and Duff. Duff first.

She ran upstairs and came back down quickly with him. He must have been waiting and listening at the top of the stairs. He was pale and even more frail looking than he had been at the jail. In fact he looked as he had two years before when he was recovering from viral pneumonia. Again, he wasn't wearing glasses and he was squinting even more than usual—to make himself seem even more helpless, I thought.

"Ride a motorbike, do you, son, as well as driving fast in your folks' car?" said the older deputy.

"I've ridden a few times on the backs of bikes," Duff said.

"Do you know some bikers in Cainesville who call themselves the Crazy Gang?"

"I've seen them, I think."

"Ever ridden with any of them?"

"Well, I don't know all of them that well—"

"Do you know Charles Romano, John McCafferty, Albert Squires—?"

"I know Al Squires."

"Were you with him last night?"

"Just for a short while."

"Where did you go?"

"Just for a short ride." Duff threw a frightened glance at me. "I don't know this area awfully well—"

"Did you go anywhere near the Waterson woods? That's a woods on this road between here and Cainesville."

"No, sir."

"You're sure?"

"Yes, sir."

Now it comes, I thought, as the deputy paused. Now he'll ask him if he killed Stephanie. But the deputy didn't.

Instead he said, "If I were you, I wouldn't hang around with that bunch. They're older than you, and most of them are no good. Also, we're pretty sure that some of them, or some like them, were involved in what happened to Stephanie Weber."

"What happened to her?"

"Your folks will tell you." The deputy turned to Jack. "There are tracks of several bikes in the woods near to where the girl was found. It's close to an old logging road, so it would've been easy for them to get in there." He looked at Duff again. "Considering who his friends are, your boy's lucky he can prove where he was last night."

I swallowed. "Can he?"

"The girl's mother and her grandmother say he was at their house from eight 'til eleven. Mrs. Reddy and Mrs. Weber say they brought him home then."

At eleven, I had been in the front room working on my mending. Was it around that time I dozed off? But even if Duff had come in the back way, surely the sound of the car and its lights would have awakened me.

The deputy closed his notebook. "Now if you'll let us have a look at Miss Weber's room, we can wind up our business here, at least for the moment."

They inspected Stephanie's belongings quickly, going through the pockets of her coats and uniforms and dumping the contents of her purse on the dresser.

"What do you think she was doing between the time she left here and the time she was killed?" I asked and instantly regretted it. If they began to wonder if the thing could have happened earlier, they might turn their attention on Duff again.

"Maybe she was out with one of the bikers," said the older deputy. "She might've slipped out of here and met him down the road aways." He swept the meager contents back into the purse. "I expect her folks will be sending for these things."

I decided to risk asking it. "How did they take it—the news of Stephanie's death?"

He stared. "How would you expect them to take it?"

"I'm sure they were upset."

"They were more than upset. The mother had to leave the room and couldn't even talk to the Sheriff." He was angry now as he and his partner threw Stephanie's lingerie back into the bureau drawers. I had offended him, I realized. I was a stranger, questioning the sincerity of some of the natives. All the same, I wondered if he shared Father Fogarty's opinion of Mrs. Reddy.

Having gone so far, I went further. "Stephanie did tell me one time that her mother and grandmother were spiritualists. I thought maybe those people accepted the idea of death more calmly than the rest of us. You know, because they believe they can keep in touch, that sort of thing."

"I don't know that much about them. I have heard that the grandmother is considered a bit queer, but harmless." He paused. "I understand she told the Sheriff that Stephanie was a wild sort and that the family had been afraid she would come to an end like this."

How could she? How could she say that about poor docile Stephanie? I was prepared now to believe everything Father Fogarty had said about Mrs. Reddy. Harmless, indeed! She was about as harmless as a rattlesnake.

The two deputies left. We all stood in the front room and watched until their car went up the road and out of sight. Then I turned and looked at Duff. He shrugged and smiled slightly and went upstairs.

"You said they were going to ask me some questions and they didn't," Franny complained.

"Be thankful they left as soon as they did," I told her.

"Why should she be thankful?" Jack asked. "None of us has any reason to fear the law officers."

I didn't comment on that. After a moment he said, "What do you think we should do? Should we phone her mother and express our sympathy?"

"You do it, if you like."

"Maggie, what's got into you?"

"I just don't like those people. Put it that way."

"But that shouldn't matter at a time like this. We ought to at least find out the time of the funeral and send some flowers.

Also, we probably ought to take Stephanie's clothes over to the Webers and not wait for somebody to come after them."

"All right, you take them."

"Maggie, I can't drive yet."

Then it occurred to me that I was being very foolish. In spite of my feelings, I ought to visit the Weber home and try to find out what the two women were up to. If they were involved in some sort of demonic activities, now might be the perfect time to learn about them. Maybe I could find out how Duff was involved—and involved he had to be, I was sure, if they were covering up for him.

I was just about convinced that he had had something to do with the death of Stephanie. It could've been accidental, maybe something done in anger like his assault on the boy at the high school and his attack on the policemen. Maybe Stephanie had provoked him in some way—or maybe he had raped her again and had been afraid she would tell of it.

Or could it have been the other person who had killed her, the man I had seen in the kitchen? He was brutish enough, seemingly capable of any horror. I was still unwilling to accept the idea that he and Duff might be the same person.

It was too awful. If it was true, it seemed surely to indicate that the whole problem was with me. Somehow, somewhere I must have seen a picture of the General (maybe Jack had shown me one years ago) and now I must be imagining that Duff looked like him.

I went upstairs to Duff's room and found him sitting on his bed, writing in his notebook. That was something I had forgotten about. Surely there was evidence there in favor of my sanity. But at what cost? Wouldn't it be better to have a slight mental aberration than to have Father Fogarty's theory proven true?

"So, Mother," said my son, smiling brightly, "you visited Saint Mary's Church today."

"How did you know?"

"How would I know? Do you think I have some sort of extra-sensory perception? Franny told me. Did you talk with Father Fogarty?"

"Briefly."

"What did he say about me?"

"He said you did something disgraceful in his church."

Duff laughed, cackled rather. Then he said very seriously, "I don't think I did." And then, "I don't think *I* did."

"Then who did it? You were caught as you were running from the church."

He seemed honestly bewildered. "I just don't know what happened, Mother." He smiled again. "What else did Father Fogarty tell you? Did he say anything about the history of this place?"

"Why?"

"You know I'm very interested in local history."

"Then perhaps you'd better go to Cainesville and talk with Father Fogarty yourself."

"Maybe I'll do that." He picked up his notebook. "Will you excuse me now, Mother?"

"Is it true what that deputy sheriff said, that you visited Mrs. Reddy and Mrs. Weber last night?"

He grinned. "Do you think they'd lie about it?"

I ignored that. "What did you do at their house?"

"Just talked."

"About what?"

"Lots of things." He paused, looking bewildered again. "I really can't remember, Mother. My memory seems to be slipping lately, along with my character."

But then he spoiled that by grinning and turning back to his work. I went out angrily and slammed his door.

He didn't come down for dinner. Afterward, without even clearing the dishes, I collected Stephanie's things and put what wouldn't fit in her suitcase into a couple of shopping bags. Then I got into the car and drove to the Weber place. I knew if I waited to think about it, I wouldn't go.

It was about seven when I turned into their yard. Emil Weber's station wagon wasn't parked in its usual place, but I assumed it was in the garage.

The small boy we had seen on our first visit answered the door. He was the only one at home, he said. Mr. and Mrs. Weber and Mrs. Reddy had gone to Ashland with the policemen in the afternoon and they hadn't come back.

"I'm sorry about your sister's death," I said.

"What sister?"

I had been assuming that he was a son of the Webers, but he only boarded with the family. His name was George Langley; he was ten years old; his father was dead and his mother was in the hospital with TB. He was apparently a foster child and I wondered what sort of court or agency would place him with people like the Webers and Mrs. Reddy.

After we chatted for a couple of minutes, George invited me in. With plenty of misgivings, I entered the living room and sat on the sofa, while the boy sat across from me, watching me gravely.

I noticed now how unlived-in the room seemed. How could I ever have thought it a pleasant place? The furniture was probably of better quality than that to be found in the average local farmhouse, but there were no books, magazines or newspapers anywhere, no pictures on the walls, or objects of any kind on the mantel. And there was no dirt anywhere, not a speck of dust on the table beside me, and around the edges of the rugs the floors gleamed. If the rest of the house was similar, I thought, it must be a terrible place for a little boy to live.

I asked how he enjoyed being with the Webers.

"Fine," he said guardedly.

"How long have you been here?"

"Since last winter."

"Do you like all the people here?"

"Sure." It wasn't convincing.

"How about Mrs. Reddy?"

"She's OK."

I realized it wasn't fair of me to raise doubts in his mind. Mrs. Reddy could be evil incarnate and still be good to the boy.

"Did they say why they were going to Ashland?"

"They had to identify Stephanie."

That shouldn't take long. They'd probably be coming back at any moment, unless they were being detained for questioning.

"I suppose Mrs. Reddy and Mrs. Weber were very shocked when they were told what happened to Stephanie." It was nasty, but necessary.

George thought for a moment. "Well they didn't cry," he said finally. "Not like I cried when my father died."

"Why do you suppose they didn't cry?"

He thought again. "Maybe they didn't really like Stephanie."

"I wonder why."

"Maybe because she wouldn't go to the meetings."

"What meetings are those?"

"The ones they have here. Would you like to see the meeting room?"

"Yes, very much." Was there time enough before they came home?

We went to the rear of the house. He opened the door of a room adjoining the dining room, switched on a light, and held the door for me. I entered fearfully, not knowing what to expect.

The room was larger than the living room and shrouded in black velvet. There was no furniture and the light was coming from recessed lamps above the velvet draperies. Then the boy turned a dimmer switch, increasing the illumination, and I saw the thing I dreaded, but strangely half-expected to see.

It was a large photograph hanging on the rear wall. It was of General Duffin Caine, and it had apparently been made from the same negative as the one in Father Fogarty's book. Evidently the priest was wrong in his speculation about graven images.

"When do they have their meetings here?" My voice was quavering.

"At night."

"How often?"

"About one time in a month. Sometimes more often."

"Who comes to the meetings?"

"Lots of people. I don't know them."

"Ten, twenty people?"

"Sometimes more than that."

"Who's in charge of the meetings?"

"Mrs. Reddy. She's in charge of everything."

"What about the Webers?"

"Mrs. Weber goes to all the meetings. Some of the time Mr. Weber doesn't go. He sits in the kitchen and drinks beer. Then Mrs. Reddy yells at him."

A sudden chilling thought struck me. "Did you ever go to a meeting, George?"

"Once."

"What happened?"

"Everybody prayed."

"Were they praying to God, do you think?"

He paused. "I think it was more like they were praying to that picture up there."

"Do you know who that man is?"

"They call him Father." He paused again. "Maybe he's supposed to be God."

"How did you happen to go to the meeting, George? Did you sneak in?"

"No, Mrs. Reddy told me to come."

"Did you pray with the rest of them?"

"No, I didn't know the words. A lot of it was in a foreign language. Also after a while it was sort of like they were praying to me." He grinned.

"Praying to you?"

"Yeah. They made me stand over there under the picture. Next to the table with the candles on it." He pointed to a folded table, black like the draperies, and resting against the wall. "Then they all bowed to me and said a lot more prayers." He was embarrassed now. "They take their clothes off at those meetings."

Another frightening thought. "Was there a meeting here last night, George?"

"Yes."

A car came into the yard. George moved quickly to turn out the lights, then grabbed my hand and pulled me out of the room.

"They can see the lights from outside if they go into the back-yard," he whispered. "There are windows behind the curtains." He closed the door of the meeting room and hurried me to the front of the house.

"They can't drive to the back, George," I assured him. "My car is in the way. Let me ask you one more question. Did you see a boy here last night—a boy with light hair, rather thin and tall?"

I was waiting for a car door to slam, footsteps on the path, the scratching of a key in the lock, but there was no sound. Were they waiting outside for me?

"Was he at the meeting, George?" I whispered.

He had only time to nod and then the door opened silently and Mrs. Reddy and Mrs. Weber were there. Both were dressed in black—coats, dresses and hats with veils.

"Mrs. Caine, how nice of you to come," said Mrs. Reddy.

"I brought Stephanie's things," I said.

"Thank you. Did our George make you comfortable?" She was watching the boy.

"Very comfortable." I hoped I was managing to control my nervousness. "I'm shocked and so sorry about what happened to Stephanie."

Rose Weber acknowledged it with a jerk of her head and hurried out of the room. She was feeling something, it seemed.

"Stephanie was a willful girl, but dear to all of us just the same," Mrs. Reddy announced. "How long have you been here, Mrs. Caine?"

"Only a couple of minutes."

"We called your home from Ashland almost an hour ago and your daughter said you had left. You must have stopped somewhere else before you came here."

"I did," I lied. I couldn't have been gone an hour. More like a half hour or at most forty-five minutes.

"Did George show you the house while you waited?"

"No," I said without looking at the boy. "What were you calling about, Mrs. Reddy?"

"Oh, Rose wanted to ask about Stephanie's things and if the Sheriff's men had been to see you."

"Yes, they came to see us." How could I have ever thought her cheerful looking? A little old Mrs. Santa Claus, I'd called her. This was a fat, evil-looking woman staring at me.

"Asked you a lot of questions, I'll bet. They did with us. We couldn't tell them anything and I don't suppose you could either."

"Very little."

"One thing they kept harping on was did Stephanie ever

mention being afraid of anyone or anything? Did they ask you that too?"

"I don't recall. What did you mean when you said Stephanie was willful?"

"Just that. She ran around with a wild crowd from over Ashland way."

"She didn't do any running around while she was with us. She seldom left the house. And the deputies mentioned some motorcyclists."

"It wasn't motorcyclists. It was some of that college crowd from Ashland that did it. They're on the dope. Most likely Stephanie was too."

"Ma!" Rose Weber had reentered the room.

"It's hard to accept these things, Rose, but we must. Stephanie wouldn't do as we told her, so she came to grief."

"What did you want her to do?" I inquired.

Mrs. Reddy looked at me for a long moment. "Why, we wanted her to stay home more for one thing. We wanted her to come home after she was finished with the job at your house, but she wouldn't do it."

"How did you know she was finished?"

"Why, she called and told us." Mrs. Reddy seemed bewildered by my questions.

"I thought maybe my son had told you."

"The only times we've seen your son is when you've been with him."

"Except for last night."

"That's right, of course. Did George tell you Duff was here?" George was still in the room, watching us.

"No, Duff told me. Also the deputies."

"Ah."

"I must apologize for Duff's dropping in on you that way."

"No need. He's more than welcome—the more so now that poor Stephanie is gone." She turned to George. "You get to bed now, sonny. School tomorrow. Say good night to Mrs. Caine."

He went off quickly, throwing one worried glance back at me. Mrs. Reddy nodded to her daughter and Rose followed the boy.

I wasn't concerned that he would say anything about our visit to the meeting room. He seemed as much in fear of these people as I was. I resolved to get him away from this house before we went back East. Surely the authorities wouldn't permit him to stay once they were informed about what was going on.

Emil Weber came in then. He, at least, had been weeping. His eyes were red and his lower lip was quivering. He had also been drinking.

"Whatever took you so long out there, Emil dear?" his mother-in-law asked.

"I was checking the oil in the car. Making sure it's OK in case we have to go back to the . . . you know . . ."

I expressed my sympathy. He took my hand, clutched it and began to sob. The poor lout was a victim here as much as young George, I thought.

"You'll have to move the car. Mrs. Caine wants to leave," Mrs. Reddy told him sharply.

I wanted to stay longer and hopefully learn more, but I couldn't think of any excuse to do it.

"Is there anything else I can do?"

"If there is, we'll call you."

"When is the funeral?"

"There won't be a funeral. We're not churchgoing people. Stephanie's body will be cremated when the coroner gets through with it."

"I think that's the best way," I said. "A funeral and the visitation time before it can be gruesome. My husband told me of the difficulties that occurred before Aunt Hannah's funeral."

"There weren't any difficulties so far as I know."

"About where she was to be buried."

"Oh, that. Just a misunderstanding." She had taken my arm and was practically pushing me out the door.

"Who *was* buried in the Caine graveyard recently, Mrs. Reddy? We've noticed some newly turned earth."

"I don't know anything about it. I haven't been near that yard for a long time. Goodbye, Mrs. Caine. We'll be in touch with you."

I went to my rented car while Emil backed out into the

road. Then it occurred to me that if Emil was sober enough, I might learn more from him than from anyone else. I backed out quickly and blocked his car before he could turn into the drive. Then I got out and walked over to his car.

He rolled down his window and stared belligerently at me. He wasn't weeping now but he had evidently had some more to drink. There was a bottle beside him on the seat.

"What do you want?" he demanded.

"I'd like to talk to you sometime, Mr. Weber."

"What about?"

"Oh, about Stephanie and other things."

"What about Stephanie?"

"Well, I know she was a good girl and I just thought—"

"She was a good girl! You're damn right she was a good girl!"

"Could we go somewhere and talk now, Mr. Weber? Maybe you could follow me back to the Caine place."

The porch light came on and Mrs. Reddy opened the front door.

"Get out of here," Weber hissed. "Get away!"

"Maybe I could help you, Mr. Weber."

He turned his head to glance at the motionless figure on the porch, then turned back to me. He was thoroughly frightened now. "Get away, get away! And keep your boy away!"

Chapter Twelve

I returned to my car and backed off. The station wagon shot into the drive, tires squealing, while Mrs. Reddy remained on the porch, watching me. Bravely I thumbed my nose at her and drove off.

It was after eight o'clock as I started for the farm, although it seemed darker than it ought to be at that time with daylight saving and on an early autumn night. The country along there is heavily wooded, and although there are a few other farmhouses, none of them seemed to be lighted that night.

It was only about a mile and a half to the Caine farm, but that night it seemed much farther than that. I was driving fast but carefully. The road was dry and level most of the way, and without many turns in it. I should've reached the farm in under five minutes, but I didn't, or at least it seemed that I didn't.

There were no other cars traveling in either direction, an oddity, because the road, although unpaved beyond the Caine farm, is a much used route to Cainesville. I was nervous, and grew more so when I couldn't find familiar landmarks. Both sides of the road were in complete darkness now. The only thing I could see was the macadam road in front of me.

I kept glancing every few seconds at the seat beside me, half-expecting the man to be there, although reason told me he couldn't be. For one thing, if he and Duff were the same person and Duff wasn't with me, then neither could the man be. But how did I know Duff wasn't with me? He could have hidden in the back of the car while I was in the Weber house.

I turned to look at the back seat, but it was impossible to see anything back there. Surely much more than five minutes had passed now and I still wasn't home. I slowed down a bit and tried to read my watch, holding it beneath the dashboard light, but the minute hand didn't seem to have moved at all.

Then I heard the voice—definitely heard it—it wasn't in my head. It was a man's voice, not Duff's voice, and not much like *his* voice as I had heard it in the kitchen either. This time it was less guttural and more resonant, and the sound rose and fell as though borne on a wind. "Maggie . . . Maggie," it called and sometimes it was loving, beseeching, and sometimes it was a question as though the caller was seeking me. "Maggie? Maggie?"

Now I saw him. He was riding beside me on a black horse, coming abreast of me now and then—unbelievably considering the speed of the car—pulling ahead. The horse was savage-looking, with wild red eyes and foam flying from its mouth. I pushed hard on the gas pedal. The horse and its rider fell back, but it was only seconds before the horse's head was up to my window again.

The man was in uniform, although it wasn't quite the uniform of the photograph. Now his dark blue coat was torn and mud spattered. His boots were even muddier and the badge on his black slouch hat was green with tarnish.

He was hunched over the neck of the racing horse, gripping the reins tightly, but he wasn't watching the road. He was watching me and grinning. The voice kept calling my name, but his lips weren't moving.

I prayed for another car to appear in his lane or mine, but the road remained empty except for the two of us. The speedometer said eighty-five, then ninety and still he kept up. It was impossible, I knew. I've ridden a lot of horses myself and I knew no horse could run that fast. It was impossible, too, that I hadn't reached the Caine farm. At that speed I should've been there in two minutes or less.

The next time I looked he was pointing with a gloved hand, not at me but at the side of the road ahead of me. I turned away and looked back and he was still pointing. He was insistent now, no longer grinning, but jabbing his finger as though he wanted me to go in that direction.

I thought he was pointing to the farm lane. I still couldn't see anything on either side of the road, but I took my foot off the gas pedal and braked, preparing to turn. Immediately the horse and rider shot ahead, led me for a moment, and then, maybe forty yards away, he wheeled the horse to face me. He was still pointing, to his left now, and a bit in front of him.

As I was about to turn the wheel—was, in fact, in the act of turning—I noticed, unexplainably, the aspirin bottle that the girl had given me in the afternoon. I reached over and took the bottle from the dashboard ledge, and then straightened the wheel quickly, heading straight at the man and horse.

I heard the horse scream as he reared. His legs and belly filled the windshield—then there was nothing. I braked to a stop a few yards beyond and sat there trembling uncontrollably for several minutes.

The night had cleared. After a while I looked in the rearview mirror, and although I could see through the rear window now, there was no sign of the horse and its rider. If I had hit them—as it seemed I had to have done, although I had felt no collision—I must have hurled them off the road.

I opened the door and looked back. A few yards behind me —surely where he had wanted me to turn—was a bridge with a rickety iron railing and a twenty-foot drop to the creek that bordered the Caine farm.

When a car came up behind me, braked and swerved and its driver leaned out and cursed me, I managed to start the Plymouth and drive the remaining couple of hundred yards to the Caine house. I got out and left the car near the front door. I couldn't bring myself to drive it out to the barn where it was usually parked.

Franny heard me and opened the door while I was fumbling with the key.

"What's that in your hand, Mother?" she said.

I couldn't speak for a moment. "The key," I said finally.

"No, the other hand."

It was the aspirin bottle. I put it in my coat pocket. "It's just an old bottle that was in the car," I said.

"Why are you trembling?"

"Cold."

"It's not that cold, is it?"

"Maybe I'm catching something. Where's Duff?"

"Upstairs. Dad's in his room writing."

"Has Duff been in the house all evening?"

"As far as I know. I've been here in the living room most of the time, so if he came down he must have done it very quietly. Oh, by the way, you had a call from Gainesville, from Father Jackson. He left his number. Golly, you're really going in for religion in a big way, aren't you."

I didn't answer her, but went out to the kitchen and turned on all the lights. Then I bolted the back door and sat at the kitchen table for a while until I had regained some composure.

I wondered if he was in the house now. If he wasn't, would bolted doors keep him out? What should I do then? Get myself a crucifix or a Bible? I already had the holy water. Had that saved me or was it my own instincts?

Shit, I thought, absolute shit. I took the bottle out of my pocket, opened the door of the wood stove and threw the bottle in. Then I sat frightened, certain I had brought calamity on myself.

After a while I went to the telephone and dialed the number

on the pad. Mrs. Guenther answered and summoned Father Jackson.

"It occurred to me that I might have seemed abrupt this afternoon," he said.

"It's all right."

"My apologies anyway." He laughed. "Your daughter told me you were visiting the enemy camp."

"Did she tell you what happened to Stephanie Weber?"

"No." And then after I told him, "My God, I didn't read the paper or watch the six o'clock news tonight from Ashland. Did the police ask any questions about your boy?"

I turned to look for Franny, but she had apparently gone upstairs. "There is no problem in that area right now," I said softly. "It seems that Duff's movements can be accounted for by the Webers and Mrs. Reddy. He apparently spent the evening with them."

"Maybe you'd better keep him away from that house."

"You're the second person tonight to tell me that. Emil Weber was the first."

Father Jackson was silent for a moment. Then he said, "I think we ought to get together and talk about this some more, Mrs. Caine. I'd really like to help you, if I can, even though I don't think there's anything supernatural about your difficulties."

"You should've been with me tonight," I said and hung up. Instantly I regretted it and wondered if I should have told him about what I had seen. Then I decided that really would have convinced him I was crazy.

Was I? Was it some sort of suicidal impulse that had almost caused me to drive my car into the creek and also run it into the ditch when Duff was with me? Was I trying to conceal my motive by imagining I saw the General?

I looked in on Jack. He was in bed, propped up with pillows and scribbling on his legal pad.

"Hi," he said, not even looking at me. "Everything all right?"

"Fine," I said and went upstairs. I'd be far better off unmarried, I thought. For one thing, I wouldn't be at the Caine farm.

And, for another, I wouldn't have Duff. Would that be good? Pass on that. Was he home? Did it matter? Based on what had happened in the past, he could have been away and come in without my knowing it. Then suddenly I remembered that he was afraid of horses, had always been afraid of them. Franny could ride as well as I could, but we could never get Duff on a horse. As far as I knew, it was his one phobia.

Feeling somewhat better, I paused by his bedroom. There was no sound and seemed to be no light. Then the door opened and he looked out.

"Did you want something, Mama?" he asked.

"I was just wondering if you were in bed. Did you go out tonight?"

"No, Mama, did you?"

"Yes, I went to see the Webers and Mrs. Reddy. I wanted to express my sympathy."

"I hope you expressed mine too." He seemed completely sincere.

"I didn't, but you can phone them if you like." Then something compelled me to say, "I wonder if the Sheriff knows about what happened between you and Stephanie."

"You didn't tell the deputies?" He was shaken now.

"No, but someone else may have. Stephanie could've mentioned it to someone in her family."

"Well, they wouldn't—"

"How do you know they wouldn't?"

"They would realize I couldn't help—" He backed into his room and tried to close the door.

"What couldn't you help, Duff?" I put my foot in the doorway. "Did you see Stephanie last night, Duff? You know I won't tell anyone. Did you see her and have an argument with her?"

There was a long silence and then he whispered, "I don't know, Mother. I just don't remember." He kicked at my foot until I pulled it away and then he closed the door.

"Duff," I called as softly as I could. "Duff, are you sure you weren't outside a little while ago."

He didn't answer. After a moment or two I went into my bedroom. Franny was in bed studying her geography.

"Feeling better?" she asked brightly. "No," she decided, "you don't look better."

"After I get some sleep I'll be all right," I said. I sat on the edge of the bed, desperately afraid. I was sure now that I was going to be the next one in the house to die.

"I must say we get more sleep here in the country than we ever did at home. Couldn't we get a TV set, Mother?"

"I suppose so. Ask your father."

"I wonder why Aunt Hannah never had one."

"Maybe she and Mrs. Reddy entertained each other."

Franny giggled. "I wonder what two old ladies like that would have to talk about."

I wondered too. And the more I thought about Mrs. Reddy, the more I wondered about Aunt Hannah. Was it possible she didn't know what Mrs. Reddy was, especially when outsiders like Father Fogarty were well acquainted with Mrs Reddy's activities? Maybe it was because of Mrs. Reddy, and not the General, that she had given the money to Father Fogarty for the building of his shrine.

"Don't just sit there, Mother," Franny said. "Get ready for bed."

I did so, going out to the bathroom, which was between our room and Duff's, and returning quickly. Then I locked the door.

"Do you think that's really necessary, Mother?" Franny grumbled. "It seems kind of silly to me. What kind of prowler would want to break into an old house that doesn't even have a TV set?"

"Maybe that's a good reason for not having one," I said. "A roof antenna might make an isolated farmhouse more tempting."

I turned off the overhead light, leaving only the bed lamp lighted. Then I went to the front window to open it and raise the shade. *He* was outside on the front lawn.

I checked a scream and turned to look at Franny. She had snuggled down with her back to me.

"What are you looking at, Mother?" she asked drowsily.

"The moonlight," I said. I thought later that I should have told her, should have called her to the window to certify my sanity, but I didn't want to frighten her. Also, I should have gone immediately to Duff's room to see if he was still there, but I was afraid to do that.

When I looked out again, the man was closer, not thirty feet away. There was enough moonlight to make him clearly visible. He was still in the same uniform and he wasn't grinning or leering at me now, but watching me gravely.

I was as frightened as before, but something compelled me to remain by the window. I pulled up a chair and sat down, and when I looked again, he had moved even closer. Franny called me two or three more times, and each time I answered that I was coming to bed. Finally she went to sleep.

I must have sat there for an hour or more, watching him as he watched me. Gradually I began to realize how handsome he was. His face was long and thin, with high cheekbones and deep-set eyes. Without the beard it was much like Duff's face.

"What do you want?" I remember whispering once, forming the words with my lips.

If he could read the question, he didn't answer it.

He began to seem more slender now too, and younger. This man I could imagine as the heroic cavalry leader; I thought he must have looked like this when he entered the army, before the tribulations of war had their effect on him. The man I had seen before was gross and he shambled when he walked. This man, I knew, would be graceful in everything he did.

After a while, still in the chair, I went to sleep and dreamed things I will not repeat.

Book Three

Chapter Thirteen

Father Jackson came to see me the next morning. It was close to eleven, and I was standing in the front room staring out the window when he drove up in an old Ford with rust holes in its panels and fenders.

Franny and Duff had gone to school, or rather I should say that Duff got on the bus with his sister. There was no way of knowing if he was actually going to school after the bus reached Cainesville, but I wasn't worrying about things like that for the moment.

Jack was fiddling with Franny's portable radio, trying to get some fresh news about Stephanie's murder. The hourly newscasts from the Ashland station had been little more than summaries of what the deputies had told us, except that the two twelve-year-old boys who had found Stephanie were identified, and on the most recent newscast Jack and I were named as her employers. It was also stated that we had failed to report her disappearance to the authorities.

"Really top-notch reporting," I said. "Why don't they say that we told her family and it was they who failed to tell anyone else?"

"We're the outsiders," Jack said. "It's easier to blame us."

I saw the rattletrap car then and went to the door. Father Jackson came in hesitantly, wearing a flashy plaid jacket that looked as if it had been selected in the dark from a rack at the Salvation Army. Jack showed his surprise when I introduced our visitor as a priest.

"I thought if you weren't busy we could take a run over to

Ashland and see a man at the college there," Father Jackson said.

"Why? What man?" Jack wanted to know.

"Father Jackson and I are doing some research on the history of the area," I said.

"I thought that was Duff's bag."

"Well I'm interested too. Do you mind?"

"Not as long as you're being accompanied by a clergyman." He winked at Father Jackson. "Of course after what I've been told lately about some of you fellas . . ."

Father Jackson reddened and grinned feebly. I took his arm and ushered him out the door. There wasn't any conversation for a while as we started off for Ashland. For one thing, talk was difficult since the car needed a muffler too.

"This is an anthropologist we're going to see," Father Jackson shouted. "Dr. Horace Tully. He's supposed to know a lot about the local weirdos. Father Fogarty suggested him." He turned to me and grinned. Left unvoiced was the suggestion that Father Fogarty was a weirdo himself.

"It can't hurt, I suppose," I shouted back. "Also, it gets me out of the house. I'll go along with almost anything that will do that."

"You and your husband don't get along too well, I take it."

"That is a subject in no way related to the one in hand. Also, it's not my husband I'm afraid of in that house."

"Tell me what you meant by that remark of yours when you hung up on me last night."

I told him what had happened on the road, not dramatizing it but just relating it in a few sentences. Then I told him about my conversation with the boy at the Webers' and about seeing the meeting room. For some reason I was reluctant to mention seeing the man outside my window.

"Well, I'm sure the meeting room wasn't a hallucination anyway," Father Jackson said.

"Damn you, I was almost killed."

"I'm sure it was very real to you, Mrs. Caine. You had an experience. I never doubt an experience, only its causes."

"One thing I forgot to mention yesterday. When I asked Duff about his nightmare the night his father was injured, he said that he had been dreaming of seeing a man on a horse." Then I knew instantly what Father Jackson's response was going to be.

"That could've suggested the horseman to you."

"Oh, to hell with it," I yelled. "Turn back, please. Why are we going to see this man if you don't believe anything I tell you?"

"I repeat, it's only the causes I doubt." After a while he added, "You know as a Catholic you don't have to believe in the devil, Mrs. Caine."

"I'm not a Catholic!"

"As a Christian then. There's nothing in the Bible that demands it. If Satan does exist, why isn't his creation mentioned in the Book of Genesis, where all the other important acts of creation are listed?"

"I don't know." My head was beginning to ache from the roaring of the motor and the bouncing of the car. It seemed to have no springs either.

"You could bring up the Apocrypha—the Book of Enoch, for example, where we read about the war in heaven and the fallen angels—but there is nothing in the Old Testament proper that can be used as evidence for the existence of devils. Moreover there is nothing in the New Testament either—including the temptation of Christ on the mountain—that can't be explained in terms of pure symbolism."

"Or the desire of the authors to entertain their readers."

He laughed. "You think you're being clever and antireligious, but there may be a lot of truth in what you suggest. The apostles were writing for simple, half-primitive people who probably believed in dragons as well as devils. Who knows, Matthew, Mark, Luke and John may have believed in them too."

"Help me, please help me," I said as he parked the car.

"I'll do my best."

"I mean other than just praying for me."

He squeezed my arm. "I don't know what else I'm good for, but I'll try."

We went up to the college administration building. It was an attractive little campus, despite the older part of it being a bit too red-brick New England. A sign said that the college had been founded in 1878. In the General's heyday, I thought.

A girl in the administration building directed us to Dr. Tully's office.

"He's expecting us," Father Jackson said. "He has a class that's over at eleven and it's after that now."

Dr. Tully was in his office, but meeting with a student, when we arrived. We waited in the hall until a fat girl in jeans came out and Dr. Tully invited us into the tiny office. It took some maneuvering for both of us to squeeze into the two chairs between the bookcase and the desk.

"This used to be a broom closet," said Dr. Tully, chuckling, "until they decided they needed a larger room for the brooms." He was a small man with a large bald head. He reminded me of the Wizard of Oz in the Denslow illustrations for the Baum book that I had read as a child.

"You are an anthropologist," Father Jackson began.

"I am an associate professor of sociology at this institution, but my academic inclinations are toward social anthropology, yes."

"You've made a study of witchcraft and magic, that sort of thing."

"In a fairly narrow and specialized way. I've been mostly concerned with the legends and superstitions of the Middle West, although some investigations have taken me into southern border states. West Virginia, Tennessee, Kentucky . . ."

"Do you believe in the devil, Dr. Tully?" I asked.

He smiled and rubbed the top of his head. "I believe there are people who have experienced devils."

Father Jackson glanced smugly at me. "We especially wanted to talk with you about a man who lived in this area many years ago. General Duffin Caine."

Dr. Tully's smile became broader and he rubbed his head more vigorously. "Ah," he said, "General Caine. A dreadful man. Positively horrifying. Of course I must apologize to this lady—"

"He was my husband's ancestor," I said, "and no apology is needed. I'm sure you know a lot more about General Caine than we do."

"I know a good deal, yes, but there's a lot more I don't know and would like to find out. Are you living in the Caine house?"

"Temporarily," I said.

"Ah. I visited there several times when Miss Hannah Caine was alive—or rather I should say I called there. She would never permit me to enter and she was never willing to answer any questions about her father."

"Did you ever talk with her housekeeper?"

"Indeed I did. Or, I should say, I spoke and she listened—very briefly. On the occasions when Mrs. Reddy answered the door, I invariably received no reply at all. The door was always instantly slammed before I could finish asking to see Miss Caine."

"Do you know about Mrs. Reddy's other activities?" Father Jackson asked.

"Oh, yes, indeed. I even attended a religious ceremony at her house, but that was before she knew who I was. When she discovered that my interest in the proceedings was of an academic nature, she urged me to leave. But now let me ask you a question, Mrs. Caine. Have you been visited by the General?"

I looked at Father Jackson, then nodded.

"Ah, ah." Dr. Tully rubbed with both hands now. "You see, I am a detective. It had to be more than curiosity or you would not have come here with your priest."

"He's not my priest."

"We're friends," Father Jackson said.

"Wonderful. Have you had lunch yet? Let me take you both to lunch."

"It will be my treat," I said.

"No, no, I insist. You can't know how delighted I am to meet someone who has seen General Caine."

He locked his office and led us out to his car, a vintage Volkswagen almost as battered as Father Jackson's Ford. He had to rearrange several stacks of books, taking those from the front seat and floor and adding them to the ones in the back. Then there wasn't much room for Father Jackson, who sat squeezed into one corner of the rear seat.

Dr. Tully didn't ask for our preference or tell us where he was taking us, but with a rattle and a roar to equal the Ford, set off in jackrabbit bounds down the exact center of the street, challenging traffic on both sides. He is known here, I thought, that is our only hope.

The restaurant turned out to be a health food establishment, The Realm of Yoga. I shuddered when I saw the sign. Those places have always turned me off. I always wonder if some of the fertilizer has been left on the vegetables, maybe in fear of losing something organic.

The Indian proprietor greeted Dr. Tully warmly—he should have, we were the only patrons—and bowed us to a table. I ordered a fruit salad (when in doubt, always stick with peeled fruit) and Father Jackson chose a vegetable curry. Our host had something that looked like dark gray pancakes, over which he poured half a large container of honey.

It was several minutes, during which we had a lecture from Dr. Tully on diet and health, before we got around to the subject we had come to discuss. I told Dr. Tully about the three times I had seen General Caine, again omitting the fourth time when he appeared on the front lawn. Dr. Tully listened with great interest, interrupting only to ask for a more detailed description of the General's features and clothing.

"This is the first time I've heard about General Caine being seen on horseback," he said when I finished, "although your description of the horse tallies with what I've learned about the General's black Arabian mare."

"He has been seen before, then?" Father Jackson said dubiously.

"Oh, yes. I've never before actually spoken with anyone who has seen him, but there are plenty of stories about appearances through the years."

"But none recently?" Father Jackson persisted.

"The last one I know of occurred about five years ago. It involved a Mrs. Henry Danforth, who used to live on your road, Mrs. Caine. Mrs. Danforth told several people that she had seen the General one night. He apparently was standing in front of the Caine house as she drove past. She described him much as you have, including the uniform. Unfortunately she and her husband sold their place and moved away before I heard about the incident. I've written her several times, but she hasn't answered any of my letters."

Father Jackson pushed his chair back. "That doesn't prove very much, does it," he said.

"I think it proves that she doesn't want to discuss the incident," said Dr. Tully agreeably.

"And where else has the General been seen?" I asked.

"Mostly on the road near the house or on the property somewhere. Very few people in this area have ever been inside that house, you know, Mrs. Caine. Your husband's aunt wasn't much for visitors of any sort. And, incidentally, if it's at all possible, I should like . . . sometime . . ."

"Of course," I said. "Come anytime—while we're there. Hopefully that won't be much longer."

"You might tell Dr. Tully about Stephanie Weber," Father Jackson suggested. "Also, about your visit to the Weber house."

I was reluctant to say anything about Stephanie, because I didn't want to talk about Duff. Of course I had mentioned that he was present the first two times I had seen the General—or that he was on the scene either before or afterward—but I hadn't said anything about the accident or his other troubles.

"Stephanie Weber, Mrs. Reddy's granddaughter, lived with us for several months, taking care of my husband after he fell and broke his leg," I said. "You've probably heard that she was found murdered yesterday." Then I told him about going to the Weber house and seeing the meeting room and the General's portrait.

"I've been in that room," Dr. Tully said. "That's where I attended the Black Mass."

"I'd like to go to one sometime," said Father Jackson. "Just out of curiosity."

"I wouldn't, if I were you," Dr. Tully said. "They're a bit obscene and also it might be dangerous for you, if it was discovered you're a priest. Whether or not you accept the supernatural, some of those people do seem to have extraordinary sensory powers. Now will you have dessert? I can recommend the pawpaw compote and the sesame pudding."

When we declined he ordered the compote himself and went on, "I saw the headline about the girl in a newspaper, but I didn't realize who she was."

I told him what the deputies had revealed about the murder, and then Father Jackson asked him if he thought it might be related to the activities of her mother and grandmother.

"It's quite possible. Human sacrifice used to be a part of the ritual in the past, and these people could have taken it up again if they thought they could get away with it. It's also possible that the girl was killed by General Caine himself, acting independently of Mrs. Reddy and her associates, although they may have summoned him."

"Summoned him from where?" Father Jackson inquired.

"Where do such beings usually reside, according to the teachings of your religion?"

"Oh, come on." Father Jackson looked at me. "I was hoping that Dr. Tully could help us make some sense of all this."

"I should like to very much," said Dr. Tully, eating his compote.

"To commit a physical act, General Caine would need some sort of physical body, wouldn't he?" I said.

"Seemingly."

I hesitated. It seemed monstrous to even consider such things. "His own body seems to have been dug up from the Caine graveyard," I said finally.

"Has it? Has it indeed?" Dr. Tully was so excited that he spilled some of his mint tea. "Now that brings us to something I've neglected to investigate, the possibility of a connection between the appearances of General Caine and the exhumation of his body. The interesting thing is that there were apparently no appearances for a number of years between the early 1920s and the early 1960s—the time when Miss Hannah Caine was in good health and able to keep a watch on the place. Then, about 1962, she became bedridden a good part of the time and it was then she employed Mrs. Reddy."

"And when was the next supposed appearance of the General?" asked Father Jackson.

"According to the stories I've collected, it may have been that same summer. I'll have to check my records, but I think it was in August, 1962, that a fifteen-year-old boy named McDaniels saw a man fitting the description of General Caine in the woods near the Caine farm. The boy was setting muskrat traps in a creek and he saw a man in a Civil War uniform standing on the bank watching him."

Dr. Tully had been mopping up his spilled tea and he waited now until the proprietor brought him a fresh pot. "Now then," he said, "it seems obvious that the General needs a body of some sort for these visits. He doesn't seem to be a spirit. It's nothing of an ectoplasmic nature. He's never diaphanous and trailing vapors, that sort of thing. Am I right, Mrs. Caine? No, he just appears in solid human form and then apparently walks away. No one has ever reported seeing him vanish into thin air."

"What about last night?" I said. "I drove my car right through the horse and rider."

"It may have seemed so at the moment, but maybe the rider pulled up the horse and avoided the car at the last instant. Maybe you closed your eyes for a couple of seconds."

I had to admit it was possible. It would have been the normal reaction, frightened as I was. But the horse had been so close. I could still see it rearing, seemingly not ten feet away and almost directly in front of me. Maybe I did close my eyes then, but could the horse have been swung away with the car that close?

"You think it was a real horse then too?"

"Oh, undoubtedly. If it was there at all, it was real. I've never heard of a ghost horse." Dr. Tully chuckled. "That's something that ought to be fairly easy to check on. There aren't that many horses around here anymore."

"And the rider?" I asked.

"It could well have been General Caine. But according to what the members of his sect believe, not General Caine in his own body. In someone else's body."

"You'd better tell Dr. Tully the rest of the story about Duff," Father Jackson said.

So I told him about the trouble in school and the car accident and the rest of it, including the attacks on Franny and Stephanie.

"But Duff can't ride a horse," I concluded lamely.

"But General Caine could, and very well too, from all accounts," said Dr. Tully. "This is very interesting. Now let me tell you something else I've learned about the apparent comings of the General. They've usually occurred in periodic sequences over the years and each sequence has been marked by other unusual happenings as well. There have been other murders like

Stephanie Weber's and other violent deaths, often explained as suicides. Most of these deaths occurred between the 1870s and the early 1900s. Most of the murder victims were young women and the crimes were usually unsolved. The suicides generally were young men, teenagers like your son or a bit older.

"Many people linked the suicides to the murders and decided that the young men had killed the girls and then in remorse killed themselves. The last such combination of murder and suicide occurred about five years ago, within a week or two after Mrs. Danforth saw the General. The body of a young girl was found in an alley in Cainesville. You must remember the case, Father. A couple of weeks later a nineteen year old boy, a sophomore here at Ashland College, cut his throat. His name was Carrothers and I think his father's farm is on the next road north of the Caine road."

"I remember both deaths," said Father Jackson, "but I don't remember that anyone ever made a connection between the two."

"I did," said Dr. Tully, "but, to be honest with you, it was only a moment ago. The conjunction of murders and suicides and visitations by General Caine has occurred to me before as a possible line of investigation, but until you told me about your son Duff, Mrs. Caine, I hadn't associated the deaths of Howard Carrothers and Lydia Graham, the girl who was murdered in Gainesville."

"And what made you think of it now?" I asked.

"Your saying that you thought Duff had been attending the ceremonies at the Weber house. You see, Howard Carrothers had been going there too, or at least he was there the night I attended. He came in late and recognized me, and that's when I was asked to leave."

"Are you suggesting that now that Stephanie has been killed, Duff will commit suicide?" In my alarm I was speaking too loudly and I saw the proprietor come out of the kitchen and look toward our table.

"No, no, I'm only telling you the pattern as I see it. You must do all in your power to prevent the pattern from being completed this time. Incidentally, there are other similarities in the two cases. I didn't know Howard Carrothers well—he was never a student of mine, although I had seen him on campus —but I remember one of his professors telling me about how Howard had changed during the last few weeks of his life. He had been a good student, but he became surly and began to neglect his work. Also, his appearance changed. He became older looking and stronger and he turned into a troublemaker. He was accused of assaulting a truck driver here in Ashland and breaking the man's jaw."

"And you think that this boy and all those who committed suicide in the past were possessed in some way by the ghost—or spirit or whatever—of General Caine?" Father Jackson asked.

"I believe that for a time they may have become General Caine—or that they thought they had, which may be the same thing in the end."

"No, it's not the same thing at all," said the priest. "Thinking it, I can accept."

"I meant only in the consequences."

"And now you believe that Duff becomes General Caine at times, or thinks he has?" I said.

Dr. Tully nodded. "How much do you know about the General's life?" he asked as he sipped his tea.

"Not much, except what Duff has told me, that he was a Civil War hero."

"That's true. Apparently he contributed a lot at times to some Union victories, and at other times helped to lessen the consequences of Union defeats. However, he was also threatened with a court-martial. Did Duff tell you that?"

"No."

"He was. For what today we call war crimes. It seems he was in the habit of torturing and killing prisoners and also Southern civilians. He was warned several times about these activities, but apparently he was so good in the field that his superiors tended to overlook the other things—until he became too flagrant, or else some of his men started to complain. Then he was captured by the Confederates and the charges against him were dropped. You won't find these things in history books, but I've read letters sent home by local boys in which some of the General's nasty

habits are described. One time during the battle of Murfrees-
boro he set fire to a barn in which a squad of Confederates was
trapped. Then he ordered his men to shoot them as they ran
from the barn trying to surrender. Another time he hanged a
farmer and his two sons because they wouldn't salute the Union
flag. There were other similar episodes, some of them mentioned in a collection of letters here at the college."

"Maybe you should bring Duff over and let him read them,"
said Father Jackson.

"I doubt it would do any good," Dr. Tully said. "If he happened
to be thinking as General Caine, he'd probably be pleased by the
letters. Anyway, after the war the General came back here to
Ashland County and continued his infamous practices. He built
the present Caine farmhouse and began conducting ceremonies
there, evidently similar to the kind Mrs. Reddy conducts today."

"Where in the Caine house?" I asked.

"I don't know that. And I don't know who else attended
the ceremonies, although I assume his mistress, Margaret
Dorn, did. There couldn't have been very many people of his
persuasion around here in that fundamentalist age. In fact, the
General's devil worshiping and his other activities soon became
scandalous. He was accused of seducing several local girls and
of shooting and killing the father of one of them.

"He was acquitted on that charge on the grounds of self-
defense, but I think his war heroics saved him. The local newspapers of his day were seemingly reluctant to say anything
but good about him. And during his lifetime there were a half
dozen unsolved murders in this area—in addition to the possible murder of his mistress, Margaret Dorn—but he was never
charged in any of those cases.

"Earlier, when he was about forty, he went to Columbus
and brought back a wife. She had two children by him and died
within a few years. The General sent the children away to be
raised in an institution—the one decent act of his life, as far as
I know, but he did it undoubtedly only to be rid of them. Then
after he died and the house had been vacant for a good many
years, his daughter Hannah went back there to live. But you're
familiar with that part of the story, Mrs. Caine."

"No, I know very little about Aunt Hannah's life. My husband didn't keep in touch with her, and he evidently wasn't told very much by his father or his grandfather."

"What do you think Mrs. Caine ought to do now?" Father Jackson asked.

"Get her son away from here."

"I've been trying to do that, but it's proving difficult. My husband has settled in here."

"Is he aware of everything that's happened?" Dr. Tully asked.

"Almost everything. And he doesn't believe some of the things I've told him. Also, how can I force Duff to leave if he refuses to go? He'd probably just move out of the house and in with Mrs. Reddy. Moreover, he has a court appearance coming up here in Ashland on the traffic and assault charges."

"Well, that should be fairly soon. The dockets here aren't that cluttered," said Dr. Tully.

"You're convinced that Duff is possessed then," said Father Jackson.

"On the evidence I've been given, yes, possessed by something—not necessarily a devil. But if you're proposing exorcism, I would very much like to attend the ceremony, Father."

"I wasn't about to propose it," Father Jackson said.

"Couldn't the police be informed of what's going on at the Webers'? Couldn't Mrs. Reddy be stopped?" I asked.

"I doubt that you could get the police to believe that Mrs. Reddy is a dangerous person. A lot of people know of her activities and some of them consider her a witch, but the general attitude is that she's harmless. The people who have been frightened of her—and of the General—have usually just moved away. And that's what the authorities would probably advise you to do—keep your son away from Mrs. Reddy or else move out of the area."

Dr. Tully paid the check, waving off the protests that neither Father Jackson nor I were about to make, and we left the restaurant. Then he drove us back to where Father Jackson's car was parked.

"I really would like to visit the Caine farmhouse," he said.

"Call us before you come," I said.

He waved and drove off, then made a U-turn and came back.

"There is one thing you can do," he yelled. "If you can find the General's remains, I would destroy them—or at least rebury them in a safe place."

"Why?" Father Jackson shouted.

"To prevent Mrs. Reddy's using them." He waved again and drove off, heading down the center of the street as before.

Chapter Fourteen

"The man is absolutely mad," Father Jackson said. "I'm sorry I brought you here."

"Well, at least there are two people who don't seem to think I'm crazy—Father Fogarty and Dr. Tully."

"You're not going to get any help from anyone who believes in the occult." We were on our way back to the farm now. "And despite what Tully says about the police, I think you should tell them what you know about Mrs. Reddy."

"I can't do that without bringing Duff into it. And I don't want the police connecting him in any way with the death of Stephanie."

"But if he did do it—"

"If he did, he did! Goddamn it, he's my son!" Then I had another thought. "Do you think Tully will go to the police with all of the things I told him about Duff?"

"I doubt it. It strikes me he's more interested in recording the legends of General Caine than in ending them. Anyway, one thing you've got to do is get psychiatric help for Duff. Even if there are outside forces at work, Duff could be helped to resist them. A good psychiatrist could help to straighten out his thinking, strengthen his will to resist."

"But where can I find someone?"

"Well, not around here certainly. However, I do know someone in Cleveland."

"But if I can't get Duff to go there—"

"You can try. And if you can't, maybe the man could come

here. Maybe he would come for at least an exploratory session. I think this man might be very interested in Duff's case."

"He'd charge a fortune."

"Should that be a consideration now? However, I think I could persuade him to be realistic about his fee, and I could arrange for his lodging. Actually, the man I'm thinking of is my brother."

"Your brother is a psychiatrist?"

"A graduate of Johns Hopkins and the Menninger Clinic. And I'm sure if he can fit it into his schedule, he'll be eager to see Duff."

"My son is a medical curiosity now?"

"Oh, come on."

"Forget Duff for the moment. Do you believe that I have seen General Caine or not?"

After a while he said, "I believe now that you saw someone. I guess Tully convinced me of that much. I still think he's a nut, though. He shouldn't be teaching at Ashland College or anywhere else."

"Why are you so afraid the devil may exist?"

"Don't be ridiculous!"

"It's true." We were shouting again, now not only to be heard above the noise of the car. "You're afraid because you don't want to have to go back to Father Fogarty's kind of traditional beliefs."

"Bullshit!"

"Such language from a priest."

"You drove me to it!"

"Why don't you say 'the devil made me do it'?"

He turned toward me, enormously angry, then suddenly laughed. "I'll go along with what Jim says. If Jim says it's the devil, I'll believe it."

"Jim?"

"My brother. Shall I get in touch with him?"

With some misgivings I agreed. "If Duff confessed anything to him, he wouldn't go to the police, would he?"

"Of course not." And then after a pause, "Although he might suggest that Duff go himself."

That was about the end of the conversation during the drive home. When he stopped the car in the yard, Father Jackson suggested that he would like to meet Duff.

"Not until after he sees your brother, if I can get him to go along with that. I don't want him to think that anyone's putting pressure on him."

"One more thing. Don't take that idiot's advice seriously."

"What advice?"

"You know, about looking for the General's body."

"Oh, that." I got out of the car.

He leaned across the seat. "Don't. You're going to need a psychiatrist yourself if you start believing things like that."

"My husband thinks I need one already."

I stood watching while he went off down the road toward Cainesville. I was angry at him and terribly afraid of what was happening to me as well as to my son. I was also fearful of going back into the ugly monstrosity of a house—and even more fearful of doing what I did. After a few minutes I walked to the back of the house and out to the graveyard.

It was a pleasant autumn afternoon. The cicadas were singing in the oak trees, and bees were swarming around the vines growing wild against the graveyard fence.

There were shoots of green coming through the new earth now. I found a fairly straight tree branch and shoved it into the soil. It went in easily, which seemed to me to indicate that if anything had been buried below, it was now removed.

Then I went to the back of the graveyard and took a close look at the general's headstone. What we had failed to notice earlier was that the stone wasn't lodged in the ground, but merely resting against a pile of rocks and small stones, evidently placed there for the purpose. In fact some of the pile was made from shattered headstones—including, I assumed, the stone from the grave that someone wanted us to think was General Caine's.

Well, if his remains weren't in the graveyard, where were they? At the Weber house? Maybe it wasn't necessary for Mrs. Reddy to have them in her immediate possession in order to make use of them. Maybe all that was necessary was to have them available to her. Therefore maybe the coffin and its contents, or what was left of them, was still on the Caine property.

But where? In the barn or the wagon shed? I walked back to the shed and squeezed in past the wagon and the buggy behind it. There was nothing in or under either one of them except curtains of cobwebs. I overcame my revulsion, brushed aside the cobwebs and lifted the cracked leather buggy seat. Nothing.

And there was nothing on the ground floor of the barn other than the rusting tools we had seen before. There was a ladder leading up to a hayloft, but it had several broken rungs and I was afraid to risk climbing it. In any event it didn't look sturdy enough to support someone carrying or dragging a coffin. Of course another ladder could have been used and then taken away.

Then another thought occurred to me. Maybe the idea wasn't to make the remains available to Mrs. Reddy. Maybe it was only necessary that they be available to Duff. Therefore maybe the coffin was somewhere in the house.

Where in the house? In the storeroom? It certainly could be concealed there easily enough among all the large articles of furniture. I went to the barn door and looked up at the back of the house. For the first time I noticed that the building was easily high enough for a third floor.

But there were no third-floor windows. Could there be another storeroom up there? Maybe that was where the General had worshiped the devil in his day, although he very likely could have held the ceremonies in any part of the house large enough to hold his congregation. Considering his reputation, he probably had never been bothered very much by intruders.

I had moved outside and was still looking up at the house when I heard a footstep on the path. I turned and there was Duff, not six feet away. He stared at me coldly, even menacingly.

"You might have called or said something," I told him when I could speak.

"Why?"

"You frightened me, coming up on me that way."

"What are you doing here?"

"What do you mean?"

"What were you doing in the barn?"

"Duff, don't speak to me that way!"

He blinked and then his expression softened. "Mother?"

"Who did you think it was?"

"My eyes . . ." He rubbed them. "It's the sunlight."

"There isn't that much sun. Where are your glasses?"

"I left them in the house. A lot of the time lately I've been able to see pretty well without them."

"Why aren't you in school?"

"I got off early. My math teacher is sick."

That I could check on. Then I thought, what difference will it make whether he's lying or not? Seemingly I couldn't do anything about it anyway.

"How did you get home?"

"Hitched. A man who lives up the road gave me a ride."

"Duff, would you be willing to see a psychiatrist?"

"What for?"

"To talk about your problems. You'll admit that you have had some, and you can talk about them—or about anything that might be bothering you."

He considered it for a moment, then smiled and said, "Okay, Mama, if it will make you happy. I'll see your shrink."

"Good, I'll have Father Jackson make the appointment." Then I regretted that.

"Who's Father Jackson?"

"The other priest at the church in Cainesville. The psychiatrist is his brother."

"Did you have to bring a priest into it?"

"I just asked him to recommend someone—"

"Did you tell him anything about me?"

"No."

"You did, you liar!" He grabbed my shoulders and shook me. Then he stepped back, horrified, and ran into the house.

I sat on the back steps until I had regained some control and then went in. As usual, Jack was in the front room, writing on his yellow pad.

"You and Duff going around and around again?" he asked without looking up. "I just heard him running upstairs."

"It was nothing unusual." I held my hands behind my back to conceal the trembling. "I got him to agree to see a psychiatrist, but then I think I blew it."

He didn't ask me how. I don't think he even heard what I said. I sat down and picked up the Ashland newspaper. After a while I managed to read that the Sheriff had mounted an all-out effort to solve the murder of Stephanie Weber. Several members of a Cainesville motorcycle gang had been questioned and more members were being rounded up.

Shortly thereafter Father Jackson called. He had spoken with his brother, and Dr. Jackson would be willing to see Duff. Moreover, he was willing to come to Cainesville the next weekend. Could Father Jackson bring him to our house?

I didn't think that was a good idea since Duff was so upset. I told him to take his brother to a Cainesville motel and I'd pay for the room. Then I'd do my best to get Duff there.

"There's something else," Father Jackson said. "I'm convinced now that you really did see a horse and rider on the road last night. I checked with the local grange and got the names of farmers who have riding horses. The fourth one I called owns a horse that fits the description of the one you saw. The man lives on Sycamore Road—that's just east of your road—and listen to this. He says his horse was taken out of his barn last night and returned early this morning."

"Could I see the horse?"

"I was going to suggest it. I'll pick you up again in the morning and we'll go over there." He paused. "Your husband is going to think we're having an affair."

"Good," I said. "I hope he does."

"What's that about a horse?" Jack yelled from the front room.

"I'm thinking of buying one."

"Great. It'll be good exercise for you. Who was on the phone?"

"My lover."

"It was the priest, wasn't it? That's a fine thing to say about a priest."

I went upstairs. Duff's bedroom door was closed, so I went to the storeroom. He wasn't there, but his notebook was on top of the pile of books where I had found it the last time.

He seemed to have written several more pages. Had he left it again for me to read? Then I heard the front door slam and Franny's voice. There was no time to read the book, but I decided to take a quick look for the coffin and also a stairs to the third floor.

There was no coffin in the room, but I did find what I took to be a stairwell. I climbed over furniture and piles of books, moving things away from two walls, before I discovered an irregularity in the third and a locked door. It could've been a large closet, but I was betting it wasn't.

Franny came in then and asked what I was doing.

"Getting dirty and ruining a Pucci pantsuit," I said.

"It's Sears Roebuck and I never liked it on you anyway. What's behind that big cupboard?"

"Tons of dust. I was just checking to see if any of this junk is worth selling. I thought maybe we could have a garage sale—or barn sale, I suppose we'd have to call it here."

"Sell these old books and newspapers too, before Duff gets some rare lung disease from them." She followed me back to the bedroom. "I thought you hated it here, Mama."

"I do."

"It doesn't seem as though you're making any great efforts to get us home."

"I am trying, dear, even though I haven't been successful." I had something else to ask her. "Franny, would you be willing to sleep downstairs for a while? I hate to leave Dad alone down there."

"Since when did you become so concerned about Dad?"

I slapped her and she cried. I told her I knew she hadn't meant the remark and that we were all living under a terrible strain. Of course I knew she was aware that I wasn't madly in love with her father.

"It might be kind of scary sleeping in Steph's room after what happened to her."

"I wouldn't worry about that. After all, it didn't happen in the room. Also, there's a key and you can lock the door."

"Can I play my radio and records down there?"

"As long as you don't disturb your father."

I had a couple of reasons for wanting her downstairs. The first was to have her farther removed from Duff. I didn't really expect him to give her any more trouble, but I thought it best to lessen the opportunities. Also, if she wasn't sleeping in the room with me, I would be freer to conduct my investigations.

Jack pretended to be disappointed that Franny was moving downstairs instead of me. "I was thinking maybe I could come in and join you one of these nights," he said, squeezing my arm.

"Join me for what?"

"You know." He tried to give me one of his slobbery kisses, but I pulled away.

"When you're ready to climb the stairs, I'll be in the first room on the left," I said. It would be a long time before he could manage the stairs, I thought, and an even longer time before he really had the inclination.

After dinner, when Franny's things were moved, I went upstairs and, for Duff's benefit, pretended to be getting ready for bed. I was hoping that fairly soon he would close his door and allow me to pass unnoticed to the storeroom.

I spent an hour or so reading a paperback edition of *The Hobbit* that Franny had left behind. Then I looked into the hallway and saw that his door was closed. I waited another five minutes, then took the key from my door and the flashlight I always carry in my luggage and went quietly to the storeroom.

I was terrified, of course, of prowling that old house in the dark—a house in which a man who had worshiped the devil had once lived, a man who seemingly was still prowling the house himself. However, I had to get to the third floor and see if his coffin was there. I'd worry later about disposing of it and whatever was in it.

But my key wouldn't open the door in the stairwell. A special lock must have been installed, I thought, and if there was a key for it in the house, my son very likely had it.

His notebook was where I had left it, so I took it back to my room. Then I locked the door, turned out the overhead light and went to the window. There was no one in the front yard.

I turned on the bed lamp, got into bed and began to read the notebook. The last entry I had seen was dated July 28. After that there were no dates and no separation of entries, except by the use of pencil and ball-point pen, which I assumed indicated that the writing had been done at different times. Moreover, the handwriting no longer resembled Duff's in the slightest.

For some reason, I wasn't surprised that I was addressed in the first sentence.

This is for you, Margaret. You remember me and I remember you. If recollection sometimes falters, we must continue to remind ourselves who we are and whom we serve.

I am Duffin Caine, late Brigadier General in the Army of the United States. I bow to no man and I acknowledge only one Master. I have served that Master for many years and he has repaid my devotion a thousandfold.

Do you know when I first discovered my Master, Margaret? It was when I was fifteen years old. I was hunting deer and came upon a party of Delaware Indians. There were five of them, and four were bathing in a pool of the creek that bordered my father's farm. Four were bucks and one was a female. The bucks were teasing the girl, trying to induce her to remove her clothing and join them in their nakedness in the pool. She was attempting halfheartedly to hide in the bushes, but she was not disinterested enough to leave the scene, nor was she too shy to peer out from between the fingers with which she was covering her eyes.

I was on a hillside above the creek, unseen by the Indians. I watched them for a while and then an inner voice told me to kill them. I will not say that I felt threatened by the Indians, nor did I think that they were a threat to my family or community. These local Delawares had been Christianized for several years and they were regarded as harmless. Also, I will not say—as it was later thought by some—that I wanted to avenge my brother, who had died at the hands of Delawares many years before. Avenging someone presumes a certain amount of feeling for that person, or at least the feeling that one's own honor has been injured. I never even knew my brother Enoch, and I have never been much concerned with personal or family honor.

No, the voice within me simply said that it would be immensely pleasing to kill the Indians and that I could gain additional pleasure from the girl if I killed her last. And so I began to pick off the bucks. I was an excellent marksman and I could pour powder and ram lead in seconds, so that none of them had the slightest chance to escape. Furthermore I kept moving behind the trees and through the underbrush so that they couldn't identify the source of their doom. Even the last buck to fall was not looking in my direction when the ball entered his heart.

Then I made my way down the hill and across the creek to where the girl crouched. I had my pleasure of her—teasing her the while with the hope that I might spare her life—then cut her throat and made my way home where I told my father that the Indians had attacked me. I had dragged all the bucks and the girl to the bank of the creek and had placed their knives and muskets near their hands, so that my story was not questioned when I returned later with my father and some of the other settlers to bury the bodies. What helped, of course, was the fact that my father and the other men hated Indians. I didn't hate them. I just had no feelings of any kind for them.

And I had no feelings for the Indians or white men I killed later, although I was always careful to avoid difficulties with the authorities. The death of Indians seldom aroused much curiosity or concern, and the white men I dispatched were usually vagabonds, local drunkards or rootless peddlers traveling alone.

Then in my thirty-sixth year the war began, offering me a unique opportunity to pursue my avocation. I had little formal education, but from books borrowed from neighbors I had mastered Latin and Greek and other subjects, and this combined with my equestrian skills and organizational abilities made me officer material. I was commissioned and rose to the rank of major before my first battle.

I made the best use of my opportunities, acquiring a great reputation for valor while at the same time experiencing some of the greatest pleasure I have ever known. Then a foolish mistake caused a charge of unbecoming conduct to be brought against me. I was usually very careful in selecting the officers and men who were to participate with me in the questioning and execution of prisoners, but in this case I picked one or two squeamish fellows who complained about me to divisional headquarters.

Fortunately, before matters proceeded further, I was captured by the Confederates. This was on the 26th of October,

1863, outside Chattanooga, my brigade then being attached to McCook's division, R. B. Mitchell's corps. I was leading a foraging party (unusual work for a general, you might say, but it was on such expeditions that I had some of my most interesting experiences) and the other six members of my party spurred their horses and escaped when we were intercepted by a large contingent of Wheeler's cavalry. I engaged the leaders briefly, felling one rider but taking a deep saber slash in the leg, and then accepted capture. Philosophically, I assumed that confinement in a Confederate prison might be infinitely more preferable than the consequences of a court-martial, and as it turned out, my life as a prisoner was not without its rewards.

After my wound was hastily attended to, I was sent east by railroad to Richmond, Virginia, and Libby Prison. The prison was an old tobacco and sugar warehouse, accommodating several hundred Union officers at the time of my residence. Many of them were badly treated, either by design or force of circumstances. For one thing, the rebels were very short of food at that time, and it could be assumed that their prisoners were faring as well as many of their soldiers in the field.

However, I must admit that I did not fare badly at all. As the only general officer in the prison at that time, I was given reasonably comfortable quarters on the third floor and a captured enlisted man to serve as striker for me. The food wasn't good, but it was better than that served to the other prisoners and, as you know, Margaret, I was never as interested in the pleasures of the palate as I was in other gratifications.

And I soon discovered that my striker had other talents. He had been a longtime follower of the Master and he began to instruct me in the ways of serving him. I then found that there were others in the prison with similar inclinations, guards as well as prisoners, and it was not long before I had organized a group that met regularly in my quarters. We even managed to arrange for the attendance of some Richmond ladies, who participated (willingly, for the most part, although some not so willingly) in our ceremonies and pleasures. Our schedule of meetings was interrupted for a short time in March of 1864 when one of the ladies passed away during a ceremony as a result of some overzealous participation on the part of one of us. Shall I admit that it was I? Unfortunately so.

Nevertheless, with subsequent caution, we managed to resume our activities, and it was with extreme regret that I learned in May of 1864 that Libby Prison was to be closed and we prisoners moved farther south. It seems that Union cavalry raiders, under the command of General Hugh Kilpatrick, were pressing close to Richmond, and Libby Prison was no longer a safe place to hold us.

During the transfer of prisoners from the building to the rail-road cars, I managed to escape. I had been supplied with civilian clothes and Confederate currency by one of our adherents, and I managed very well for several days in Richmond, residing for a time at the Spotswood Hotel, where I passed myself off as a cotton planter come to the capital to deal with military buyers.

Then I made my way to Washington, where I cannot say I was welcomed with open arms. I was questioned several times by Secretary of War Stanton and by several officers in his department. Finally it was decided that, in the interest of national harmony and support of the war effort, it would be best not to pursue and thereby publicize the charges against me. It was stated therefore that since I was now physically incapable of continuing my long and valiant service to my country, I would be honorably discharged and sent home to Cainesville.

My brothers and sisters having died or relinquished their claims on it, I was now the sole owner of the Caine farm. With the help of my Master I soon made it prosper, and engaged in other prosperous business ventures as well. Then in tribute to the one who now ruled my life, I had the old log farmhouse torn down and a new house built, choosing as my model the place where I had first sworn to serve my Master.

I spent many gratifying years in the house, and my Master succored me. He came to me many times there, as he still comes to me. He has insured that I shall never die, and he has made it possible for me to return to the place where you wait for me, Margaret. Even as you desire me, I will come.

The notebook entry ended with that chilling statement. I got out of bed, unlocked the door and went quietly to the store-room and put the book back where I had found it.

Before returning to my room, I paused by Duff's door and listened, but I could hear nothing, not even his breathing. I wanted to open the door and see if he was in the room, but I was afraid to do it—afraid maybe to find out that he wasn't there.

I'm sure I locked my door again. My mind is in such a turmoil lately that I can't really swear to it. However, I was so nervous at the time that I'm sure I would have been certain to lock the door. Anyway, I then went to the window.

General Caine was standing on the front lawn, closer to the house now than he had been the night before. There was a good bit of moonlight and I could see him even more clearly. His arms were folded and he was staring at me, but there was no malevolence in his expression. I stared back at him for a moment, then pulled the shade down and got into bed.

I tried to tell myself that there had to be a natural explanation, but my teeth were chattering and I was trembling so much the bed was shaking. Then I had a somewhat comforting thought. If I had to desire him before he could come to me, then I was sure he would never come. But then after a long while I went to sleep, and in my dream I did desire him and once again he came to me.

Chapter Fifteen

In the morning I again told myself that we have no control over our dreams. I knew that subconscious minds can play tricks, distorting our true instincts and inclinations. Then I noticed the indentation on the other pillow and the way the covers were rumpled on the other side of the bed.

Maybe Jack had come upstairs, after all, or maybe I had rolled over on that side myself. But I never did that at night, or at least I never had until now. Then Franny must have come back during the night. But the door was locked now, although the key was on the floor. Could it have been slid under the door?

I put the whole thing out of my mind and had a quick soak in the tub. Then I dressed and rapped on Duff's door and he answered immediately and cheerfully.

Indeed, we were a cheerful company at breakfast that morning. No mention was made of Stephanie's death, or any other unpleasantness. Duff and Franny jabbered about their school activities (listening to Duff, one might have thought he was spending a lot of time at the high school) and even Jack was jolly telling us how good he had begun to feel and how well his work was going. He had decided to quit depending on his crutches and to try his luck with a cane. He gave us a demonstration after breakfast, and he really could get around better than I had expected.

"What do you think, old lady?" he asked. "Should we go back East now?"

"I thought you wanted to stay here."

"It occurred to me maybe I ought to talk with some publishers about my book. I'm far enough along now to show them something."

"On that yellow pad?"

"I'll get a typist to work it up. Actually, maybe you could do it. You used to be a pretty fast gun on the old Underwood."

"No, thanks. But you go to New York for a few days if you think you can manage all right. Duff and Franny and I can get along here."

"I thought you wanted to leave."

"I do, you idiot, but the kids are in school!"

"No problem," said Franny. "I'll be glad to go to school somewhere else."

"We could probably find schools in Manhattan," Jack said.

"Are you crazy? Decent ones would cost a fortune. And what about the danger to your children on the streets?"

"I wouldn't be afraid," Franny piped.

"Will you shut up? And what about Duff's court appearance?"

"It can probably be advanced if we tell them we're leaving town. Maybe the authorities will be glad to be rid of us, eh?" He punched Duff playfully. Duff didn't react.

"We're not going to ask for any favors. Duff will go to court when they call him."

"I can't understand you. A couple of weeks ago you would've been willing to do anything to get away from here. What about you, Duff? What are your feelings?"

"I'll go along with whatever Mother wants," Duff said quietly.

That was the end of the discussion. Duff and Franny went out to wait for the school bus, and Jack, highly irritated, went to his room to take up his writing. I don't think he was serious at all about leaving. I think he was just trying to bait me. I still wanted to get away from the Caine farm as soon as possible, but there just didn't seem to be any reasonable way to do it immediately.

Shortly afterward Dr. Tully called and asked if he could visit us. I'm afraid I was rather abrupt with him, telling him that my husband wasn't feeling well and that I didn't expect him to feel better for some time.

Then a few minutes later Father Jackson came along. I saw his car and went out to meet him.

"You seem gloomy," he said as we drove off. "More visitations?"

I hesitated. "No."

"What then? Not that it's any of my business."

"You're right. It's none of your business."

Priest or not, he wasn't my confessor. This was only my third meeting with him and he seemed to feel entitled to pry as much as he wished. On the other hand, I thought, he was supposed to be trying to help me.

"I did see the General again," I said.

"I thought so. Where?"

"On the lawn in front of the house last night."

"He didn't come in the house?"

"I didn't see him come in." I paused. "I also managed to read some more in Duff's notebook. It definitely wasn't Duff's handwriting anymore."

"We ought to be able to find something in the General's hand. A deed or some other legal paper in the Ashland courthouse maybe. Go on."

"In the notes he just talked about his life. His Civil War experiences and so forth."

"Could I have a look at the book?"

"Sure, sometime."

"Maybe after we've seen this horse."

"I'm not sure it would be a good idea to try and sneak the book out today. I don't know where Duff is."

"Isn't he in school?"

"You never know with Duff."

"Well, you don't have to sneak it out. Why can't I just come into the house and have a quick peek at it?"

"Duff has probably hidden it again. Also, he'd be very upset if he caught you looking at it. I do want you to see it, though, if only to give you some evidence of my sanity."

We arrived at the horse owner's farm, which was on the next road—nearly opposite the Caine place, Father Jackson thought, on the other side of the woods. If a person knew a path through the woods, it seemingly would have been no trouble to lead a horse from one farm to the other.

We walked out to the barn and met the owner, Fred Dobbs. Mr. Dobbs was a lean and weathered seventy or so, and he watched me silently as Father Jackson explained that I was living in the Caine house and that someone had been riding a horse on the Caine property.

"I didn't know any of it was cultivated, so's it would make any difference," Dobbs said.

"Actually, the horse and rider were on the road," I said, "but the horse was being ridden too hard. I love horses and I don't like to see them mistreated."

Dobbs relaxed. "Are you going to keep horses on the Caine place?"

"Maybe later."

"I've got a nice young hunter I can let you have cheap. Also, a couple of gentle ponies, if you've got children."

"Could we see the horse that was stolen?" Father Jackson asked.

Dobbs took us into the barn, where there were several horses in stalls. He opened a stall door and led out a beautiful black mare.

"That's the horse," I said.

"You're sure?" Father Jackson said.

"There can't be that many black Arabians with white patches on their right forelegs around here. She's a beauty," I told Dobbs.

"Ain't she? She ain't full Arabian, but she's got plenty of good blood. Look here how she was spurred." He turned the horse around so we could see the gashes on both flanks. "That's how I knew she'd been taken out. Whoever did it must've come around after dark. She'll make up with anybody."

"Don't you keep this barn locked?" Father Jackson asked.

"Yes, but it's an old padlock that would be easy to spring. Look here, whoever was on her must've ridden her into a fence or something."

There was a long scratch on the mare's right hind leg.

"Could she have been scraped by a car?" Father Jackson asked.

"Sure, that would've done it too. Did you get a good look at the fella riding her?" Dobbs asked me.

"Only a quick look. It was dark."

"Was he young or middle-aged or what?"

"Reasonably young."

"Probably some punk from Cainesville. I don't know any-body around here who'd pull a trick like that. If it had been some thief stealing her for gain, I could understand it better." He led the horse back into the stall. "I'd consider selling this baby too, if you're interested."

"I'd love to have her, but not right now."

Dobbs walked back to the car with us. "You ever have any trouble over there at the Caine place?" he asked.

"What sort of trouble do you mean?"

"Oh, you know. If you're a member of the family, you must know the reputation that place has."

"Oh, we've heard stories."

"They're more than stories, according to some folks. Lots of folks have moved away from here."

"But you've stayed," said Father Jackson.

"Yep. I won't say I haven't seen and heard a few strange things though in that woods back there."

"What sort of things?" I asked.

"Well, I was hunting a dog in those woods one time and I saw a procession of people, all in black, coming out of the Caine graveyard."

"A funeral?"

"Weren't no funeral. They were taking a coffin out, not putting it in."

"When was this?" asked Father Jackson.

"Sixty years ago. It was before old Hannah Caine moved into the house."

"But you haven't seen anything similar since?"

"I never went over there again. I've heard screaming and sobbing, though, in that Caine woods late at night."

"Why haven't you investigated?" Father Jackson asked.

Dobbs sniffed. "I tend to my own affairs. And I won't be scared off valuable land. Whatever goes on over there at Caines', I figure it's people of today are causing it, not any creatures out of the past."

"That's exactly my judgment, Mr. Dobbs," said Father Jackson.

We got in the car, and Dobbs leaned in the window on my side. "They say old General Caine used to ride an Arabian like that one of mine."

"Is that so?"

"Yep. Some also say that General Caine was the old Nick himself."

"There's a little of that fellow in all of us, Mr. Dobbs," said Father Jackson. When we were back on the road, he said, "Well, there's your horse. Now where's the rider?"

I was tempted to say, "In Cainesville High School, or at least that's where he's supposed to be." In a way, I was sorry to learn that I had seen a living horse on the road. It may have been evidence of my sanity, but it offered a terrible alternative.

Father Jackson read my thoughts. "It needn't have been Duff, you know. In this instance you didn't see Duff immediately before you saw the General. It could've been a local kid just as Dobbs suggested. A kid dressed up like the General."

"Why would he try to make me wreck my car?"

"Who knows why kids act as they do nowadays. Why was Stephanie killed?"

"That wasn't the work of kids. Or if it was, I'm sure there were others involved too."

"Let's try something else. Let's go over to the Waterson

woods where Stephanie's body was found. Maybe we can poke around and uncover something."

"Uncover what? You already have evidence that it wasn't the devil I saw—unless the devil likes to use local transportation."

"Maybe we can stumble on something that would indicate Duff wasn't involved," said Father Jackson patiently.

"Leave it to the police. They don't suspect Duff."

"They may begin to suspect him, if they decide to investigate Mrs. Reddy."

We went back to our road and down it to the Waterson farm. It seemed that the Watersons were parishioners at Saint Mary's in Cainesville. Father Jackson introduced me to Mrs. Waterson and explained my relationship with Stephanie. He said that I thought if I could look around the place where her body had been found, I might see something that had escaped the eyes of the police—I was so close to Stephanie and all. He was becoming as much of an operator as I was.

Mrs. Waterson, who may have been around my age but was (I hoped) considerably more haggard, sent her twelve-year-old daughter to guide us. Ruth Ann knew the location from listening to the conversations of the deputies, but until now her parents hadn't permitted her to visit the site. Consequently she set off at practically a gallop.

There wasn't much to see once we reached the place. And getting there by the girl's route resulted in a number of scratches on my arms and legs and a rip in the back of my cashmere sweater.

"Here's where they found her," announced Ruth Ann, beaming. "At least I'm pretty sure it was here. The Sheriff said it was near that big oak tree."

"It was here," said Father Jackson. He indicated some pegs in the ground on an open slope of grass. The pegs made a rough outline of a body.

"No motorcycle could have been brought in the way we came," I said. "Even a person walking would've had a terrible time at night."

"I brought you the quickest way," said Ruth Ann. "The logging trail where the motorcycle tracks are is over there." She pointed to the other side of the slope.

"Then let's go back that way," I said, "or any way other than the one we came."

Father Jackson had picked up a stick and was walking up the slope, whipping the grass.

"What do you expect to find?" I called.

"Nothing probably," he yelled back. "This area must have been gone over by experts."

"I've never known anyone who was murdered," said Ruth Ann shyly. She was a skinny, unattractive child with dental braces.

"Didn't you know Stephanie?"

"Not really. She wasn't a Catholic, you know. I saw her in her yard a couple of times when we passed her house, that's all. Her mother and her grandmother are supposed to be witches."

"Really?"

"Yes. Maybe Stephanie was a witch too."

"I rather doubt that."

Father Jackson came back, waving something. It was a pair of silver-rimmed eyeglasses with large lenses. Duff's glasses, I thought immediately.

"How could the deputies have missed those?" Ruth Ann wondered.

"They were pretty well buried in the grass, but I saw a flash of sunlight on them," Father Jackson said.

"I wonder if you'll get a reward, Father." Ruth Ann seemed disappointed that she hadn't found them.

"They may have nothing to do with Stephanie's murder," I said. "They could've been in the grass for a long time."

"Any person I know, if he lost his glasses, would have looked for them until he found them and probably had his whole family looking for them too," Ruth Ann said.

Father Jackson was watching me. "Of course it's always possible they belonged to Stephanie."

"Let's get out of here," I said.

Father Jackson put the glasses in his pocket, and Ruth Ann led us out of the woods by a less hazardous path than the one we had taken in. When we reached her house she invited us in, but I declined. I didn't want her mother asking questions about the glasses.

"Are they Duff's?" Father Jackson asked as we drove off. He handed the glasses to me.

"Yes," I said.

"I thought so from your expression. I'm sorry I didn't put them in my pocket as soon as I picked them up. When was the last time you saw Duff wearing them?"

"I can't remember. He used to wear them all the time, but lately—I just can't remember." I thought of the previous afternoon when he seemed to have difficulty recognizing me when he came upon me in the yard. However, at other times he was obviously able to get along very well without glasses.

"Shouldn't you turn these over to the Sheriff's office?" I asked Father Jackson.

"You can do that, if you like."

"God, I don't know what to do. What do you think would happen if I did?"

"They'd undoubtedly take a good hard look at Duff again, despite any alibis provided by Mrs. Reddy."

"Do you think he did it, Father?"

He didn't answer until we reached our drive. Then he said, "You're sure he's always been afraid of horses?"

"It's more than fear. He's allergic to them, or was. When he was little, he would break into a rash and choke up if I even took him out to watch me ride."

I'm sure he wasn't listening to me, because he went on, "He must have the clothes hidden somewhere—the uniform you saw the General wearing."

I screamed, "Goddamn it, you just suggested that it was a local kid!"

"That was before I found the glasses. Take it easy, Margaret."

"Mrs. Caine!"

"I'm sorry, Mrs. Caine." He started the motor.

"Wait . . . please wait, Father. You're the only one I can talk to."

He turned the ignition off again.

"It must be someone else," I said carefully. "The size and age are so different. There is a kind of resemblance in some of the features, but in others—"

"Stage makeup."

"I would've noticed it. I was so close in the kitchen and in the car."

"It's all scientifically possible, maybe even without makeup. Changes in appearance have been known to coincide with changes in personality. My brother Jim can tell you about that. Changes in physical capacity aren't so rare either, which would account for Duff's strength that time at the high school and in the fight with the police. You've heard of instances in which it took a dozen men to overcome a hundred-pound madman."

I began to cry. Then I told him about the two dreams.

"Dreams are nothing to worry about. You can't control your dreams."

"But can anybody else control them?"

"Hardly. Anyway, I don't know anything about dream interpretation. You can ask Jim. I think he's a Jungian rather than a Freudian, and he'll probably tell you your dreams have nothing to do with sex. You saw the man on the lawn, so you dreamed about him, that's all. Maybe you were punishing yourself for some reason—or punishing someone else."

"One other thing. It looked this morning as though I had company in bed last night."

"Your husband?"

"He would have had difficulty with the stairs. Also, the door was locked."

He was silent for a while. Then he said, "I think you and your family have to get away from here."

"Duff will refuse to go. And there's his court hearing."

"You don't have to go that far," said Father Jackson impatiently. "Just get away from this house. I know a place you can stay in Cainesville. There's an old couple who're going to Europe for three months and they'd be glad to have someone reliable in their house."

"I'll think about it." I leaned over and kissed him gently on the cheek. I don't know why I did it, but it embarrassed him. Then I got out of the car. "Don't worry. I'm sure everything will turn out all right."

"Are you going to show Duff the glasses?"

"Maybe."

"You'd better be prepared for trouble. That Waterson girl will tell her mother and there's a good chance it will go on from there."

"I'll cross that bridge when I come to it."

He sighed. "I'll phone you as soon as Jim gets to town. And if anything else happens, please call me."

"I will."

He took something from his coat pocket, concealing it in his fist, then reached out and put it in my hand. It was a pair of rosary beads.

"Keep them," he said. "Maybe they'll do you some good."

He drove off, even more embarrassed now, and I went into the house. Jack, seemingly exhausted after his morning literary labors, was taking a nap while waiting for me to fix lunch. I took a package of cold cuts and a carton of milk out of the refrigerator and put them on the table with a loaf of bread. Then I opened the door of the old wood stove and threw the rosary beads in where I had thrown the bottle of holy water a couple of nights before.

Afterward I went upstairs to Duff's room and searched his closet and bureau drawers, but I couldn't find any part of a Union army uniform. The notebook was on top of the bureau, but nothing had been added to what I had read before. I wondered if it was possible for Duff or anyone to write consistently in a hand so different from his own. I also wondered if Duff knew that I had read his most recent notes.

Also on the bureau now was a key, similar to the one that fitted my bedroom lock. I tried it in Duff's door, but it didn't work. Then I went to the storeroom, pulled aside the wardrobe that concealed the door and tried the key.

It unlocked the door. I opened the door and ahead was a flight of stairs. I went back to my room, got my flashlight and then, without waiting to think about it, went back to the storeroom and up the stairs.

I advanced cautiously, shining the light on each step. If anyone had preceded me recently, they had done so without leaving footprints on the dusty treads or dislodging a lot of cobwebs. That was one consolation and another was the thought that spiders probably couldn't live long in that almost airless passage.

At the top was one large, windowless room, piled high with the same kinds of things that filled the second-floor storeroom. There were many more pieces of antique furniture, more chests and trunks and hundreds more books stacked on the floor. Most of the things were collected at the far end of the room, leaving plenty of open space near the stairs for the General's meetings, if they had been held there.

I moved toward the furniture, the beam of light creating a tunnel in primeval darkness. With only that narrow light and all the things in the room, it could've taken forever to find what I wanted, had it been hidden. Instead it was laid out directly in front of me on a leather-covered settee.

There was a dark blue coat with shoulder braid, lighter blue trousers, a gray flannel shirt and a black slouch hat. On the floor beneath, black boots with spurs.

The cloth was old, there was no doubt of that. What I had taken for mud was grayish mold. There were holes in the coat lapels, and the edge of the collar crumpled as I touched it. The gold buttons and the braid were tarnished and so were the crossed sabers on the hat. Wherever the uniform had come from, it had not been made recently by any costume house.

It had obviously been intended that I see it. There had been no attempt to conceal it, and the key had been left in plain sight in Duff's room. Why? Why, after several seeming attempts to make me believe in the supernatural, was this evidence of a natural explanation laid before me?

Was the intention now to convince me that Duff was the General when he really wasn't? There was one way to find out. Gingerly I picked up the uniform coat and rolled it up. If it hadn't been taken from a grave, stripped from the bones of a man who died a hundred years ago, then it had been in some similar place of decay for a long time.

Before leaving the room I aimed the light at several other cluttered areas, but I couldn't see a coffin or anything else that looked as though it might have been taken from a coffin. Then I hurried downstairs with my dank bundle, closed and locked the door in the storeroom and returned the key to Duff's bureau. I took the glasses out of my pocket and put them on the bureau too. Finally I went to my bedroom and put the uniform coat under my mattress.

Now let's see if General Caine shows up tonight without his coat, I thought. What I would have done if he had—or if he had appeared wearing another coat—I don't know. The fact is I didn't see him again for several nights and I didn't dream about him either.

Chapter Sixteen

As the end of the week approached I was beginning to hope that the whole nasty business was over. Maybe revealing the uniform to me marked the end of it, I told myself. Maybe they were giving up—Mrs. Reddy, her daughter and whoever else was involved. Maybe the death of Stephanie had frightened them into quitting.

And hopefully they would no longer try to involve my son in their filthy practices. That was the main reason I didn't say anything to Duff about the glasses. He must have found them, although he still wasn't wearing them. Nevertheless I had no intention of reporting the matter to the authorities, and I wasn't going to confront my son with it either. If he had killed Stephanie, I didn't want to know it. If he had done it, the others had caused him to do it, and I was hoping—and as a couple of peaceful days went by, beginning to believe—that nothing like that would ever happen again.

On Friday morning I mentioned to Duff that the psychiatrist would probably be in Cainesville the next day. Actually, I was wondering if I shouldn't call Father Jackson and cancel the whole thing.

"He's coming to see me?"

"Well, he hopes to see you, but that's not the only reason he's coming. Father Jackson says he and his brother haven't gotten together for a long time, so that's probably the main reason."

"I sure can't understand why he'd want to bother with me. After all, it's just a simple behavior problem, isn't it? You think I haven't been behaving as I should lately and you want to know why. Any good shrink must see a dozen such cases every week."

"That's right. Dr. Jackson has probably agreed to see you only because he doesn't play golf or tennis and there's nothing else to do in Cainesville on a weekend."

"He could go riding."

I turned and stared at him.

"There are plenty of riding stables around here, aren't there?"

"I don't know, are there?"

"I would assume so. This is the country, after all. Plenty of open land around here." He grinned and then said, "All right, Mother. I don't have anything else to do this weekend either."

That night Father Jackson called to say that his brother was in town. He had suggested seeing Duff at his motel the next morning if I could arrange it. Also, Jim would like to talk with me before the meeting with Duff. Could I come to the motel and have a drink with them in an hour or so? Maybe Jack would like to come too, Father Jackson suggested.

I didn't even mention it to Jack. I was sure he would only laugh at the idea of meeting with a psychiatrist and a priest to talk about his son, whom he considered to have very minor, if any, problems. I told Franny I was going for a drive when I left for the Siesta Time Motel about eight-thirty, and she didn't question it. I don't know whether Duff was in the house or not. I was getting sick of always looking for Duff anyway.

When I arrived Father Jackson and his brother were in Jim's room which was large enough to turn around in if you did it carefully. They were drinking Scotch. Father Jackson was wearing his bookie jacket again.

Jim was older, heavier and handsomer than his brother. He offered me the one chair. "Couldn't we go somewhere else? Isn't there a bar or something?" he asked.

"I can't very well patronize the bars around here," Father Jackson said. He fixed me a Scotch and water and then sat on the bed with Jim.

"Am I supposed to begin?" I asked. "First may I say I'm rather surprised that you've consented to this sort of arrangement, Dr. Jackson."

"Your problem sounded very interesting."

"It's not exactly my problem. I mean, not in your sense. I hope your brother assured you of that."

Dr. Jackson nodded. "Tell me about your son."

"Hasn't your brother told you?"

"I'd rather hear it firsthand."

So I told my tale again. Everything, even about the dreams. Father Jackson got up a couple of times to replenish his drink, but Jim sat watching me attentively, seldom even sipping his Scotch.

"Well, what do you think?" I asked when I finished. "Is Duff a schizoid, or is he possessed by the devil?"

He took a long swallow now. "Well, I don't think he's the former. Not from what you tell me. And as for the other, there's been entirely too much emphasis on that kind of thing lately. Books, movies . . ."

"Duff seldom goes to movies or reads fiction."

"But he has seen Mrs. Reddy," said Father Jackson.

"Yes," Jim said, "that could be what triggered it. Have you ever heard of multiple personality, Mrs. Caine? Jekyll and Hyde. Two or more distinct personalities in the same person. Each personality has its own way of thinking, feeling and acting, its own habits and mannerisms. Multiple personality differs from schizophrenia in that the personalities in most cases are completely different and not split aspects of the same personality."

"And could something like that come on suddenly?"

"It could reveal itself overnight. It's very rare, however. I've never encountered a case before in fifteen years of practice."

"Would the person know what was happening? Duff doesn't seem to realize. He could be lying, of course, but when the General appeared in the car and in the kitchen, Duff honestly didn't seem to know about it."

"That's possible. Almost always one personality is stronger than the other, and sometimes the stronger one is aware of the actions and thinking of the other. In this case, the General might be the stronger. From your description, it sounds as though he would be. Consequently he could be aware of what Duff is doing and thinking and not the other way around."

"That's it, I'm sure of it!" I was elated, but then I remembered my dreams.

I must have blushed because Dr. Jackson smiled. "You've been dreaming about the General, not Duff," he said reassuringly. "And now that you have a possible explanation for the visits of the General, I'm sure you won't have any more such dreams."

"Or, if you do, get up quickly and take a shower," said Father Jackson, grinning.

I ignored him. "Could the appearances of the two be so completely different?"

"They might just have seemed very different on a quick glance, and while you were emotionally upset. One face could have been very distorted, for example. And the General may be much stronger than Duff, possessing strength that would be unimaginable in Duff."

"But he seemed so much heavier. And his hair is darker and sparser. And his beard . . ."

"How about that, Jimmy? Can you lose and grow hair with multiple personality?" Father Jackson asked. "Maybe we should try it."

I finished my drink and put my glass on the dresser. "It's time for me to go," I said. "I've told you all I can."

Dr. Jackson was staring at me. "Is something wrong?" I asked.

"No, no."

"Then why are you looking at me that way?"

Father Jackson giggled. "Maybe he finds you attractive."

Dr. Jackson escorted me out to the car. "I'm sorry about Pete. He never could handle his liquor."

"Do you think you can help Duff?"

"I'll know better after I talk with him."

"Supposing it isn't a case of multiple personality?"

He shook his head. "I don't know. But let's wait and see."

I hesitated. "Can a psychiatrist believe in the devil?"

He laughed. "We all, in one way or another, believe in the devil. That's not to say there is a devil, but in the collective unconsciousness there are still demons and dragons and witches flying around. Deep down, some people think, we're still very primitive, but the normal conscious mind can control all that." He started to close my door, then held it. "Are you normally left-handed, Mrs. Caine?"

"No, why? What's that got to do with Duff?"

"Nothing. Good night."

I slammed the door and drove off, showering him with gravel as I left the parking lot. Why had he asked a question like that? I kept wondering all the way home. I had given him my right hand, I was sure, when his brother introduced us. Did left-handed mothers sometimes produce children with mental problems?

Jack was at his literary labors in the front room when I let myself in. Franny was in her room, maybe reading, and probably brooding over the lack of a television set.

"Why don't we get her one tomorrow," I said, "as long as we're going to be here for a few more weeks."

He looked up briefly. "Wonderful," he said without expression. "Why don't you go into Cainesville and get it."

"Is Duff upstairs?"

"He could be. If he didn't go out."

"Did he tell you he was going out?"

"No." And seemingly my husband was disinclined to say anything more than that.

I went upstairs and found Duff's door closed. There was no response when I knocked. I opened the door quietly. He was sitting on his bed with an impish grin on his face.

"Mama, Mama." He admonished me with his finger.

"Why didn't you answer when I knocked?"

"Because I knew you'd come in."

"I just wanted to see if you were covered properly. It's chilly tonight."

"Bosh, it's warm." He patted my hand. "Never mind, Mama. I know you have my best interests at heart. Did you make an appointment for me with the shrink."

"Yes, for tomorrow right after breakfast."

"Okay. I hope some good comes of it for your sake."

"You must be honest with the man, Duff. You must answer all his questions truthfully as best you can."

"Right on, Mama."

I wanted to kiss him—he seemed such a child again then—but I was afraid to. Instead I just nodded and went to my room and soon after to bed. Of course, I checked to see if the uniform coat was still under my mattress. It was, and I went to sleep certain that I wouldn't be troubled by the General for another night.

Chapter Seventeen

The next morning Duff was up before me and downstairs waiting for me. He had made pancakes, burning them slightly, and the two of us had breakfast, not waiting for Franny and Jack.

We didn't talk about the coming session with Dr. Jackson, but about other things, old times in Scarsdale mostly, and about his last birthday and his approaching one. For his sixteenth birthday several of his pals had come to dinner. I wondered now if he wanted a dinner party this year. He declined.

"Isn't there some girl in your class you'd like to invite?"

He studied me for a moment. "No, there isn't any girl."

"Are you sure?"

"Quite sure." He went and got his coat and mine. "Do you think I ought to find myself a girl, Mother?"

"I think you ought to do what you want to do."

We did very little talking on the way to Cainesville. As we approached the motel I said, "You mustn't worry about this. It's painless."

"Don't you find it painful to talk about certain things, Mother? Or sometimes to even think about them?"

There was a sly note in his voice. I turned, half-expecting to see the General, but it was only my son looking very serious and completely innocent.

"There are things in all our lives that we don't like to be reminded about," I conceded. "But sometimes by talking about them we can relieve the unhappiness they've caused us."

I parked in front of Dr. Jackson's room at the motel. He must have been looking out the window, because he came out to the car and shook Duff's hand warmly. I thought maybe I should have told him that Duff wouldn't be impressed by a hearty reception. He usually mistrusted overly enthusiastic people.

Nevertheless he went along to Dr. Jackson's room without even looking back at me. I sat in the car for a while, wondering what they were talking about, and then decided to kill some time in the motel coffee shop.

The Reverend Peter Jackson was sitting at the counter, drinking coffee. I took the stool next to him. He greeted me and apologized for any remarks that might have offended me the night before.

"Forget it," I said. "I've said and done worse things at parties. One time—"

"Maggie, I think maybe this isn't going to do any good."

"Duff's session with your brother? Why?"

He shook his head. The girl brought my coffee then and I waited until she moved away. "Listen," I said, "this was your idea. If you're suggesting now that your brother isn't competent—"

"Maggie, the church was vandalized last night. Someone broke the lock on the door and got in. The large statue in the shrine was knocked off its pedestal and broken, and there's other damage. Broken windows, defaced walls ... Father Fogarty is pretty upset."

"I don't wonder. Do the police have any idea—?"

"No."

"Well, it wasn't Duff, I'm certain. I'm sure—or reasonably sure—that he didn't go out last night. He was in bed when I got home."

Father Jackson didn't say any more until I finished my coffee. Then he asked me to drive him back to the rectory.

"I walked over here this morning," he said. "Whoever wrecked the church did a pretty good job on my car too."

It would have been hard to improve on what age and the elements had done already, I thought, but I was wrong. The car was in the rectory drive with all its tires flat, its windows smashed and its radiator punctured.

"There's something else," Father Jackson said. He led me to

the front of the car. The windshield was still intact, but someone had written on it with a grease pencil, "Shit priest, stay out of it."

"Someone doesn't like your association with the Caines," I said.

"So it would seem. I can't think of anything else I've been doing lately that would lead to this." He hesitated. "What time did you get home last night, Maggie?"

"A little after ten. Why?"

"I stayed with Jim and had a couple of more drinks. I left about eleven-thirty, and when I drove past the church there was someone standing in front. As I pulled in the drive here, the person turned and went up the church steps. I got out of the car and walked over there, but there was no one around."

"Don't tell me the person you saw was Duff."

"No." He paused. "The person I saw—or thought I saw—was you."

"You were drunk!"

"I'd had a lot to drink, I'll admit."

"I was in bed at eleven-thirty. Do you want to check that with my family?"

"Please, Maggie, don't shout. It's illogical, I know. It must have been another woman, dressed as you were. The same kind of raincoat."

"And you think that person wrecked your church and car?"

"I have no way of knowing. The church door was locked when I tried it. Then I came back to the rectory and thought about calling you."

"Calling my husband and children, you mean, to ask what I was doing wandering around Cainesville!"

"Please, Maggie, keep your voice down. I decided it couldn't have been you and went to bed."

"If you decided that, why do you bring it up now?"

"Please, please, Maggie . . ." He looked toward the rectory, I suppose hoping that Father Fogarty and Mrs. Guenther would come out and rescue him from me.

"Why did your brother ask me if I was left-handed?" I really was shouting now.

He didn't reply, but suddenly his expression changed. He had been embarrassed before, but now he was staring at me in horror.

"Go inside, you weak little shit!"

I don't know what made me say that, but I was so angry I couldn't help it. I went back to the Plymouth and drove away, leaving him standing there with his mouth hanging open.

I drove around for forty-five minutes or so, trying to calm down. Then I went back to the motel and knocked on Dr. Jackson's door.

The session was over and Duff had gone to the coffee shop to get a hamburger, Dr. Jackson told me. He was packing his bag.

"So how is he?"

"Fine. Nothing wrong as far as I can determine."

"What about the multiple personality?"

"Nothing like that emerged. I gave him a Rorschach and a TAT, and both tests indicated that he's as completely well-balanced as any boy his age ought to be. No overly aggressive tendencies. He's imaginative, although he doesn't fantasize. He's highly intelligent, and he shows a strong degree of independence. You ought to be happy that you have such a son, Mrs. Caine."

"But what about his fighting in school? What about assaulting his sister?"

"He denied those things happened—at least in the way you described them to me. He said he was wrestling with the other student and the boy slipped and fell."

"What about his sister?"

"He said he was teasing her. He told her that the sweater she was wearing belonged to him, ordered her to take it off, and she did it."

"Franny wouldn't lie about it!"

Dr. Jackson shrugged. "Maybe, thinking about it later, she saw something sinister in the incident. Girls approaching puberty and with only a vague knowledge of sexual matters are often apprehensive in such circumstances."

"What about his raping Stephanie!"

"I doubt that it was rape. Given the opportunity, most boys his age—"

"Can't you see he's been lying to you?"

"If he was, he's very clever."

"Of course, he's clever! What about the car accident? What about his hitting the policemen?"

"He admitted driving recklessly, but that sort of behavior in a teenager isn't pathological, or even unusual. It would be more surprising if a normal teenage boy didn't speed when he had the chance and was alone in a car. He denied hitting the policemen. He said they pulled him out of his car and shoved him around, but he didn't retaliate beyond some talking back to them. That apparently angered them. You know as well as I do, Mrs. Caine, that some policemen are prone to be excessively aggressive."

"You're on his side, aren't you? Duff has captivated you."

"I'm not on anyone's side, Mrs. Caine. Duff is a personable youngster, but I think I've been in practice long enough—"

"That's just the point, don't you see? He never was personable before! He didn't care what people thought of him!"

"Mrs. Caine, it's very difficult, if not impossible, to conceal the true state of one's mind in psychological testing."

"Duff could deceive you, I know he could."

"Not unless he had seen the whole series of pictures and inkblots before and knew exactly what the normal responses ought to be in each case. Then he would need to know how to vary the responses just enough off the norm in a few instances to make the total personality seem plausible. And that would almost demand someone with professional training. More than that, I can usually tell by physical signs, as can any trained person in my field, when a patient is lying."

"Can you, Doctor? Well you muffed one this time."

"All right, Mrs. Caine."

"What about the man I saw? Do you think that was all in my head?"

"I couldn't think that without further evidence—"

"What about his pissing in church?"

"I asked him about that and he denies it. He said—"

"Send me your goddamn bill!"

"I shall certainly do that." He held up a few sheets of paper. "I can go over some of Duff's written responses to the Thematic Apperception test if you like."

"Stick them." I went to the door.

"Perhaps you really did see another person, Mrs. Caine."

"Thanks. If I were you, I'd try some of those tests on my brother."

I went out to find Duff sitting in the car. He greeted me with a grin, nothing anxious about it either.

"Well?"

"You're sane." I started the car and moved out onto the road before saying anything else. "Duff, you promised you'd cooperate with that man."

"I did, Mother."

"You lied to him."

"No, I didn't, Mother."

What was the use in arguing? I thought about turning around, taking him back to the motel and making him go over his stories again, but then I thought, what's the use? He'd only come up with more explanations and Jackson would drag out his tests results again.

And wasn't it a good thing that the psychiatrist had found no trace of mental illness? Even if Duff had deceived the man, maybe he had also decided to mend his ways. Whatever the explanation for the General, maybe he would never appear again and Duff would become his old self once more. Of course, I was only kidding myself in thinking that things might get better, because they almost instantly got worse.

I had turned onto our road and we were nearing the Weber place, when strangely the car and the world outside seemed to change. The windshield melted away and the steering wheel disappeared under my hands. Instead of a wheel I was holding reins and there was an old gray horse plodding along in front of me. The road that had been macadam when we drove to Cainesville was now hard-packed earth, high in the middle and with deep ditches on both sides.

The Weber house, a wood-shingled colonial with a one-story addition in the back (the meeting room, I realized later), had become a smaller house. The addition was gone and the sides were now clapboarded instead of shingled. Moreover the station wagon that had been earlier parked in the yard was also gone, and in its place was a new-looking, leather-topped buggy with a handsome brown horse hitched to it. For some unexplainable reason I felt that the new buggy would soon be mine and that I lived in the house.

I was about to cry out to Duff when I heard a guttural cough and I knew it was no longer Duff who was seated beside me. I was afraid to turn my head and look, but I knew.

It lasted only ten seconds, maybe less. Then I heard Duff shouting, "Watch the road, Mother!"

The macadam road came back, and the windshield and steering wheel. I had strayed out of my lane and was headed for an approaching, and very modern, farm tractor. I pulled back with just about half a car's length to spare.

"Mother, Mother, you take chances," Duff murmured. I looked now and it was certainly he. Then I looked in the rearview mirror at the Weber place we had just passed. The house was as it had been before and the station wagon was in the yard.

"The Webers and Mrs. Reddy must be back from the cremation," Duff said.

"What?"

"Stephanie's body was to be cremated today. I saw it in yesterday's paper. I guess they had to wait this long because the coroner wasn't finished with his tests."

"You don't sound awfully sympathetic," I was finally able to say.

"Oh, I am. But maybe she's better out of it, don't you think? You're a former Catholic, Mother. Don't Catholics believe in an afterlife that's preferable to this one? If one makes the right preparations for it, I guess I have to add, don't I?"

I stopped the car by the front of the house and let him go inside before me, pleading that I had a headache and wanted to rest for a few minutes.

When I did go in, the phone was ringing. It was Father Jackson. I hung up on him.

"Who was that?" Jack yelled from his room.

"Wrong number," I said.

A minute later he called again. "Before you hang up, I just want you to know I'm praying for you," he said.

"Would you mind telling me why, you bastard?"

"I asked Jim if he'd see you, but he's upset now with both of us. He thinks I'm crazy too."

He hung up. I thought about calling him back but decided against it. For one thing, Jack had come out of his room and was watching me. I went upstairs without offering any explanation. Duff was standing in his bedroom doorway, but I didn't say anything to him either.

I went into my own room and closed the door. Then I looked under the mattress. The uniform coat was still there. I lay on the bed until dinnertime, trying not to think about any of it.

Chapter Eighteen

Nothing unusual happened the rest of the weekend. I kept waiting for the General, but he didn't come. Then on Monday afternoon Dr. Tully paid us a visit. I wasn't pleased to see him, to say the least, but I was civil to him.

He stood in the front room, beaming with delight. "This is the first time I've been in this house," he said.

"Does it fulfill a longtime ambition?" Jack asked jovially.

"Oh dear, yes."

"Dr. Tully is an anthropologist at the college in Ashland," I said quickly. "He's making a study of old local families."

"Then he and Duff ought to get together."

"I should very much like to meet Duff," Dr. Tully said.

"Some other time. He's in school now."

"He ought to be home soon," Jack said.

"Not for a couple of hours possibly. And Dr. Tully probably can't stay that long."

"Oh, I have plenty of time," Dr. Tully assured us. "I have no more classes today and since I'm a bachelor with no family ties, it doesn't matter how long I stay."

It matters to me, I thought. I didn't want him asking a lot of questions and possibly upsetting Duff. I was sorry I had ever let Father Jackson get me involved with him.

I took him upstairs, mainly to get him away from Jack, and showed him the bedrooms.

"Marvelous," he said. "This house is supposed to resemble Libby Prison, you know."

"Yes, I've been told that."

"But have you been told why?"

"I've read part of a journal that mentions it was at Libby Prison that General Caine first took up the practice of Satanism."

"A journal kept by the General? I should very much like to see that."

"I'm not sure it's in the General's own hand. And I don't know where the book is right now."

"If you find it—"

"Of course."

We were standing in my room and Dr. Tully said, "I imagine this was the General's bedroom."

"Why?"

"Well it's the larger of the two bedrooms on this floor. The two downstairs bedrooms are much smaller and were probably conceived as servants' rooms, although possibly never put to that use. Yes, I'd say he slept in this room and in that bed, and died there too, probably."

"What happened to him?"

"There is a legend that he was poisoned by his mistress." Dr. Tully rubbed his head. "I think I've mentioned her—Margaret Dorn. Apparently she was a local siren, a widow who was also suspected of having murdered her husband. He had a farm somewhere on this road, I think. Margaret is said to have been a member of the circle of worshipers, and after her husband was out of the way, she took up with the General. He may have been involved in the death of Margaret's husband too. This was a year or so after his wife died and he sent his children away. Margaret evidently moved in here, which so incensed some of the more respectable local citizens that they burned down her house and barns. Then later she and the General seemingly had a falling out. Anyway, it was suspected that he did away with her."

"I thought you said she poisoned him."

Dr. Tully chuckled. "That came later. She died very suddenly in the summer of 1890, but no investigation was made. There was a local physician in the group, and he apparently signed the death certificate. Then a week or so later some local children found the front door here open and they decided to explore the house. The General's body was here on the bed, dressed in his uniform. He had evidently been dead for several days. Some slices of fruitcake containing arsenic were found on a downstairs table, and it was assumed that Margaret Dorn had baked the fruitcake for him."

"And he ate the cake after she was dead and buried."

"Very possibly." Dr. Tully gave a mock shudder. "I've often thought if I had to be confronted by one of them on a dark night, I would prefer it be the General. At least the General never killed any of his relatives."

We went to the storeroom. "Some of this furniture may have belonged to Margaret Dorn," Dr. Tully said. "She may have brought some of it here before her house was burned. I imagine a lot of the other things were picked up on the cheap by the General. He may have bought them at auction from the homes of people he frightened away from here."

Our visitor wanted to see the third floor, but I told him there was no key for the door. Naturally, I didn't say anything about the uniform I had found. We went back downstairs then and he prowled around some more in the kitchen, and then we went outside and he looked at the barn and the sheds.

"And here's the graveyard," he said as we came upon it. "I've visited here before. As I told you, I could never get into the house while Miss Hannah was alive, but I did manage to explore the grounds."

"You probably know that this is—or was—General Caine's grave, then," I said as I indicated the place where the soil had recently been overturned.

"I'm sure it isn't. Or at least I'm sure he wasn't buried here originally."

"But Father Fogarty told me—"

"Father Fogarty is wrong. Unless, of course, the stones here have been misplaced for a long time." He was searching the long grass, kicking through it until he found a small stone, only a rectangle of slate really. Some letters were crudely scratched on it. "M. E. D."

"There you are," said Dr. Tully. "Margaret Edith Dorn. She was buried here, or so I always assumed, because the stone was here. I imagine that the General dug the grave himself, since few of his neighbors would've been likely to help him. He probably cut the initials on the stone too. Then a little more than a week later he was buried over here." He led me to where the General's stone was standing.

"But you can see how that stone has been propped up recently."

"Oh, not so recently, I think. It was like this the first time I saw it several years ago. Of course, it was probably taken down a few times when the General's coffin was removed, although it doesn't seem as if the earth here has been disturbed for a long time. I imagine the stone was knocked down a few times too, by some of the General's ill wishers." He moved back toward the gate. "Here's where his poor wife is resting, do you see? Hannah Caine's mother. Really bad taste, wasn't it, to later put his mistress next to his wife."

The small stone, almost hidden in the grass, was engraved ADA DANVERS CAINE 1850–1881.

"Do you think Margaret Dorn's coffin has been dug up?" I was very nervous, for some reason.

"It looks like it, doesn't it. That's a new twist." He went back to Margaret's grave, stopped and picked up a handful of the soil. "There are several possibilities," he said finally. "One, Margaret is still here. Two, her body has been removed. Three, Margaret and the General are both here. Partners in evil resting together. Four, perhaps the General was put here with Margaret a long time ago, and has only recently been disinterred. Five, if Margaret and the General were both here, maybe both were recently taken away."

"But why would anyone want to dig her up?"

"She was an important figure too—maybe even second-in-command of the group during her lifetime." Dr. Tully took my arm and we left the graveyard. "There's another point of which I'm sure you're unaware. I only discovered it myself after your recent visit to my office prompted me to do some research into county records. I think I have found that your Mrs. Reddy is a granddaughter of Margaret Dorn."

"And the General?"

"No, I don't think she ever bore any children by him. But she had a daughter before she came to him. The girl was put in a county home, and in the Ashland courthouse there is a record of her marriage in 1899 and the birth of a daughter named Hazel in 1901. Then in 1930 the marriage of Hazel and a man named Steven Reddy was recorded."

"And that's Mrs. Reddy down the road?"

"I'm reasonably sure of it. She was away from this area for a long time, and then came back with her daughter Rose in the late forties or early fifties. Then Rose married Emil Weber, and later Hazel took the job here with your aunt. I'm sure your aunt knew nothing of Hazel's connection with Margaret Dorn, or she would never have taken her on."

We were at the front of the house now, and I saw the school bus approaching. I steered Dr. Tully toward his car.

"I've tried to ascertain your Mrs. Reddy's first name in order to confirm my theory," Dr. Tully went on, "but so far no luck. She has apparently never voted here, nor has she any bank accounts in Cainesville or Ashland. Is that your son?"

The bus had stopped and Duff and Franny were getting off.

"Why don't you just call and ask her," I said. "Pose as a census taker or an Internal Revenue agent."

Duff and Franny had crossed the road and were coming toward us. Why was I afraid to have him question Duff? It might've been better if I had permitted it. Maybe he could've found out something that would've saved us. Instead I opened the door of his Volkswagen.

"Would you mind, " I said. "I don't feel well."

"I'd like to say hello—"

"Please, some other time." I was pushing him into the car. Then I closed the door.

"May I come again?" he shouted.

"Call us first."

Duff and Franny had reached the house and were watching with great curiosity. I took their arms. "This is Duff, this is Franny," I called. "Duff, Franny—Dr. Tully." Then I took them inside.

"Who was that?" Franny wanted to know.

"A salesman," I said.

Duff grinned and went upstairs. Jack didn't even lift his gaze from his yellow pad. I watched through the window for several minutes until Dr. Tully finally gave up and drove away.

Then I went upstairs. Duff's door was closed. I went to my room and lifted the mattress. The uniform coat was gone. I ran into the storeroom and pulled the cupboard aside. The door to the third floor wasn't locked.

Without the flashlight, it was almost impossible to see anything as I groped my way up the stairs, biting my tongue to stop from screaming every time a cobweb brushed my face.

At the top I called, "Duff? Duff?"

There was no answer. I made my way through the darkness to the other side of the room and found the settee. The rest of the uniform was gone too. I got down on my knees and felt around on the floor, but I couldn't find the boots either.

Then before I could get to my feet, I heard the door in the storeroom slam. I did scream then and stumbled in what I thought to be the direction of the stairs. There had been a faint light from below before, but now there was nothing.

I missed the stairs and ran into the opposite wall, then coming back, I missed the stairs again and ran into some furniture. I thought I heard the guttural laugh. Was he here?

Then reason took over. I dropped to the floor and crawled until I reached the far wall again and then crawled back obliquely until I found the stairs, went down them, half-falling, and threw myself against the door, screaming Duff's name.

He opened the door.

"Mother, what have you been doing? You're a mess."

"You locked me up there," I sobbed.

"Mother, the door wasn't locked. Look, there's no key. An air current must have blown the door shut."

"The key is on your bureau."

"No, it isn't. I did find it a few weeks ago and I went up to the third floor once, but then I misplaced the key."

"You lie, you lie, just as you lied to the psychiatrist!"

"Mother, Mother . . ."

He tried to put his arm around me, but I pulled away from him and ran to his room. There was no key on the bureau now, but the eyeglasses were still where I had left them.

Duff picked them up. "These are yours, Mother."

"They're yours!"

"Try them on."

I refused to try them. I was sure they weren't mine. They looked like a pair of mine, it was true, a pair I seldom wore. In fact I never wore them except for sewing.

"Where are yours, if these are mine?"

"Here." He took another pair of glasses from his shirt pocket. They were very like the other pair, although the lenses were thicker. Duff had switched them, I was sure. He had gone to my purse or my sewing basket and gotten my glasses and then put them on his bureau in place of his.

"Liar," I said softly. "You're a liar, as well as something worse." I walked away from him and went into my room and closed and locked the door.

He came and knocked at the door later, and so did Franny and Jack, begging me to come down to dinner, but I refused. In fact, after a while I didn't even bother answering them.

General Caine came to me again that night while I slept. Shortly after dawn I awoke and he was gone, but again there was evidence that he had been there.

I got out of bed and went to my dresser and picked up my brush. Then I stood in front of the mirror, and began to brush my hair. I think I had only just lifted the brush when I fainted.

Book Four

Chapter Nineteen

A pounding on the door brought me back to consciousness. I grabbed the end of the bed and pulled myself up, not remembering anything for a moment. I went to the door and unlocked it. Duff came in, wearing pajamas.

"What's wrong, Mother?" He switched on the light.

"Nothing," I said.

"You were screaming and then I heard a thud. Did you fall out of bed?"

"I guess I must have."

"Did you have a nightmare?"

"Yes. What time is it?"

"Six o'clock or so. Aren't you hungry, Mother? You didn't have any dinner."

"I'm fine. I have a headache, that's all."

"That's from not eating. Can't I get you something?"

"No, thanks. Go back to bed."

"What was your nightmare about?"

"I don't remember. What was yours about, the one you had the night of Dad's accident."

He smiled. "I've forgotten now."

"There you are. Nightmares are so ridiculous and meaningless that they don't even stay with us for very long. Did I wake your dad and Franny too?"

"I don't think so. I haven't heard them moving around down there."

"All right. Try and get another hour's sleep."

I touched his cheek. It was smooth. Had he shaved recently?

He was shaving once or twice a week then. My own cheeks were still burning, as though they had been in contact with rougher ones.

"Do I seem any different to you, Duff?"

"You look a bit feverish. Do you want me to get you some aspirin?"

"No, I guess not."

"Why do you lock your bedroom door, Mama?"

"Nerves. A strange house."

"It shouldn't be that strange now."

"I'm still getting used to it."

He left and I closed the door, but didn't lock it again, afraid that he would hear. Then I sat on the edge of the bed for a long time, trying to work up enough courage to go to the mirror.

What I saw when I managed it was not much different, I was certain, than what I could have seen eight hours before. My cheeks were reddened, and my chin, but that could've been because of my state of excitement. Also, there were the marks of a restless night—bloodshot eyes with bags under them. But there was nothing else, nothing like what I had seen before in the mirror.

What had I seen then? Was it really someone so unlike me? The nightgown was the same—even in my terror I had noticed that—though it hadn't fitted me as well as it did now. The woman who had worn it then was bigger boned, with broader shoulders and larger breasts.

Her face was nothing like mine either. Hers was wider and her nose was longer and less tilted. Her lips were fuller, more sensual, her eyes were dark brown and so was her hair. Also it was longer, much longer than mine.

It was Margaret Dorn, I was sure of it. I wondered if there was a portrait or photograph of her anywhere in the house, but then I knew I didn't want to find any such thing. I didn't want proof. I told myself I couldn't be certain. Probably I had been thinking of Margaret Dorn, worrying about her possible presence in the house, and then my fear could have caused the hallucination.

If it happens again, I thought, I'll begin to worry. Right now

I'll put it out of my mind. And I was able to do that for a few minutes at least. I showered and dressed and went downstairs to drink coffee and read old newspapers. Then I heard the alarm clock go off in Franny's room and I knew I couldn't face the others.

I decided to drive to Cainesville and see Father Jackson. Despite my difficulties with him, there was no one else with whom I could talk. It was only a bit after seven, but I was hoping that he might be saying early Mass.

I went down the road at a highly unsafe speed, fearful as I approached the Weber house that I would see what I had the last time I passed. But I didn't. The house looked the same as always and Emil's station wagon was in the yard. I did have the sensation that I was being watched as I went by, but I didn't see anyone.

Mass was in progress when I reached Saint Mary's Church and Father Jackson was the celebrant. There were only five or six people in the pews ahead of me as I knelt in the back. Boards had been put over several of the windows, I noticed, and there was evidence that the walls had been scrubbed in several places.

Father Jackson saw me when I entered. He was reading the Gospel and he paused briefly, then continued. He didn't look at me again during his short homily that followed. He spoke eloquently and reverently, I had to admit, about charity and tolerance. I wondered for a moment if he was addressing the remarks to me, but then I realized he must have prepared them earlier.

After Mass I waited in church, wondering if he would come back out to see me. The rest of the congregation had gone, except for a couple of women who had moved into the shrine in the apse. In a few minutes he came out through the sanctuary door and down the aisle. He had removed his Mass vestments, but he was still wearing his cassock.

"Come outside," he whispered as he passed my pew.

I got up and followed him out, then waited on the church steps with him while a couple of elderly women came up and complimented him on his sermon. He nodded graciously, puffing a cigarette and glancing nervously at me.

"I'm sorry about Saturday," I said when the women were gone.

"I'm sorry too."

"It wasn't your fault. Did you get your car fixed?"

"Yes, and the statue has been put back in the shrine. Father Fogarty won't have it repaired though. He wants to leave it the way it is as a reminder that Satan is still around in the world."

"When I left the other day you had a strange expression on your face. You seemed frightened of me."

He nodded. "You looked like you were ready to kill me. I've never seen such hatred in anyone's eyes."

"But it was still me?"

He hesitated. "Who else would it be?"

I told him, all of it, starting with what I had seen going home with Duff. I was interrupted several times by people going in and out of church, stopping to chat with him.

When I finished he said, "Don't panic. Come over to the rectory and have some coffee."

"And go through an inquisition by Father Fogarty?"

"He has the next Mass. He won't have time to bother you."

I went along to the rectory dining room. Mrs. Guenther brought us coffee and rolls, silently indicating her disapproval of my being there. Then Father Fogarty came in. He didn't seem overjoyed at seeing me either.

"How are you coming with the devil business at her place?"

Father Jackson winced. "I've been trying to help Mrs. Caine—"

"She could help herself if she'd get down on her knees. Does she know how her trouble has been passed on to us?"

"I don't think you have any evidence—"

Father Fogarty shook his finger under his assistant's nose. "When you leave an ungodly loophole anywhere, then that fella can slip in and do his dirty work in even holy places." Then he left without even a nod in my direction.

Father Jackson sighed. "Now about this new development."

"Skip it." I finished my coffee. "I'll go back to my ungodly loophole."

"Forget that. And you're not Margaret Dorn."

"Not now."

"None of the time. It's all just the result of a subconscious suggestion."

"What about what you saw Saturday?"

"I'll admit you seemed changed, but it was only because you were so angry." He sighed. "I wish Jim could've stayed another day."

"Tell me now what he meant when he asked if I was left-handed."

"When we were having drinks at the motel it seemed to him that you were acting strangely. You'd pick up your glass with your right hand, but then your left hand would snatch it away. The same thing happened a couple of times when you picked up your purse."

"She must have been left-handed."

"Forget it, Maggie. There's probably no way of finding that out anyway."

"I'm going to find out one thing about her. I'm going to find out if she's still buried in that graveyard."

"Maggie, you can't do anything like that!"

"I have to know if they're using her remains the way they're probably using General Caine's."

"Jim said you had the problem and not your son."

"You son of a bitch!" I went to the front door.

He followed me. "Maggie, I still want to help you."

"You haven't done much so far." Outside on the steps I turned to him. "If you think, as your brother evidently does, that I'm psychotic, why did you call up and tell me you were praying for me?"

"It's not unusual to pray for disturbed people."

"Thanks!"

"Wait." He caught up with me when I was halfway to the car. "It did enter my mind Saturday that there might be something ... unexplainable, I guess. I've truly never seen such evil anywhere as I saw—or thought I saw—on your face. Anyway, don't do anything about Margaret Dorn today. I have to work on the parish budget today with the old man, but I'll come to your place tomorrow."

"Make it before my children get home from school. I don't

want them to see that their mother is reduced to needing a priest."

I drove out of town, angry at him and more angry at myself for having gone to him. For some reason it seemed to infuriate me to have him think that the strange things happening to me were all inside my head, even though I had tried to convince myself of that very thing earlier in the morning.

Be happy you're crazy, I told myself now. None of it has happened. You're not Margaret Dorn, you haven't been visited by the General, and there's nothing wrong with Duff. You have had a temporary mental illness, and now that you're aware of it, you're going to get over it.

Then I thought of something I hadn't mentioned to Father Jackson. The glasses he had found and that Duff insisted were mine. If Duff wasn't lying, what did that mean? Could Stephanie have taken my glasses either by mistake or by design?

I was approaching the Weber house again, certain that nothing strange was going to happen this time. I was wrong. As I reached a point a hundred yards or so from the Weber drive, the car disappeared and I was in a buggy again, but not the same buggy as before. This was the one I had seen in the yard. The upholstery was rich-looking leather and the wood and metal were highly polished. The horse in front of me was the handsome chestnut, trotting briskly along.

I wasn't afraid now because I was no longer Margaret Caine. I didn't even remember Margaret Caine, but afterward I remembered what I did as Margaret Dorn. The horse went up the graveled drive and stopped beside the house. I got out of the buggy, holding up my long black taffeta skirt, and went to the door. It wasn't locked, as I knew it wouldn't be.

The parlor was filled with heavy, dark Victorian furniture, including an upright piano that I knew had been bought for me. I didn't hesitate, but continued to the stairs and then up to the second floor.

I went into a bedroom where a man was lying in bed. He had a full gray beard and he looked about sixty. He also seemed ill. His eyes were closed and his face was beaded with sweat. He opened his eyes now and smiled at me.

I went to a night stand, picked up a bottle and a spoon and poured out some liquid. The man had raised up now and he took the dose I gave him, then fell back and closed his eyes again. I knew he was my husband and I knew I was poisoning him.

I recorked the bottle, put the spoon in its glass, left the room and went back downstairs and out the front door. General Caine was standing in the drive beside his Arabian. He wasn't wearing his uniform now, but instead a well-cut black suit. He was watching me intently, and when I nodded my head he came forward and embraced me. Then he helped me into the buggy, which I knew he had bought for me, got on his horse and rode down the drive. When he reached the road, he waved to me to follow him.

I had picked up the reins and was about to start the chestnut when a voice below me asked, "Why did you come back?"

Chapter Twenty

The buggy disappeared and I was sitting behind the wheel of the Plymouth. I was Maggie Caine again, although I remembered everything that had happened. George Langley, the boy who lived with the Webers, was standing by the car door watching me solemnly.

"Why were you in the house?" he asked. "Did you want to see the meeting room again?"

When I was able to speak I said, "Yes, that's right. Where were you?"

"Walking on the road. I saw you drive in here so I came home."

"You saw me drive in?"

"Yes."

"In this car?"

He studied me briefly, then nodded. "Yes."

So there it was. I was losing my mind.

"Where are Mrs. Reddy and the Webers?"

"Mr. Weber went away a little while ago. Mrs. Weber and Mrs. Reddy were in the parlor when I went out."

"How long ago was that?"

"About ten minutes ago. I just went out for a walk."

How could they be in the parlor? Wouldn't I have seen them? They would have prevented me going up the stairs, wouldn't they?

"Did you see me go in the house too, George?"

"Yes, and then you came out a couple of minutes later."

Was he lying? Had they sent him out to lie to me? But to what purpose? And how could they have managed the rest of it—causing me to see the house as it was. Even if they had brought in old furniture and put an actor in the upstairs bed, they couldn't have made the car disappear, and changed the road, and put me in a black taffeta dress in a buggy. Or could they?

Could they have hypnotized me and made me see things that weren't really there? But how could they have managed that if I hadn't even seen the two of them first? Didn't you have to look into a hypnotist's eyes and listen to his voice in order to be put under his spell?

"Do you want me to fetch Mrs. Reddy and Mrs. Weber?" the boy asked.

"No, thank you, George." I wondered if they were watching me from the house. "Why aren't you in school?"

"I don't go anymore. Mrs. Weber gives me lessons."

What kind of lessons? I wondered. "You ought to go to school. Do you have anyone to play with around here?"

"No."

"Why don't you ride your pony?"

"I don't have a pony."

"But I saw you riding one. The first day we came here. You were in the yard and you were on a pony."

He nodded. "His name was Ginger. But I only had him for that day. Mr. Weber went and got him in a trailer and then took him back the next day."

"But why?"

He shrugged. "I don't know. Mrs. Reddy told him to do it."

I had a sudden thought. "Where did Mr. Weber get Ginger?"

"From Mr. Dobbs on the next road. He rents out ponies."

Was Dobbs in on it too? I was terrified of waiting there any longer. Whatever power they had over me, it seemed obvious they could put it to work again.

"Do you know where I live, George?"

He shook his head.

"It's a mile and a half or so down the road. It doesn't look like a house. It looks more like a warehouse or a factory. If you ever have any trouble here, you can come and stay with me."

"What kind of trouble would I have?"

"You'll know when it happens."

I backed out on the road, tires screeching, and then looked at the house again. I was half-expecting one of them to come out, but it didn't happen. The boy was still standing in the yard as I drove off.

It had been window dressing, the pony rented for George, I was sure. We were supposed to think they were a typically happy farm family. But how did Mrs. Reddy know we were coming the day we arrived from the East? The real estate agent in Ashland could have phoned her, but that wouldn't have given her much time to arrange for the pony. I should have asked the boy what time of the day the pony had been delivered.

Still, no phone call might have been necessary. If she could make me think I was Margaret Dorn, she could easily have telepathic powers as well. And, on the plus side, if Mrs. Reddy was responsible, then I wasn't crazy after all.

It seemed all the more urgent now that I find the remains of Margaret Dorn and the General. Whether or not Mrs. Reddy could use them in some supernatural way, if she *believed* she could use them, then they had better be destroyed before something worse happened to Duff or me.

By the time I reached home, however, I was in a state of terror and incapable of searching for anything. I ran from the car without even closing the door, went into the house and up the stairs, refusing to answer any of Jack's questions, and locked myself in my room.

I heard him hobbling up the stairs around noon. He knocked on my door and then went back downstairs again. After a while I opened the door and found a cup of tea and a cheese sandwich on a tray. I made a deliberate effort to eat the sandwich and drink the tea, using my right hand, but it was impossible. My left hand kept grabbing the cup and the sandwich and I was powerless to stop it. After a while I quit fighting it.

I went to the mirror occasionally to see who I was, but I remained Maggie Caine, at least in appearance, for the rest of the day. (I brushed my hair several times, using my left hand, and remembered that I had been doing it that way for several days.) When they returned from school Duff and Franny came to my door, but I ignored all their rappings and pleadings.

That night I became Margaret Dorn again in body. I didn't have to look in the mirror to know it. My face became longer, my cheekbones more pronounced, my breasts swelled, and my fingers became thinner and more tapered. And the General came to me again.

In the morning I was awakened by Jack hammering on my door. He was yelling, "Get up, Maggie! You have a visitor!"

I found my watch on the dresser. It was nine-thirty. I calculated that I had slept fourteen hours or more. I hadn't done that in years—not since college, and then only after a couple of all-night pre-exam sessions.

"Your priest friend is here to see you," Jack shouted. "Your children are disgusted with you, Maggie, and I am too. Locking yourself in a bedroom like this. Have some consideration for your family!"

"Fuck my family," I said, but not loudly. Then I was horrified. How could I have even thought anything like that?

"Tell Father Jackson I'll be down in five minutes."

I waited until I heard Jack clumping away before going to the bathroom. Then I dressed quickly and was downstairs in not much more than my announced time.

"I'm sorry to break in on you like this," Father Jackson said. He was wearing his Roman collar.

"I invited you, didn't I? Or at least I knew you were coming. Have some breakfast with me."

I steered him out to the kitchen and into a chair while I prepared an enormous breakfast—bacon, eggs, sausage, five or six pieces of toast. Jack came to the doorway a couple of times to look in on us suspiciously, but I didn't speak to him and the second time I thumbed my nose at him. Father Jackson was embarrassed, so I went over and ruffled his hair and kissed him. Then he was even more embarrassed.

"Are you going to eat all that food?" he asked.

"I am if you're not going to help me."

And I did. He had a cup of coffee and watched me gorge myself. Then, when I had eaten all I had cooked, I went to the refrigerator and polished off some cold roast beef and a bowl of tapioca pudding.

"Now I feel better," I said. "I'm ready to go out and do some digging."

"It's illegal," Father Jackson said.

"Nonsense. This is private property. Our graveyard belongs to us."

I left the dishes on the table and went out to the barn, Father Jackson following reluctantly. As a matter of fact I knew what I proposed to do was foolish. I was sure I wasn't going to find anything. However, I was enjoying Peter Jackson's discomfort.

I found two long-handled shovels and a pick among the rusting tools. The blade was half gone on one shovel and the handle was cracked on the other.

"These will do," I said. "There isn't much clay in this ground."

I led him to the graveyard and the place where Dr. Tully had said Margaret Dorn was buried. Without preamble I went to work, driving my shovel into the earth.

"You'd better take off your coat if you're going to help," I told him.

He didn't know what to do. He stood by the fence for a while, watching me and growing more agitated. Finally the gentleman in him prevailed. He took off his coat, draping it carefully over a tombstone, picked up the shovel with the broken blade and lifted about a tablespoonful of earth.

"We'll be here 'til dark at your rate," I said, shoveling at a speed of which I would never have dreamed I was capable. I was a good two feet down by that time. At about four feet, I found a couple of rusty nails and a piece of rotting board that could have been part of a coffin.

Jack came down the path shortly after that, limping along with his cane.

"What in the name of God are you doing?" he yelled.

"Getting some exercise," I said, not pausing. Father Jackson grinned feebly.

"This is desecration, Father! I'm surprised that you'd take part in it."

"You're right. I'm sorry." Father Jackson threw away his shovel and climbed out of the hole.

"Maggie, for God's sake, a member of my family is buried there."

"Not here. There's no one buried here." I was ready to quit anyway. "And apparently there's no treasure chest either," I added as I threw out the shovel and reached up to let Father Jackson pull me out of the hole.

"What treasure chest?"

"I found a letter upstairs that said General Caine had buried some money here."

That grabbed my husband. "How much money?"

"I don't know. There's supposed to be a box or chest with a lot of gold coins in it, but it's not here, as you can see."

"Where's the letter? Let me see it."

"I'll show it to you later. Go back to the house now. And don't say anything about this to Duff or Franny. We don't want them out here desecrating your graveyard."

He went. Father Jackson stood watching me unhappily as I began to fill in the hole.

"Why couldn't you have told him the truth?" Father Jackson asked.

"Too complicated. Also, he wouldn't have believed it. Are you going to help me or stand there and criticize?"

He picked up his shovel again and in a few minutes we had the hole filled and leveled. Then we took the tools back to the barn. I showed Father Jackson the ladder to the loft.

"Climb up and see what's up there," I told him.

"Will that thing hold me? It looks shaky."

He went up cautiously, hesitating a couple of times. I had to keep urging him on, but he finally made it into the loft. He disappeared for a couple of minutes and then came back.

"There's nothing up here but a lot of mice and a few more old tools," he said.

"All right, come down." He did and then I added, "I knew there wouldn't be any coffins up there."

"How did you know?"

"I just knew. What's left of General Duffin Caine and his mistress, Margaret Dorn, is at the Weber house. They were in the cellar, but I think they're in the meeting room now."

I looked at my fingers. They were growing longer. I felt my cheeks. The bones were more prominent. Couldn't he see the difference? Then I was completely Margaret Dorn and I could no longer remember Maggie Caine.

I reached for him and he yelled and ran out of the barn. I knew he would return, so I sat on the floor and waited for him. In a minute or two he came back wearing his stole around his neck and carrying a prayer book. Then he stood some distance away from me, reading from the book and raising his hands occasionally to make the sign of the cross while I shouted obscenities at him. At least I know now my words were obscene. Then I thought they were amusing.

After a while I went up the ladder to the loft and invited him to come with me. I had it in my mind to seduce him and then afterward kill him. I was sure I was strong enough to strangle him. However he paid no attention to my repeated invitations, and after a while I stretched out on the loft floor and went to sleep.

When I awakened, it was much darker and for a moment I couldn't remember where I was. Then I looked over the edge of the loft and saw Father Jackson. He was seated on a wheelbarrow, still reading his prayer book.

"Hi," I called softly. He looked up cautiously. "It's me, Maggie." I came down the ladder. "What time is it?"

He glanced at his watch. "Four-thirty."

"God. Are the kids home from school yet?"

"Your daughter is. She looked in here a while ago, but then she went away again without saying anything."

"Did she know I was up in the loft?"

"I don't think so."

"Why didn't you tell her?"

"I didn't think you wanted her to see you. Did you?"

"Maggie Caine didn't." He didn't reply. "Do you believe me now?" I asked.

"I believe there's something wrong with you," he said carefully. "Maybe you're the one who's a multiple personality."

I was angry, but then I thought, maybe he's right. My God, I hope he's right. At least it would be something treatable.

"I don't suppose your brother would want to see me."

"I could call him. I don't think he'd want to come here again, but we would drive up to see him."

"No, I'll go alone." But then I thought, what if I get halfway to Cleveland and find myself in the buggy again.

"I don't think I ought to go anywhere, Peter. I ought to be guarded and not let out of the house." Then I told him what had been in my mind when I was up in the loft and also what had happened when I went in the Weber house.

"Don't tell me again I'm not Margaret Dorn."

He smiled wanly. "Well, you're not now at any rate."

"Didn't I really change this time?"

"Your personality surely changed."

"Goddamn it, my features, my hair, my body. My complexion is lighter, I'm shorter, my tits are smaller than hers!"

"That's what you see. I saw only a person who seemed demented."

"Goddamn it!"

"Maggie, what difference does it make? I agree there's something wrong with you."

"And will you agree that it could be caused by an outside source?"

"Oh, I don't know—"

"Peter, how could such things possibly happen to two persons in the same family at the same time? Wouldn't the odds be astronomical on the same thing happening to Duff and me?"

"Well, we have only your word about things happening to Duff."

"Goddamn you, Jackson, go to the high school, go to the police in Ashland! Go and ask his father!"

"Still, no one but you has seen the General!"

I flew at him and hammered his chest. He caught me and held me tightly. He was stronger than I had expected him to be. After a while I was exhausted, and then I just stood there sobbing and letting him hold me.

"Stay with me. I mean stay in the house tonight, Peter."

"But I can't—" He hesitated and then said, "All right. If it's all right with your husband. I'll have to think of some excuse to give Father Fogarty."

"Tell him the truth. Tell him I'm possessed."

"He'd love that. That's what he'd like to hear. Why do you want me to stay tonight?"

"I just feel that something might happen and someone who knows about me ought to be around. I haven't been able to talk to Jack about it."

"I think you should."

"I can't. You're the only one I can trust, Peter."

He realized he had been holding me for a long time and he released me then. Was there still something of Margaret Dorn in me? I think even when she wasn't in complete control of me, she had begun by that time to influence me greatly.

We went into the house and I told Jack that Father Jackson was going to spend the night. His bedroom at the rectory was being painted, I said, and paint fumes always made him ill. Peter looked uncomfortable during this but he didn't protest.

"Where will he bunk?" Jack asked. "Maybe you could move downstairs with me, Maggie, and Father Jackson could have your room."

"The sofa here is good enough," Father Jackson said. "I'm small. I can manage all right for one night."

"It could be more than one night," I said. "It takes a while for a newly painted room to air out."

Duff and Franny came downstairs then. I was wondering how Duff would react to the priest, since it was supposedly he who had stopped Duff after the first church incident.

"Do you know Father Jackson, Duff?" I asked casually.

"No, I don't think so," Duff said and shook hands. He didn't react either to the news that Father Jackson was spending the night.

"Do you play Scrabble?" Franny asked. "I'm afraid that or poker is all we can offer you for entertainment, since we don't have a TV set."

"I'm a champion Scrabble player," Father Jackson assured her.

"You have to watch Dad. He makes up words that you can never find in a dictionary. And Duff uses four-letter words."

"Untrue," Duff said and smiled at me.

I didn't pursue it, and I silenced Franny when she wanted to give us some examples. And we did play Scrabble after dinner —a dinner over which I labored somewhat more than usual, partly because we had a guest, but mostly because I was afraid of night coming on and prolonging dinner seemed to be keeping it at bay.

Then the Scrabble game. All of us except Duff played. I don't know whether it was because of Franny's remark or not, but he refused to participate, although he stayed in the dining room and kibitzed to an annoying degree.

Father Jackson didn't seem to mind and had more fun than any of the rest of us. I suppose it was a welcome change from his usual evening at the rectory. Jack enjoyed himself too—mainly because Duff was helping him, suggesting words when Jack was stumped and supplying longer and better-scoring words in place of Jack's often feeble ones.

After a while I began to lose control. The first indication was when I picked up letters to build on a word of Franny's. I had intended to spell "Jacobin," but after I had picked up a "J" and a "C" to build on Franny's "A," it was impossible to pick up any more letters with my right hand. Instead my left hand picked them up and spelled out "jackass."

"I guess that shows what Mother thinks of me," said Franny.

"Jackass is male. She must be thinking of someone else," murmured Duff.

Then on my next turn I wanted to add "history" to a word of Father Jackson's. Instead my left hand spelled "him." Father Jackson was watching me closely. I winked at him.

"You'll never pile up points that way, Mother," Franny told me.

The next time I built on Jack's "initial" to spell out "incest." My right hand wanted to prevent it, but it couldn't.

"Mother," Duff said reprovingly and grinned.

"This is a stupid game," I said. "I'm going to quit."

"No, don't," Father Jackson said sharply. "Play a while longer."

"That's right," said Jack yawning. "Scrabble usually gets more interesting as it goes along."

"When all the players have learned to spell at least simple words," I said. He had just reversed the "I" and the "E" in "receive."

On my next turn I added "kill you" to his word. I wasn't disturbed by it any longer. I just smiled.

"Single words only, Mother," said Franny.

"Who will?" Father Jackson asked softly.

My left hand put down an "M" and then an "E." Then I swept the board and all the letters off the table and ran upstairs. I locked myself in my room and sat on the bed. At that moment I did want to kill Jack. I wanted his death more than anything else, even more than I wanted General Caine.

After a while I went and sat in front of the mirror. I couldn't wait to become Margaret Dorn and fulfill whatever mission was destined for me. I believed completely now in the General's Master, and I was willing to serve that Master as he had.

Chapter Twenty-One

Franny knocked on my door after a half hour or so and said petulantly that I had spoiled the evening for everyone and that her father had sent her up to get some sheets and a blanket for Father Jackson. I told her to take whatever she needed from the linen cupboard in the hallway.

"Why does your voice sound so funny?" she asked.

"I have a cold," I said.

"Why did you spell what you did on the board, Mama?"

I didn't answer that. In a little while she went away. I disrobed, turned out the light and lay on the bed, waiting for the General to come. After a few moments I began to hear voices calling me. First his voice, then others I recognized out of the past, but I was still too much Maggie Caine to put names to them.

"Come," the voices called. "Come to us, Margaret."

Still I waited. I wanted to obey, but I knew it was better to wait until those downstairs were asleep. I wasn't concerned about Duff. I suppose he came upstairs when Jack and Franny went to their rooms and Father Jackson made ready to sleep on the sofa. Or maybe he didn't bother with any pretense.

The voices continued, more insistent now and louder. Old voices, young voices, even the voices of children calling for Margaret to come and join them. There seemed to be dozens of them calling plaintively, wistfully, but never commanding. It was as if those who were calling really loved Margaret and wanted her to be with them.

At last I knew it was time to go. I had become Margaret Dorn in body as well as spirit, and I was immensely happy. As Maggie Caine I had never had the same feeling of happiness and fulfillment.

There was a large cupboard in the room that I had never used. I went to it now and found Margaret Dorn's clothes and put them on—the drawers, the corset, the under blouse, the black silk stockings and the black taffeta, high-collared dress. Last I put on the black patent leather shoes with the aid of a buttonhook that I found on the dresser.

Then I unlocked my door and went downstairs. There was a light in the parlor. I went in and saw a man I didn't recognize, nor did I recognize some of the furniture in the room. The man was on his knees and he had fallen asleep with his head on the horsehair sofa that General Caine had bought for me. He awakened now and arose and started toward me, but I went quickly out of the room and to the kitchen. There I unbolted the back door and was into the yard before the man could reach me.

I went down the path past the graveyard to the woods. I looked back once and saw the man behind me, but he stopped pursuing me then, although he continued to call my name. The other voices had stopped now that I was on my way.

Even though the woods was dark I kept on without hesitation. It was a chilly fall night, but that didn't bother me either. When I came to the creek I moved along it until I found a place to cross by stepping on the rocks.

It must have taken me a half hour or more, because the path meandered around thickets and followed the lower side of hilly ground. I saw no house lights until I came out of the woods, crossed an uncultivated field and found another path. Ahead was the rear of a house with one lighted window. It wasn't my house, but it stood where my house had once stood.

I could hear singing and chanting as I approached the door. When I was a few feet away, the door opened and a woman called out, "Welcome, Mother. Welcome to this house." She had white hair and she seemed much older than I, although I knew she was my granddaughter.

She led me to the back room, where the congregation waited. There were twenty or more people in two lines, and they all bowed low and murmured, "Welcome, Mother," as I passed between the lines and went to the head of the room.

There was an altar over which hung an inverted crucifix and behind the altar on a platform were two chairs. General Caine in his uniform was seated in one chair. He arose and beckoned to me to come around the altar and take the other chair. I did, and then saw that on the floor between the chairs were three wooden coffins.

The middle one was newly made and the lid was on it. The other two were old and the wood was rotten and crumbling. Inside each of them was a skeleton. The skull of the one next to my chair had vestiges of long black hair.

The General raised his hand and an elderly man wearing priestly vestments came forward and began a kind of Mass. The rest of the congregation knelt down.

"I came from the altar of God to the altar of my Master," the priest chanted. He was speaking Latin but I understood him. He continued with the opening prayers that I now know were perversions of the rite Maggie Caine was familiar with when she was young.

When the time came for the Offertory of the Mass, two

women moved forward. One was the white-haired woman I had previously recognized. The other was her daughter, my great-granddaughter. They walked around the altar, paused and bowed before the General and me, and then reverently they lifted the lid of the middle coffin. Inside was the body of my great-great-granddaughter. It was clothed in black as I was, and as were all the members of the congregation.

"Master, we offer thee this child. Let her be united with thee," the women chanted to the General. Then, turning to me, "Mother, we offer you this child. Let her be born again, if it be your will and the Master's will. Let her be born again, as you have been born again to serve the Master."

Then I stood up and stepped forward. I knew I was supposed to do that. The two women began to undress me, and at the same time several other women came out of the congregation. The first was carrying a basin of water and a towel. The others were carrying bottles and jars. I knew they were to prepare me for the climax of the ceremony in which the General and I would couple on the altar.

They bathed me and anointed me with various kinds of ointments and fragrances. Then another woman came forward, carrying a black velvet robe embroidered with gold. She was a small, dark old woman with wrinkled cheeks, and she went behind me to help put on the robe. After she had tied the sash, she held her right hand up before my eyes. In her palm was a small silver medal.

"Begone, unclean spirit," she said loudly. "I command you in the name of the Mother of God!"

Several of the others grabbed her and pulled her away from me, but she continued to hold the medal up and shout the same denunciation. The General remained seated, seemingly unaffected by the disturbance.

I was bewildered. For a moment I didn't know who or where I was. Then I became Maggie Caine, and in terror I ran around the altar, down the aisle and out of the room, evading those in the congregation who reached out for me. I went out the back door into the yard and then down the path to the woods.

I expected to be pursued immediately, but I wasn't. Once

inside the woods I stopped and looked back, but there was no sign of anyone coming after me. I set off again as fast as I could, but I wasn't as sure of foot now, as I had been as Margaret Dorn. I kept straying from the path and bumping into trees and bushes, until finally I had to slow down and grope my way.

Then I saw lights, first on one side of me and then the other. They were faint and flickering at first, but they became stronger as those carrying them moved closer. Now I saw two lines of people carrying lanterns and torches and walking parallel to me.

They were dead, I knew, most of them dead a long time. There were men and women dressed in tattered ancient clothing. Men in buckskin, soldiers in uniforms of long-ago wars, Indians in ragged, beaded garments. Women in dresses like Margaret Dorn's, others in dresses of an older time, still others in dresses made of rough handwoven cloth. Even though they never turned toward me, the lines kept coming closer.

I was frantic but I kept moving, ignoring branches and brambles. For some reason I felt if I could only reach the Caine yard, I would be safe. I felt that the things wouldn't pursue me where others could see them. I was also sure that if the lines ever came together, or if I was ever touched by one of them, I would be dead—and, dying in their company, I would be damned like them.

The lines weren't ten feet apart now, less than four feet away on either side of me. Some of the heads were only skulls. The flesh on the others was dried and shriveled or else hanging in blackish green decay. Many of the hands that held the lanterns and torches were nothing but bones.

Several of those closest to me could have reached out now and touched me, but they seemed to ignore me. They didn't seem to be trying to keep pace with me either, although they never all fell behind me. At one moment something dressed in the remnants of a Revolutionary War uniform would be on my right, and something in a frock coat and gaiters on my left. Then the next time a turning in the path caused me to look, the soldier might have been replaced by the bones of a woman in homespun, and the other by something in rotted silk or brocade.

Then I broke out of the woods and began to run toward the

Caine house. Suddenly I heard the General's voice calling my name and heard his running feet behind me on the path. I didn't look back but kept running, stumbling often on the uneven path.

At that moment the line on my right began to move ahead of me. By the graveyard gate the end of the line turned and blocked the path. I couldn't continue toward the house. I could only go back or turn into the graveyard.

There was nowhere else to go. I ran toward the fence on the far side of the graveyard, hoping to be able to get over it, but I tripped on a headstone and he caught me and turned me around. He was like he had been the first time I saw him. His eyes were bloodshot, full of hate and not desire. He wanted to kill me now, I knew.

I screamed once, I remember, as his hand went to my throat. Then as I stumbled backward, I saw Jack standing behind him holding a flashlight, and behind Jack was Franny. In that instant the General fell on me, bearing me to the ground. I felt a crushing blow on the back of my head and then I remembered nothing.

Chapter Twenty-Two

I don't even remember dreaming. There was just nothing. When I regained consciousness I was lying in a bed and Father Jackson was bending over me. He was wearing his stole and he had his prayer book in hand. He was murmuring a prayer and making the sign of the cross over my lips.

"Is it the sacrament for the dying?" I asked weakly.

He nodded, startled. "It's just a precaution, Maggie. Thank God, you've come around."

"Stop it. I don't want it. Where am I?"

"In Ashland Hospital. You've been unconscious for a long time."

"How long?"

"Twelve hours or more. You had a concussion."

I looked beyond him and saw Dr. Fowler at the door. He was

wearing a white coat and he smiled at me and came forward, adjusting his stethoscope. Then I remembered that he had been the celebrant at the Black Mass.

"Get him out of here," I screamed. "He's one of them!" I suppose it was more of a croak than a scream, but it was the best I could manage and it made my head feel as though it had been hit by a sledge hammer.

Dr. Fowler continued to smile. "She's hallucinating. It's not abnormal under the circumstances." He took my wrist firmly and checked my pulse. I struggled for a moment and then I thought, he can't do anything to me with Father Jackson as a witness.

I relaxed and let him shine his flashlight in my eyes and then use his stethoscope. I even went along with his tests, counting his upheld fingers and giving the proper responses.

"She'll be all right," he said. "We'll keep her here for a few days though, just to be on the safe side."

"I'm leaving now," I said. I tried to sit up, but the room began to spin.

I lay back again as Father Jackson took Dr. Fowler's arm and drew him to the door. I heard the word "funeral."

"Will it be on Friday?" asked Dr. Fowler. "We should be able to release her then." Then he left the room without looking at me again.

"What funeral?" I was afraid to hear the answer. I tried to sit up again, but Father Jackson pushed me down gently.

"It was God's will, Maggie," he said.

"Bullshit! Whose funeral?"

"Your husband's."

I sighed. Was I relieved? I had been thinking of Duff.

"He had a heart attack last night. It was evidently a massive attack. He died instantly. And he didn't suffer at all, Maggie."

Fine, I thought. Great. The poor devil. Then I cried a little, at first because I thought it was expected of me, but then some genuine tears came.

"What about Duff?" I asked.

"Duff is at home." Father Jackson hesitated. "But Franny's not too well, Maggie."

That shook me. "What's wrong with her?"

"She had a seizure of some sort. She was unconscious for a couple of hours, but she's awake now although she doesn't seem to recognize anyone. Her room's down the hall."

"Let me see her!" I tried to get up, but again I couldn't make it.

"In a little while, Maggie. She'll be all right. She's in no danger. You were, though. Dr. Fowler was very concerned about you."

"He belongs to the group, you idiot!" It was all coming back to me now, my flight through the woods and the rest of it.

"Maggie, you mustn't say those things."

"Where did Jack die?"

"In the graveyard. We were out looking for you and he was the first to find you after you fell and hit your head on a stone. The shock of seeing you there on the ground evidently caused his heart attack."

But Jack had seen me before I fell, or at least as I was falling. He also must have seen the General, and so must Franny, who had been standing behind Jack.

"And Franny had her attack at the same time?"

"Then or seconds later. All three of you were on the ground when I got there."

"Where were you earlier?" I asked bitterly. I remembered leaving the house and his coming after me a short distance along the path.

He shook his head. "I was afraid, Maggie. I'll admit it. I should have followed you, but instead I went back to the house to get Jack."

I let him stew for a minute or two and then said, "Forget it. You couldn't have caught me anyway. I wasn't Maggie Caine then."

"Oh, Maggie, don't start that again."

"You mean you didn't see any difference in me, not even in my clothes?"

"When you went out, you were wearing an old dress you must have found in one of the trunks in your house."

"And when you found me in the graveyard?"

"You were wearing a robe. I assumed you must have slipped

back into the house to get it without any of us seeing you. Or else you had it stashed away in the barn."

"Where's the robe now?" I asked as calmly as I could.

"Here in the hospital somewhere, I suppose. Maybe in your closet." He looked. It wasn't there.

"Never mind the robe. What did you do when you found the three of us—call Dr. Fowler?"

"No, Duff did."

"Naturally."

"He was in bed. Evidently he didn't wake up until he heard you screaming, and then he was only a few steps behind me when I reached the graveyard. I tried mouth-to-mouth on Jack but it didn't do any good. Then Duff went in and called Dr. Fowler and he sent the ambulance. Someone at the hospital must have called the state police too, because a couple of them showed up and asked us a lot of questions. It was finally decided that you had been sleepwalking."

"You know better than that."

"No, I don't, Maggie. That's exactly what it could have been. Anyway, Duff and I followed the ambulance here in my car. He stayed here for several hours, alternating between your room and Franny's. Then, when your vital signs seemed to be improving, I took him home and suggested he get some sleep."

"And you came back to pray over me. I wish you'd use your brains once in a while instead of your prayer book. How long was it between the time you saw me leave the house and when you found me in the graveyard?"

"Ten minutes, maybe fifteen."

"Bullshit! I must have been gone over an hour!"

"You weren't, Maggie, honestly."

Could they compress time like that? My head was aching too much to think about it.

"Where's Jack now?"

"His body is at the morgue. The coroner will have to do an autopsy, but Dr. Fowler says there won't be any difficulties, considering Jack's medical history." He paused. "Duff says his father wanted to be buried in the family graveyard, Maggie."

"Oh, my God! When was he supposed to have told Duff that?"

"Shortly after you came here from New York, Duff says."

I closed my eyes. "I'm sure he's lying," I said, "but on the other hand what difference does it make? Jack wasn't one of them."

Father Jackson ignored that. "Duff and I arranged for the Nichols Funeral Home in Cainesville to handle everything."

"Good for you."

"Duff also asked me to conduct the services at the grave. Even though Jack wasn't a Catholic, we can do that sort of thing now, you know, since Vatican II."

"Terrific."

He arose. "I'll let you get some sleep now, Maggie."

Something occurred to me. "Is Duff the person you caught after someone committed an indecency in your church?"

He grimaced. "I've been thinking about that, and I can't give you a flat answer. Duff does seem to resemble him, but on the other hand, that fellow was struggling so much I didn't really get a good look at his face."

"Great. Do you want to hear about what happened to me last night?"

"You'd better not talk any more right now, Maggie."

"Are you concerned about my health, or is it that you don't want to listen."

He sat down again and I told him everything, beginning with my leaving the Scrabble game and ending with my falling in the graveyard.

"It could've been seeing General Caine for the first time that caused Jack to die of fright," I said.

"General Caine attacking you?"

"Yes, that's what he must have seen."

"Sexually attacking you?"

"Well, I don't know how far things went along that line."

He reddened. "Can you tell me a bit more about the woman you saw at Mrs. Reddy's house? The one you say broke up the proceedings by exhibiting the medal."

"Small, dark, withered ... She could have been seventy, or maybe even eighty."

"Italian?"

"Possibly."

"Did you know Mrs. Scaravelli, the woman Father Fogarty told you about?"

"No."

"I called the rectory a while ago and Father Fogarty said that Mrs. Scaravelli's body had been found in her backyard this morning. Like Jack, she apparently died of natural causes. There was no sign of a struggle or other violence. Of course, there may be no connection." He waited for a moment before going on. "Father Fogarty said she had a medal in her hand, a small Miraculous Medal. Do you remember what that is from your Catholic days? It commemorates some supposed appearances of the Virgin Mary to Saint Catherine Labouré in 1830. Since that time some superstitious people have ascribed miraculous powers to the medal, which is about the size of a dime, sometimes gold or silver—"

"What do you want me to say? Yes, the woman I saw could have been Mrs. Scaravelli and, yes, she could have had such a medal in her hand?"

"If you're well enough to be released before she's buried, I'd like you to go to the funeral home and take a look at her."

"Just to convince you I'm telling the truth?"

He threw up his hands. "Maggie, I don't know what to think anymore, what to believe. Anyway, I'm sure you'll be glad to know that Father Fogarty is happy again. Mrs. Scaravelli's death will take some pressure off the shrine, he thinks. Maybe she wasn't cured of cancer, after all. And the fact that she died with a medal in her hand proves to him that good old-fashioned devotion pays off in the end. He thinks the Blessed Mother has put Mrs. Scaravelli on a direct flight to heaven."

"I hope Jack got on the same flight."

"I hope so too, Maggie." He sighed and went out of the room. In a few minutes he was back. "I checked with the head nurse on this floor. Dr. Fowler was here all night. He has another patient who is critically ill and he's been here since about eight o'clock last night."

"Was someone watching him all the time?"

He patted my hand. "You rest now, Maggie, and I'll come back and see you later."

I tried to sleep but couldn't. I looked for the call button, intending to ask for something to relieve my headache and help me sleep, but then it occurred to me that sleep might not be a good idea with Dr. Fowler prowling around. Taking an unknown sedative might not be so wise either.

I had to get out of the hospital immediately, I thought. I couldn't take a chance on spending another night in the place. It didn't seem to me that Franny was in any present danger, but, on the other hand, if she had really seen the General, she might be considered a threat to the security of Dr. Fowler and the others.

But if it wasn't the General, could it have been Duff that she and Jack had seen? That pulled me up and onto my feet. I lurched for the door as it was coming around and fell out into the corridor.

"Mrs. Caine!" A nurse came running up.

"I have to see my daughter."

"But you can't walk around in your condition."

"Watch me . . ."

I fell again, but then she realized it was useless to argue with me. There was a wheelchair nearby. She got it and helped me into it, then wheeled me down the corridor to another room.

"You can stay for just a moment," she said. An elderly woman with a tube in her nose was in the nearest bed, and Franny was in the bed next to the window.

"Push me closer."

She did. Franny seemed to be awake. She was very pale. Her hands were motionless at her sides and she was staring rigidly at the ceiling.

"Franny, look at me!" I tried to pull myself out of the chair to bend over her, but I was too weak and the bed was too high. "Franny, it's Mama!"

Her eyelids might have flickered, but otherwise she didn't move.

"Franny, what did you see last night? You have to tell me!"

The nurse pulled me away. "Mrs. Caine, I'll have to take you back now. Excitement isn't good for you with your head injury. Your daughter is going to be all right. There's nothing physically wrong with her."

She wheeled me back to my room and helped me into bed. Then she went away and left me in mental agony. My head was pounding more than ever, but that was nothing compared with the torture I was going through in my mind.

Chapter Twenty-Three

After a while Dr. Fowler returned with the staff neurologist, a Dr. Gustavson. Dr. Gustavson examined me quickly and pronounced me practically recovered.

"Your concussion was a mild one," he said. "I think it was shock that kept you unconscious so long. That may be your daughter's problem too, a psychological shock of some kind."

"What could have caused it?" I asked warily, glancing at Dr. Fowler.

"I don't know, but I think maybe Frances isn't coming out of it because she doesn't want to come out of it. Is there any situation that has been giving her difficulties, something she doesn't want to face?"

"Not that I know of."

"Why were you wandering around in the dark at that time of night, Mrs. Caine?"

"I'm told I was sleepwalking."

"I understand you were found in the family graveyard."

"Apparently so."

He waited, but I didn't say anything more. He shook his head and went away with Dr. Fowler. Shortly thereafter a nurse came in with some medication and persuaded me to take it. It relieved my headache and put me to sleep for a couple of hours.

When I awakened, Duff was sitting in the bedside chair. He was definitely the old Duff—thin and frail and looking now as though he needed a week's sleep as well as a good meal.

"Hi," he said, smiling wanly.

"Hi. How did you get here?"

"Father Jackson brought me. He's visiting some other patients now." He paused and then his eyes filled. He couldn't have been faking it. "Father Jackson says he told you about Dad."

"Yes."

Another pause while he sniffled a little. "Well, I guess it had to happen sometime. At least he got the chance to do what he wanted, coming out here."

"That's right. Where were you when it happened, Duff?"

"Didn't Father Jackson tell you? I was in bed when I heard you scream. Then I rushed out and got to where you were almost as soon as Father Jackson did."

He continued to weep. I began to wonder if he felt responsible for Jack's death, assuming that what he had just told me was a lie. On the other hand, if he was the General and he knew it, he was probably as powerless to do anything about it as I was about my situation. I felt a rush of sympathy for him now, and also remorse that I had been blaming him for a long time for things he very likely couldn't control.

"Is there anything you especially regret about Dad's death, Duff?" I asked as gently as I could.

"What do you mean?"

"Do you think there might have been any way you could have prevented it?"

"I don't see how. Father Jackson said Dad was pretty upset when he went looking for you. Maybe you could have prevented it if you hadn't gone out, Mother."

"I couldn't help it." I waited, but he didn't respond. I wondered if, as Duff, he knew that I was sometimes Margaret Dorn.

But he didn't ask me any questions. He just said, "Well, it probably wouldn't have made any difference anyway. Dad might have died even if we stayed in Scarsdale. Maybe even sooner."

"Are you sorry we left Scarsdale, Duff?"

"Sometimes I am."

"Why?"

He hesitated. "Sometimes I seem to be a different person than I was in Scarsdale."

"What sort of person, Duff? Tell me about it."

"Oh, I'd better not get into any long-winded discussion now, Mother. The nurse said I was to stay only a few minutes."

"Are you still forgetful, Duff? You said one time you thought your memory was slipping."

"I was joking, Mother."

Father Jackson rapped and came in then.

"Am I disturbing you?" he asked.

"Yes," I said.

"No, you're not," Duff said, standing up. "I'm going down the hall and sit with Franny for a while. I think Mother should get some more sleep."

"What do you think is wrong with Franny?" I asked. "What could be causing her not to recognize us?"

"Oh, I think she recognizes us," he said. "I think she just doesn't want to talk with us."

He went out and Father Jackson took the bedside chair and gave me a lot of platitudes about things getting better and relying on the mercy of God.

"What am I supposed to do if they don't get better?"

"They will."

"Crap."

"You must have faith and you must pray."

"Pray for what? My husband's dead and my daughter's in a catatonic state. And I don't think General Caine and Margaret Dorn are going to remain quiet just because I pray that will happen."

"Try it and see, Maggie. We'll both try."

"Get out of here."

"Maggie, Maggie." He took my hand.

I snatched it away. "Do you think you can start pawing me now that I'm a widow?"

He stammered something and got up and left the room. I was only trying to make a joke, admittedly one in poor taste, although I was prompted partly by exasperation. Then I began to wonder if I was still being influenced by Margaret Dorn.

I called the nurse and asked for more sedation. She brought it and I took it and went to sleep again. That was the last time, however, that I took any sleeping pills while I was there. I kept asking for them, but I always saved them, concealing them in my hand and then taking a big gulp of water while the nurses watched.

That was the first time I thought of suicide. I was in the hospital four days, and by then I had collected eight sleeping pills in a handkerchief. I don't know what kind they were or what their potency was but I decided I needed more than eight if I was going to use them to put an end to myself.

The autopsy on Jack's body revealed that he had died of a massive myocardial infarction. His remains were then taken to the funeral home in Cainesville to await my release from the hospital.

Duff came in to see Franny and me every day, but we didn't get around to discussing any supernatural problems. We talked about notifying Jack's relatives and mine, but I finally decided against it. He had only a few cousins, all of them in the East, and I was sure none of them would come to the funeral. The same applied to my relatives.

Duff kept assuring me he was getting along splendidly at home. He wasn't going back to school until after the funeral, but he was driving the rented car for grocery shopping and visiting Franny and me. If he was stopped by the police, I told myself, I would take the blame.

The morning I was released Father Jackson showed up again. He apologized for his conduct and I apologized for mine. Then he waited while Duff and I went to see Franny.

As on the first day I visited her, her eyelids seemed to flicker briefly and she made a slight motion toward clenching her fist. I don't know whether the latter was an emotional reaction or just an involuntary thing. I still don't know, even after all this time, what she feels about me, except sometimes I think she's afraid of me.

Following Father Jackson's car, Duff and I drove to the Nichols Funeral Home in Cainesville. The proprietor, a fat, cherry-faced man who seemed on the verge of a coronary himself, conducted us to a small room where a gray metal casket rested on a stand. There was a large basket of red roses near it. On the basket handle was a gaudy ribbon inscribed "Dear Father."

"I hope you find the casket suitable," Mr. Nichols wheezed.

"It's fine."

"Good quality, but not ostentatious. We could have given you something much more costly, but my feeling—"

"It's fine, wonderful."

"Would you care to view the remains?"

I nodded. I didn't care to, but I didn't want to say so in front of Duff and Father Jackson.

Mr. Nichols bowed, then reverently lifted the lid of the casket. What was in there didn't look much like Jack, although it was wearing Jack's navy blue knit suit and Countess Mara red and white striped tie that I had given him last Christmas.

I looked for perhaps ten seconds, then turned away. Duff had left the room.

"I hired two local men to go out to your farm and dig the grave, Mrs. Caine. Your son showed them where it was to be," said Mr. Nichols. "I also obtained the necessary county burial permit."

"Fine."

"A limousine is included in the cost, if you would like to ride in it."

"Thank you. I think my son and I can find our way home in our car."

The hearse was already parked on the street and we waited until Duff had pulled the Plymouth up behind it. Then Father Jackson parked his Ford behind the Plymouth, while Mr. Nichols took my arm and walked me slowly out to it and helped me in. I felt like kicking him.

After an interminably long time, four men, including Mr. Nichols, carried Jack's casket down the steps and slid it into the hearse.

"How much is he charging for all this?" I asked Duff.

"Two thousand dollars."

"That's outrageous."

"The flowers are included."

"They cost him twenty dollars maximum. Where in the yard is your Dad being buried?"

"Where you and Father Jackson were digging the other day. I thought since that place was empty—"

"Who told you we were digging there?"

"Dad. And Father Jackson admitted it when I asked him. Dad said you were looking for some money that was supposed to have been put there."

Two of the pallbearers got into the hearse. Mr. Nichols went back into the funeral home and returned with the basket of flowers, which he deposited solemnly in the back of the hearse beside the casket. Then he closed the doors and walked past us to get into the limousine that the third pallbearer had pulled up behind Father Jackson's Ford.

"Do you know who was supposed to have been buried in the place you're putting your father?" I asked Duff after we started off.

"No."

"Margaret Dorn."

"Who was she?"

I turned to look at him, but he was sober-faced and carefully attending to his driving.

"She was supposed to have been your great-great-grand-father's mistress."

"Really? I've never read anything about her in my research. I haven't read anything about any buried money either."

I didn't believe him at the time, but now I think it is possible he was telling the truth. Maybe knowledge of Margaret Dorn was restricted to those times when he was possessed by the General. That he had been possessed I no longer doubted.

We reached our drive, and the hearse pulled up and stopped in front of the barn. There was a stake truck already parked there, with picks and shovels in it. Getting out of the hired limousine behind us were Father Fogarty and Mrs. Guenther.

"That's a lot of bloody nerve," I told Duff.

"What difference does it make, Mother? We're paying for the car anyway."

The pallbearers carried Jack into the graveyard, where the gravediggers began attaching ropes to the handles. There were none of the trappings I had seen at other burials—no canopy, no green carpet to hide the grave and the mound of earth.

Father Jackson glanced questioningly at Father Fogarty, and the old priest waved him on. Then Jackson took a stole from his pocket, put it on, opened his prayer book and began to drone some prayers. When he was finished, he took a fountain-pen-like device from his breast pocket and sprinkled the casket with what I assumed was holy water.

Then he led us all in the Lord's Prayer and stepped back, assuming that the ceremony was over. It wasn't. Father Fogarty decided that Jack's soul needed more attention. He took the holy water sprinkler and gave the casket a liberal dousing.

"Dear Lord," he intoned, "we ask you to protect the departed, John Caine, from all evil spirits and take him with you into heaven."

Then he walked around the graveyard, sprinkling holy water everywhere and ordering Christ and the Blessed Virgin to get rid of any diabolical things that might be inhabiting the place. Finally he came back and emptied the sprinkler in Jack's grave.

"Whoever or whatever was in here before or may be in here now, I say to thee leave the soul of this man alone. Let it go on its way to paradise and eternal happiness."

That moved me. It really did. Jack had never really been very happy during his life and a lot of it was my fault. Father Fogarty came up to me then and took my hand. I guess it pleased him to see me weeping.

I blotted my eyes with my handkerchief, and then something compelled me to turn around. Mrs. Reddy and Mrs. Weber were standing by the graveyard gate.

Chapter Twenty-Four

They were both dressed in black, with black veils, as I had seen them the night Stephanie's body was found. They were watching me, I thought, although I couldn't be sure because of the veils. They didn't approach or make any gesture at all, just stood there.

I don't know whether anyone else noticed them or not. I turned to say something to Father Jackson, but he was listening to something Father Fogarty was telling him. When I looked back again, the two women were gone. It would have been easy enough for them to walk up the drive and out of my sight, considering the cars parked there and the trees, but they would have had to move very quickly. I couldn't see Emil's station wagon anywhere, but perhaps they had left it on the road.

Father Fogarty and his housekeeper got in the limousine now and the driver backed out. The gravediggers were preparing to lower Jack's casket. Father Jackson took my arm.

"It's locked and it will be covered by a cement vault that will be locked too," he said softly. "Come away now."

He ushered me into the house. Duff remained behind and continued to watch.

"Do you have anything to warm us here?" Father Jackson asked in the kitchen.

I poured us both healthy slugs of bourbon. He downed his, then reached into an inside pocket and took out a small color photo. It seemed to be of the head and upper torso of a sleeping woman. Then I noticed the casket lid.

"That's Mrs. Scaravelli," he said. "She was buried yesterday so I took that Polaroid shot before the funeral."

"I think it's the same woman," I said, "but I can't swear to it."

"Anyway, you'll be interested to know that Father Fogarty gave her a rousing send-off. He even called her a saint. Incidentally, her autopsy didn't reveal any sign of cancer. The cause of death was listed as a coronary occlusion, like Jack's."

"It could have been brought on by fright too, couldn't it?"

"Any kind of excitement. She was an old woman, remember. Anyway, it's over now and you have to do what's best for yourself and your children. I think you should get away from here now and go back East."

"My daughter happens to be in a hospital in Ashland."

"Then you and Duff go to Ashland and stay in a motel. You can afford it, can't you? And it shouldn't take you long to arrange for Franny's care back in New York."

"We don't have a house there, remember?"

"You have relatives somewhere, don't you? Or you could rent another place. Anyway, I'll bet your tenants will give up your house once they're aware of the circumstances."

"The circumstances being that this house is haunted."

"That your husband has just died and your daughter needs the kind of medical care she can only get in the East. Listen, I'll call the people for you. Maybe a clergyman's voice will help convince them."

"They're Texans and probably anti-Catholic."

"I'll say I'm a Baptist minister. For God's sake, Maggie, you've got to get away from here!"

"You mean you're beginning to believe my story now?"

He poured himself another drink. "I believe it would be dangerous for you to continue living in this place."

"Still hedging," I said. "Well, Duff won't want to leave. Besides, there's still his court appearance."

"That can be moved up on the docket. Father Fogarty knows a lot of people around the courthouse and there's a good lawyer in Cainesville, Dave Southworth, who handles all the parish legal affairs. Incidentally, you should have contacted a lawyer before this."

"I should've done a lot of things."

"Well, do something positive now. Take Duff with you and move to Ashland this afternoon."

"And if he won't go?"

"Then go without him. He's been alone here for several days already and he seemed to get along all right."

"You mean when I'm not here he doesn't have problems?"

He looked at me steadily. "It's possible, Maggie."

I refused to get angry. I just wanted to get him out of the house.

"Let me wait a couple of more days. I have a lot of things to do here. Jack's papers to go over, deciding how much of the junk here I want to take with me."

"I'll help you."

"I appreciate that, Peter. I'll let you know if you can."

"Maggie, I don't want you to spend another night in this house."

"Don't be silly. Nothing's going to happen. I'll call you if I need you. By the way," I said as I moved him toward the door, "it was pretty nervy of Mrs. Reddy and her daughter to show up, wasn't it."

"Were they here? I didn't see them, although I don't think there's anything unusual about it. After all, Mrs. Reddy was close to your husband's aunt, wasn't she, and Stephanie was here for quite a while. It might be more odd if they hadn't come to pay their respects."

He went away, assuring me he'd phone later. I watched as he backed out of the drive. The gravediggers were putting their ropes and tools in the truck, then they drove away too.

The graveyard was at least a hundred yards from the house, and the view was blocked by trees, but I could see Duff—standing, it seemed to me, not by his father's grave but farther away by the back fence where General Caine was supposed to be buried.

After about five minutes he walked toward the house. I moved away from the window and busied myself at the sink. Apparently he hadn't washed any dishes all the while I was in the hospital.

When he came in, I fixed ham and cheese sandwiches for both of us. Surprisingly I was hungry. Duff had a good appetite too.

"I've never really thought of that place out there as a cemetery," I said, "but now with Dad there it makes it different, doesn't it?"

"I guess so."

"Do you think that means we have an obligation to stay here?"

"What do you think, Mom?"

"Well, let's not worry about it for a while. We can't leave anyway until Franny is better."

He was silent for a while and then he said, "Mom, do you think you might ever get married again?"

"Come on, Duff."

"Why not? You're attractive and young looking."

"Thank you. Would you like me to get married again?"

"No, I guess not."

"Well, then, I won't." Then I said, "It was nice of Mrs. Reddy and Mrs. Weber to come today, wasn't it?"

"I didn't see them," he said.

I was sure he was lying, but I didn't pursue it. He helped me with the dishes and then we drove to Ashland to see Franny. She was as unresponsive as ever, so after a while we drew our chairs away from her bed and conversed in low tones about a lot of unrelated things—vacations, holidays, funny experiences we had had. I said "low tones," but after a while we were giggling so much a nurse came and looked in at us.

Then we said good-bye to Franny and went to a supermarket where we bought enough food for a dozen people, enough to last us a month or more. In fact, much of what we bought that day is still in the refrigerator or on the kitchen shelves. I also bought a box of cake mix and managed to hide it from Duff. His birthday was coming up very shortly.

Nothing out of the ordinary happened that night. After a good dinner we went to bed early and I had a wonderful ten hours sleep with no dreams I could remember. Father Jackson called twice before we went upstairs, wondering if he ought to drive out to see us. I told him positively not and the third time the phone rang I refused to answer it.

On Monday Duff went back to school. I let him take the car and he brought it back on time without incident. The General was evidently leaving him alone, as Margaret Dorn seemed to be leaving me alone. Duff brought several textbooks with him and spent a couple of hours that night at the dining room table doing his homework.

I had spent that day writing neglected letters, including one to our lawyer in Scarsdale. Although there was quite a lot of money coming from Jack's insurance, I said I wanted to sell the Scarsdale house as soon as possible, since Franny's care would be a continuing expense.

I was contented—I don't know how else to put it—and I grew more contented as the days went by. Father Jackson called every day and I was civil to him, but I kept telling him that I wasn't ready to leave yet, that I had many more things to do.

I did ask one favor of him. I lied and said I was having trouble sleeping and asked if he could get something to help me. Despite the period of calm, suicide was still in the back of my mind. I felt I would have to go through with it if things turned for the worse again. For the moment however, I would just keep the medicine on hand.

"You should go to a doctor and get a prescription," Father Jackson said.

"Call your brother and ask him to write one."

"He won't do it. You're not his patient."

"Please, Peter, isn't there someone you know? I just need a few, just until we get back East. I'll go to our family doctor then, if I'm still having trouble sleeping."

"There's a pharmacist in town who might give me something."

"Oh, Peter, ask him. Just a dozen or so tablets, or a few more if you can manage it."

"I'll see what I can do. But I don't like it."

I determined that if and when I did use the pills, I'd leave a note stating that I had brought them from Scarsdale. I certainly didn't want to get Father Jackson and his pharmacist friend into trouble.

Chapter Twenty-Five

A couple of days later a notice came ordering Duff to appear in Ashland Juvenile Court on the following Monday. Having heard nothing for so long, I had been hoping the authorities were going to drop the charges. Now I began to wonder if I shouldn't call the lawyer Father Jackson had mentioned.

"Why call him?" Duff asked. "Why not the lawyer Mrs. Reddy told you about—Oliver Matson?"

"Impossible."

"Why? I know you don't like Mrs. Reddy, but that doesn't mean the lawyer isn't any good. I am sure Mrs. Reddy likes me, so wouldn't she want me to have the best possible legal help?"

He was probably right, I thought, insofar as Mrs. Reddy and her friends wouldn't want him to be sent to some juvenile institution if he was of value to them in their ceremonies. Therefore Matson might be a better bet for us than Father Jackson's man. It didn't occur to me that I might be opening a door again, incurring a debt that might be hard to pay.

I looked up Oliver Matson in the Ashland phone book and called him. His secretary put me through immediately, without questioning me, almost as though she had been expecting the call. Mr. Matson was most cordial and sympathetic when I told him about Duff's problems.

"Boys will be boys," he said chuckling. "I remember when I was a sprout I caused my folks lots of worrisome times." His cracker-barrel way of talking was irritating, but I supposed it might go over big in the local courts. "I don't think you need fret too much, Mrs. Caine. Judge Sinclair, who's sitting in Juvenile Court now, is an old friend of mine and he's generally guided by a boy's appearance and his family situation. Long as your boy ain't a long-haired hippie, and long as he's repentant, I think things will go all right for him."

How did he know what Duff was like? Of course Mrs. Reddy could have told him. All in all, I was sure I had done the right thing, although I wasn't happy to be dealing with a friend of Mrs. Reddy's. Also, I suppose I was thinking that no judge in the world could treat my son too badly and therefore the choice of lawyer wasn't going to make a great deal of difference.

I made sure Duff looked his best the morning of his court appearance. I pressed his most conservative suit—a gray flannel that was really too small for him, but I felt might help to make him look more boyish. I made him wear a white shirt and a dark tie of Jack's, and finally I put a towel around him and trimmed his hair a bit. When I was finished, I was satisfied he looked incapable of assaulting policemen.

Then we drove to Ashland, arriving a good forty-five minutes before the scheduled ten o'clock appearance. I had arranged to meet Mr. Matson outside the courtroom at a quarter to ten, but I hoped he would be early. He hadn't asked me any questions at all on the telephone and I was worried about what kind of a defense he was planning to offer.

Promptly at a quarter to ten he came down the corridor, a sprightly little old man with a string tie and a great shock of white hair, much longer than Duff's. I recognized him immediately. He had been in the congregation at Mrs. Reddy's the night Jack died.

He pretended not to recognize me. He squeezed my hand warmly and then Duff's. In answer to my offer to tell him something about Duff he said, "Don't need to know any more about him. I got all the facts in the case from the records, and I'm sure Duff's a good, responsible boy. Nothing to worry about here."

"But the record certainly doesn't show he's responsible."

Mr. Matson winked. "You have to read between the lines."

He ushered us into the courtroom, where several groups of parents and teenage children were waiting.

"I'll have Duff taken care of in a hurry," he assured us, guiding me to a seat in a row ahead of the others. "You'll be home in plenty of time for lunch." Then he opened a gate in the railing and led Duff to a seat at a front table. An elderly bailiff looked up questioningly, but he didn't protest.

Shortly thereafter the judge came out. No one stood up. I was tempted to do so to gain a few points for Duff, but Judge Sinclair didn't seem to be paying any attention to us. He sat down and rearranged some papers on his desk and repositioned two small American flags, then looked over and nodded to the bailiff. The bailiff arose and summoned Duff.

Duff and Mr. Matson went forward and stood in front of the judge while the bailiff read the charges. Then Mr. Matson announced that Duff was pleading guilty and the judge studied some papers for a couple of minutes. Then he said, "Referred to probation," and the bailiff called another name.

Smiling, Mr. Matson ushered Duff through the gate and I got up and followed them. At the rear of the courtroom a toothless old woman who looked like a habitual visitor reached out and caught my sleeve.

"He ain't our regular judge, you know," she whispered.

"Our regular judge is out of town. This fella was sent in from someplace. You're lucky. Our regular judge would've locked your boy up."

I pulled away and joined Duff and Mr. Matson in the corridor. "What does the probation involve?" I asked.

"They're supposed to check on Duff and make recommendations before the judge hands down a sentence."

"I thought you said there wouldn't be anything like that."

"It won't be a jail sentence. The judge will likely order Duff to report to the probation officer once a month or so for a while. I'll arrange to have it on Saturday mornings, if you like."

"And that's all there is to it?"

"That's all."

"Well, thank you, Mr. Matson. Can I give you a check?"

He smiled. "No, you'll be billed."

"But I'd just as soon pay you now, if your fee isn't too high."

"Oh, I don't think you'll find it excessive. And I'd prefer it this way, if you don't mind. If you gave me a check, I'd probably just lose it. I'm very careless." He took my hand. "I hope we meet again, Mrs. Caine, under other circumstances."

I certainly didn't share that hope but I nodded. He shook Duff's hand, then bowed slightly to both of us.

"It is my duty to serve you," he said softly. Then he went down the corridor and out of sight.

"Far-out," Duff said.

"He's a kook," I agreed, "but he seems to have done the trick for us."

We had hamburgers and coffee at a nearby restaurant (neither of us had eaten much breakfast) and then went home. Despite my relief, I was vaguely disturbed by Mr. Matson's assurances. It didn't seem to me that charges that serious could be dismissed so lightly. I was also concerned about what form his billing might take, considering what I knew about him.

On the other hand what did I really know? Maybe I had never seen him before. Maybe I was going around looking for people to match those I had seen in my hallucination.

On Friday afternoon Father Jackson brought me the sleeping pills. He apologized for taking so long about it, but his pharmacist friend had been away.

"It's all right," I said. "I haven't needed them lately."

"Throw those away then. Or I'll do it."

"No, no, I might need them again." I opened the vial. There were about twenty white pills in it. "What kind are they?"

"I don't know. I didn't ask. And he was very reluctant to give them to me. He said not to take more than one or two a night."

"Don't worry, I'll be careful. And I'll never say where I got them."

"When are you going back East, Maggie?"

"One of these days. I still have lots of things to do around here."

Why didn't I want to go? For God's sake, why didn't I?

Because Margaret Dorn was telling Maggie Caine that nothing was going to happen and everything was going to be all right.

The next day, Saturday, was Duff's birthday. I had asked him again if he wanted to have a party and invite some of the kids in his class, but he refused. I don't think he ever made any friends at Cainesville High School. He apparently never participated in any after-school activities and I don't think he ever met with any of his classmates away from the school either.

I told myself (Margaret Dorn told me) that next year things would be better. He would be at Yale and we would be living in a house in New Haven and I would have a big surprise birthday party for him. This year there would be just a small party for the two of us.

That night I became Margaret Dorn again in body and the General came to me.

Chapter Twenty-Six

I awakened early that Saturday morning and got up and showered for a long time. Then I opened Duff's door quietly. He was still sleeping. I went downstairs and began to mix the ingredients for his birthday cake. Around nine he came down, and after I had put the cake in the oven, I made breakfast.

"When we go into town we'll buy your present," I said. "What would you like?"

"Let's get something for all of us, but especially for Franny," he said. "A television set."

I agreed and he laughed and clapped his hands. We went to the hospital and afterward to a nearby furniture store where I bought the largest portable color television set the two of us could carry. We took it home and Duff watched part of a football game while I frosted the cake. He was pretending he didn't know anything about it, and I went along with that, putting the cake in a cupboard before I called him to dinner.

After dinner I went out to the kitchen, lit the seventeen candles on the cake, and brought it into the dining room. He reacted with convincing surprise. Then he blew out the candles and made a wish.

"Do you want to know what I wished for?" he asked.

"The wish won't come true if you tell it," I said.

"I'll take a chance. I wish we could be together like this for always, just the two of us."

"You know that's impossible, Duff."

"Well, for a long time anyway."

"It can't even be for very long. You'll be going away to college next year."

"Maybe I won't go."

"Now you're being silly. In any case even if you didn't go to college, you'd go somewhere else. You'd get a job and eventually find a girl and go away."

He just shook his head and grinned. We didn't say any more on that subject, but instead moved on to more pleasant things —again the old days in Scarsdale mostly, but I also talked about my girlhood, telling him things I had never told Jack. Lately I've been wondering why I didn't tell him about some of the recent things that had happened to me—the times I had seen the General, for example, and the things that had happened at Mrs. Reddy's house. Maybe that would have made a difference. Maybe it would have persuaded him to run, to make him make me run.

Anyway, we cleared away the dishes and moved into the front room, where we watched some inane television programs until ten o'clock or so.

Just after he turned off the set Duff said out of the blue, "I've done some bad things, I know, Mother, but I didn't kill Stephanie."

"All right, Duff, I believe you," I said.

"Good night, Mother. Thank you for the nice birthday."

He went upstairs. In a little while I heard him playing his flute —a Bach minuet, I think. Then I went into Jack's room and got his yellow legal pad, the one he had been using most recently to write his novel. The first page was half filled with his scribbling, but the only thing I could make out was the page number—five hundred and something. I never could read Jack's handwriting.

I found a ball-point pen and went out to the kitchen, where I tore off the uncompleted page, crumpled it and threw it away. Then I sat at the kitchen table and wrote some letters of instruction, one to our Scarsdale lawyer, Bill Levitt, and another to my sister Marilyn in Albany.

Jack and I had made wills at the same time, and mine specified that in the event of his preceding me in death the estate should go to the children, with Marilyn as guardian and Bill Levitt as executor. I asked Bill to see that the terms of the will were carried out, and I asked my sister to be loving in the care of my children.

Finally I wrote a note to Duff, asking him not to try to understand what I was doing, but to be assured that it was necessary. I told him to look after his sister and see that she was moved to a good hospital or nursing home near his aunt's home in Albany. Last, I asked him to have my body cremated—I didn't want any part of the Caine graveyard, although I didn't tell him that—and then to go to his aunt's home immediately and make the arrangements for Franny. For some reason, I had the notion that once I was out of the way, Franny would quickly return to normal. Sometimes I still think that.

Then I went upstairs, got the pills from the drawer where I had hidden them, returned to the kitchen and made myself some cocoa. All together I had twenty-eight pills, and I thought that many ought to do the job. I put them in the cocoa, and after they had dissolved I tasted the mixture. It was slightly bitter, but not unpleasant. After a couple of more sips it didn't seem to taste any different from ordinary cocoa.

Then Duff came downstairs again. "I was wondering what you were doing," he said.

I turned my letters over quickly. "Nothing," I said. "Getting ready to go to bed."

"Could I have some cocoa too?" he asked.

"Sure."

The water was still hot. I made more cocoa in a large cup that matched the one I was using, being careful to take mine with me when I moved away from the table. Then I brought both cups back with me. The one I held in my right hand was the one with the dissolved sleeping medicine. I put both cups on the table, the one with the fresh cocoa in front of Duff. I know that. There is no doubt in my mind at all.

He sipped his cocoa. "Good," he said.

I don't remember what I replied, because I was getting sleepy. I closed my eyes for an instant, and when I opened them again General Caine was seated across from me, grinning at me. I screamed, I guess, and jumped up and covered my face, and then Duff was beside me with his arms around me.

"What is it, Mother?" he was saying.

"Nothing, nothing . . ." Why couldn't I have told him then?

He led me to a chair, the same chair I was sitting in before. And my cup of cocoa was in the same place, or seemed to be.

"Drink up, Mother, and let's get to bed," he said. "This whole thing with Dad and Franny has just been too much for you."

So we drank our cocoa. Mine tasted the same as before. Then we went upstairs together. At my door he gave me a hug.

"I'm really groggy," he said, smiling. "Hard day, I guess. Good night again, Mama."

I went into my room, undressed and got into bed and waited for the barbiturates, or whatever they were, to take effect. I remember thinking it a bit strange that Duff hadn't asked me any questions about what I had been writing.

I lay awake for a long time, thinking after a while that I hadn't taken enough medication. Then at last I fell asleep and didn't die, but slept the night through.

In the morning when I remembered what I had tried to do, I was unexplainably glad to be alive. I had been saved, I thought, and maybe that meant my troubles were over. Whatever power had come to my rescue might now move in between me and my enemies.

And I'll help myself by moving away, I resolved. I'll do what Father Jackson advised. I'll take Duff and Franny and go back East. Then I thought of the letters I had left on the kitchen table, got up quickly, put on my robe and went out into the hall.

Duff's door was ajar. I was going to ignore it and had started down the stairs, but then I wondered if he was up already. I went back to his room and found him on his bed. He hadn't undressed, hadn't even taken off his shoes. I touched his hand and I knew.

Chapter Twenty-Seven

In the afternoon Father Jackson came and found me sitting on the stairs. He had called several times and then drove out to the farm and found the back door unlocked.

He took me to Ashland Hospital—apparently I went along without protest—and they gave me something that put me to sleep. A week or so later when I was rational again, he came to see me.

He sat down beside my bed and shook his head, unable to say anything.

"Just don't give me any shit," I said. "Don't tell me it was God's will."

"Maybe it was, Maggie."

"Bullshit! You don't even know what I was trying to do."

"I read your letters."

"Bastard!"

"The police read them too. I had to let them. They'll be in to see you shortly. Dr. Fowler has managed to keep them away from you until now."

"Where's Duff?"

"Buried. The coroner hasn't given a verdict yet except for the cause, but he let us—"

"Buried where!"

"Next to his father. Mr. Nichols had his men probe and there was room—"

"Goddamn you!"

"Maggie, we didn't know how long it might be before you were capable of handling things, so the court appointed—"

"Appointed whom, some friend of Mrs. Reddy's?"

"Your lawyer. Mr. Matson came forward and said he was your lawyer—"

"Goddamn them! You could've made them wait!"

"I couldn't, Maggie. And there were no addresses on those

letters. I didn't know how to reach your sister or your Scarsdale lawyer."

"You could've called long-distance and found Bill Levitt in two minutes, but you didn't have the guts."

"I didn't think it mattered that much, Maggie."

"It matters this much. I'll have him dug up and cremated."

"I guess you can do that eventually if you like. Meanwhile you'd better consider what you're going to tell the authorities. You could be charged with murder, you know, despite the letters."

Then he apologized for that. He said he didn't mean to imply that I had deliberately harmed my own son, but the police didn't know me, didn't know how close Duff and I had been. They might find it hard to understand how I could have let such a thing happen.

Shortly thereafter a sheriff's deputy and an Ashland detective came in to ask me questions. I told them the truth, that I had been trying to commit suicide and I didn't know how the cups of cocoa became switched.

Did I think my son knew what I was attempting? Could he have deliberately switched the cups? No, absolutely not. He couldn't have known. It had to have been an accident. He had no reason to kill himself. He was happy, he was getting along well in school and looking forward to college.

They didn't bring up the matter of the recent juvenile court action, but they did ask about Duff's relationship with Stephanie. I said they had been friends, that's all. Duff and Franny had both been very friendly with Stephanie.

Afterward Father Jackson came in and said there was a good chance I was going to be charged with involuntary manslaughter, if not something more serious. But it didn't happen. I remained in the hospital for three weeks and the authorities didn't bother me anymore. Maybe they thought that as a mother I'd had enough grief.

I was on the same floor as before and this time my room was even closer to Franny's, but I didn't go in to see her, didn't even walk by her room. I didn't know what to say to her. I visit her now in the nursing home and I've tried to explain what happened to Duff, although it doesn't seem to matter to her.

I was trying not to think of any of the things that had happened and, to an extent, with the help of the drugs I was getting, I succeeded. At first I refused psychiatric care and there was no attempt to force it on me. However, Father Jackson said something one day that gave me second thoughts.

"There's a possibility you may be declared insane, Maggie, or at least legally incompetent. Apparently you've been saying what the staff considers nutty things. Also, you attempted suicide and that's enough to get you put away if it's thought you'll try it again."

So I began to cooperate. I made it known that I would be willing to see the psychiatrist and when he came to visit me I answered all his questions. I told him that anything I might have said earlier about supernatural happenings was just the result of wild dreams. I said I had tried to commit suicide because of grief over the death of my husband, but now I realized I had made a terrible mistake and I would never do such a thing again.

After a week or so of that I was released from the hospital. Father Jackson came to drive me to the Cainesville motel where Duff had met with his brother. I promised everyone who seemed interested that I was going to leave for Albany and my sister's home within a few days and would make arrangements to have Franny transferred to a medical facility near there.

As a matter of fact, I had no plans beyond the one of trying again to kill myself, but I didn't have the energy to work on that immediately. Most of the time I just sat in front of the TV set in my motel room. Once in a while, mainly because it was expected of me, I'd go over to the coffee shop for a sandwich.

Father Jackson came every day and droned his platitudes. I seldom listened to him, but I learned to interpret the rise and fall of his voice so I could nod wisely and with apparent acceptance at appropriate moments.

Then one day he said something that caught my attention.

"By the way, Maggie, it may comfort you to know that the boy has been taken away from the Weber home."

"George?"

"Yes. Apparently he wasn't going to school and someone must have complained about it. He was placed with another family. Then the other day when I drove by the place I noticed that there was a lot of junk mail in the box. I asked the mailman about it and he said he thought the Webers and Mrs. Reddy had gone away for a while."

That night I thought for a long time about what he had said. Mrs. Reddy and her daughter might not be in the house, but the coffins of General Caine and Margaret Dorn were undoubtedly still there. It seemed to me I had a great opportunity to make certain that the contents of those coffins could never again be used by Mrs. Reddy in her ceremonies.

The following Friday afternoon I went to a nearby liquor store and bought a fifth of Scotch. I was expecting Father Jackson to visit me about four and I was hoping he would drive his car. Sometimes he walked over from the rectory. My rented Plymouth had been returned to the agency while I was in the hospital. I could have rented another car, I suppose, but considering what I was planning, I preferred it be thought I had no access to a car.

He parked his old Ford in front of my room shortly after four. I fixed drinks for both of us, making his considerably stronger than mine. Then I let him talk, refilling his glass regularly but not mine. There was only one chair in the room and he usually sat in that while I sprawled on the bed. I didn't tonight, but sat on the floor near him, pretending to be fascinated by everything he said.

Ordinarily he went back to the rectory in an hour or so, but this time I persuaded him I needed more words of comfort. About six we went over to the coffee shop and had some vile fried chicken and then came back to the room. I kept asking him leading questions that enabled him to show off his theology and quote Thomas Aquinas.

Around seven-thirty the bottle was almost empty and he was becoming incoherent. At close to eight he passed out in the chair. I took off his coat, his shoes and his trousers and toppled him on the bed. Then I covered him with a blanket, took his car keys and went out.

It was dark by then, a chilly fall night. There was no one in the motel yard when I got in the Ford, which I managed to start after a few attempts. If the car was heard, I thought, it would be assumed that Father Jackson was returning to the rectory.

I don't remember everywhere I drove. I know I went thirty or forty miles from Cainesville before I stopped at a gas station and filled the tank of the Ford and then bought a five-gallon can of gasoline. The attendant refused to sell me any more.

"What do you want it for?" he asked. "It's dangerous to carry it in the car."

"I'm afraid of running out when stations are closed."

"That five gallons will get you to one that's open."

I drove another twenty miles or so, stopping at several more stations and buying another five-gallon can and several single gallons. It was shortly after ten when I started back toward Cainesville. I didn't go into town but took a byroad to the farm road.

The Weber house was completely dark when I drove by it. I turned around and went past it several times before pulling into the drive. As Father Jackson had said, the mailbox by the road was overflowing with advertising circulars.

I parked close to the house, doubting that my car could be seen from the road or, if seen, identified. At any rate traffic would be sparse, particularly since the Cainesville High basketball team had no game scheduled. I had checked that on the poster in the motel office.

I sat in the car and watched the house for a few minutes. The shades were drawn in the front windows and there wasn't a glimmer of light anywhere. In addition the front screen door was loose and flapping in the wind.

I got out of the car and took the cans of gasoline from the trunk, lifting the five-gallon ones with difficulty. Then I opened them all and walked around the house, splashing gasoline on the wood, pouring a couple of gallons on the porch floor. Finally I tore some motel towels into strips and tied the strips together to form a length of six or seven feet.

I put one end of the cloth strip on the porch, weighed it down with a stone, stretched the rest of it into the yard and soaked it with the remaining gasoline. Then I struck a match, lit the strip and ran to the car.

I was behind the wheel as the porch exploded in flames. By the time I had backed out on to the road, the whole front of the house was burning. I waited there for maybe half a minute while the flames climbed and then I heard screaming. Even though my windows were closed and I was at least a hundred feet from the house, I could hear voices screaming in agony. I covered my ears, but I could still hear them. And I could hear them for at least a mile on the way to Cainesville.

Chapter Twenty-Eight

I pulled off the road somewhere and sat there until I had regained some control. There was nothing human in the house, I thought, and what I had heard had no human origins. Whatever it was, it was nothing for me to worry about now.

I threw the empty gasoline cans in a ditch, drove back to Cainesville and parked the Ford in front of Saint Mary's rectory. I didn't want anyone to hear a car being driven up to the motel. Then I walked back to my room and let myself in. Father Jackson was still unconscious on the bed, snoring loudly. I undressed, put on a nightgown and got in beside him. Despite what had happened, I went to sleep almost immediately.

He was awake before I was in the morning, dressed and sitting in the chair. From the way he looked, he had a monumental hangover and he was also in an extreme state of anxiety.

"Forgive me, Maggie, I was drunk," he said miserably.

"We both were. Relax, nothing happened. You passed out and I put you to bed. I wouldn't have let you do anything even if you wanted to."

"Where's my car?"

"I took it back to the rectory so no one would know you spent the night here."

"Thank you, Maggie. You're really a good person."

He left and I went back to sleep. Around noon I got up and

had some coffee, then came back and turned on the television set. An hour or so later Father Jackson returned.

"Do you know what happened last night?" he said.

"What?" I kept my eyes on the soap opera.

"The Weber house burned down. It was completely destroyed."

"It's lucky there was no one—"

"Two bodies were found. They were badly burned, but it's thought they're the bodies of Mrs. Reddy and Mrs. Weber."

"But you told me they'd gone away!" It couldn't be they. The searchers must have found the remains of General Caine and Margaret Dorn. But those were only bones, and could hardly have been mistaken for anything else. On the other hand, Stephanie's body might still have been in the house.

"The Sheriff has evidence that the fire was deliberately started." Father Jackson moved between me and the television screen. "Were you here all last night, Maggie?"

"You know I was! You were with me."

"I was out for more than ten hours. And there are a hundred more miles on my car now than there were yesterday afternoon."

"Some kids must have borrowed it. Get away from me. I don't want to be interrogated."

He went, but he wasn't satisfied. The next day he said, "Did you ever show those glasses to Duff, the ones I found?"

"Yes, I gave them to him."

"What did he say?"

"Nothing that I recall."

Then I had a horrible thought. If I was guilty of the murder of Stephanie—and now of Mrs. Reddy and Mrs. Weber—was I also responsible for leading Duff into evil? Could he have taken the sleeping pills knowingly because of that?

The next day I asked Father Jackson if I could go to confession. He looked at me for a while, then nodded and went to his car and got his stole. He put it around his neck and sat on the bed while I knelt beside it and told him about setting fire to the Weber house. It disturbed him, but he didn't say anything. I also told him it was possible I had killed Stephanie, since it was my glasses he had found. I didn't remember going out of the house that night, but I did remember a terrible dream that was somehow related. Then I said I was sorry for having attempted suicide.

"Is there anything else?" he asked.

"No."

"About you and your son?"

"I had intercourse with someone several times, but I swear it was not my son."

I said the Act of Contrition. He sighed and made the sign of the cross over me and pronounced the words of absolution. Then he took off his stole and sat for a while without speaking.

"You ought to go to the authorities and tell them what you've told me about the Weber house and about Stephanie," he said finally. "But I can't make you do it or even penalize you spiritually for not doing it. I also think you should go back to the hospital or to some institution where you can get help. But I can't make you do that either."

"I'm not crazy, Peter! I was made to do those things!"

"That, I would think, is as good a definition of insanity as any other."

Whatever it was, I was sure that if my enemies were really dead, I would never be afflicted again. After a while I would even be able to get along without Duff. I would take Franny and we would go somewhere and live again.

The next day I went to Mass. I couldn't make myself walk up the aisle and receive Communion, but I thought it would only be a matter of time before I was able to do it. In any case, Father Jackson was pleased that I had come, and afterward he let me take his car to drive to Ashland and see Franny.

I might have been kidding myself, but I thought she smiled a bit —just a hint of movement at the corners of her mouth—when I entered her room. Anyway, that day I made arrangements to have her transferred to a nursing home in Cainesville near the motel.

Then one afternoon a couple of weeks later I borrowed the car again and drove out to the farm. Father Jackson didn't want me to go, but I persuaded him that it was necessary therapy, that I had to be able to face the place again.

I parked in the yard and stayed there a long time, staring at the monstrous old building. But then the sun came out, sparkling the frost on the oak branches, and the place didn't seem so bad. I drove away, but in a few days I came back again and this time unlocked the front door and went into the parlor.

Nothing had been changed. One of Jack's legal pads was on the table near his customary chair, and Franny's rain boots were on the floor near the stairs. I went out to the kitchen and found nothing unusual there. The cocoa cups must have been taken away, and if I had left other dishes in the sink, someone must have washed them and put them in the cupboard.

Nothing was wrong now, I thought. Whatever evil had been in the house was no longer present. I could go away with Franny and put it all out of my mind. There was just one more thing to do. I had to decide whether or not to leave Duff's body in the graveyard.

It shouldn't make any difference now, it seemed to me. If the evil was gone, then why disturb the grave. I had to look at it though, just once. I would do that, then take what I wanted out of the house and never come back here again.

I went out the back door and along the path to the graveyard. I wasn't frightened. There didn't seem to be anything to be frightened about. The sun was still shining, and though it was almost winter some blue jays were chattering on the fence as I approached the gate.

Then I opened the gate and saw the hole. It was where Father Jackson had said Duff was buried, next to his father. The empty cement vault was below, and its lid was on the pile of earth next to the hole.

My first reaction was anger, rage at those who had dared to steal the body of my son. That was instantly followed by sickening horror at the thought of the purpose for which the body was surely to be used.

The Weber house was destroyed. The casket couldn't be there. Could they have taken it into the Caine house? I ran back to the kitchen, slammed the door and bolted it.

Then I looked through all the rooms downstairs, but there was nothing in them that hadn't been there before. Upstairs? More likely, despite the weight of the casket. The storeroom possibly, or maybe the third floor.

But I couldn't make myself go up the stairs. What good would it do anyway if I found it, I thought. I couldn't move it without help, couldn't take it away with me. I would leave now and come back in the morning with Father Jackson. If we found it, I'd have the undertaker come and get it and cremate the contents—as should have been done in the first place.

I had picked up my purse and was at the front door when I heard music coming from upstairs. It was the Bach minuet being played on a flute. I was terrified, but I tried to convince myself that I wasn't really hearing it but only remembering it.

I fled out the front door to the car and for a couple of awful moments couldn't find the car keys. Then when I did find them, I couldn't start the car. In my panic I flooded it, but I kept bearing down on the pedal anyway. The cranking sounds became slower and slower and then there was nothing. The battery was dead.

Then a slight movement on the lawn caught my eye, the wind fluttering black cloth. I turned my head and looked out the side window, and there by the front door of the house were Mrs. Reddy and Mrs. Weber.

They were standing there staring at me with their hands clasped as though in prayer or supplication. As before, they were both dressed in black—black dresses and black veils. I closed my eyes and screamed and screamed and when I looked again they were gone.

I had never been more frightened. It was growing darker outside and I knew I ought to get out of the car and run somewhere to a telephone, but I couldn't move. The phone in the Caine house had been disconnected, but even if it hadn't been I wouldn't have been able to go back into the house.

I sat for a long while until the sun went down and it grew very dark. I couldn't even turn my head to look at the house now. I thought I was going to die. I hoped I could die quickly and get away from the horror.

But it wasn't over for me yet. I sat there in the darkness, trembling, unable to think coherently, sure that the General would come. Maybe he was in the car already. In the back seat or maybe even sitting beside me. Then I had an even more terrible thought. Maybe Duff would come.

There was a knock on the car window. My heart stopped. I opened my mouth to scream again but now I couldn't make a sound.

Then a voice called, "Don't be scared, lady. Is anything wrong? Can I help you?"

I opened my eyes and turned my head. A young man—a perfectly normal-looking young man—was standing there staring anxiously at me. He seemed to be about Duff's age.

"I can't get this car started," I managed to shout.

"Let me try."

I got out and he got in and turned the key.

"Battery's dead. Do you live here, ma'am?"

"I used to."

"I'm Jeff Duncan. I live up the road. I could get my car—"

"No, no, don't leave!"

"It's raining, ma'am. Is there anyone in the house?"

"No." No?

"Does anyone know you're here?"

"A friend of mine in Cainesville."

"Do you think your friend might come after you?"

"Probably in a while." It was raining hard now.

"Maybe we ought to wait inside until your friend comes." He took my arm and I went with him to the front door and into the house.

We took our coats off. He sat on the settee and I sat in Jack's chair. He told me he was a senior at Cainesville High and that he had known Duff casually. He said that even though Duff had been at the school only a few months, all the kids seemed to like him and that a memorial service for him had been held in the gymnasium. He knew that would please me.

He said that when the rain stopped we could both walk up the road to his house. Then he would get his father's car and drive me back to Cainesville. I didn't ask him how he happened to be walking on the road in the rain.

I suggested a cup of tea. I couldn't have made cocoa. He said he usually didn't drink tea, but it might be nice now. I went out to the kitchen, filled the kettle and waited for the water to boil. When I turned back to the table, the General was sitting there, grinning at me.

I shrieked, I think, and ran into the front room. Jeff Duncan was gone. Mrs. Reddy and Mrs. Weber were standing in front of the door, blocking it.

There was nowhere to go but up the stairs. I went up slowly and fearfully, looking back at the two as they began to follow me. And now the flute music began again.

I reached the upstairs hall. Duff's door was closed but the music was coming from his room. Soft music now, plaintive music, calling me.

I went to his door, had my hand on the knob, but then couldn't turn it. No matter what was behind me, I couldn't make myself open the door.

He called me, softly at first, "Mother, please come in, Mother." Then crying, "I need you, Mother, I beg you to come in." Then, groaning as though in pain, "Oh, Mama, only you can save me! If you love me, Mama, come in and help me!"

The door opened without my touching it. The room was dark and there was an overpowering stench of corruption. But that vanished as I began to change. I was no longer Maggie Caine.

I took one step into the room. I could see a figure in a gray suit stretched out on the bed.

Then a voice behind me cried, "Maggie, don't go in there!"

I was grabbed from behind and pulled back. But not before I saw his face.

Epilogue

The young priest had borrowed his pastor's car to drive to the farm. He managed to get Maggie into the car and then took her to the motel where, with the help of the motel manager's wife, she was put to bed. Then a local doctor came and gave her a sedative.

When the priest came the next morning she said, "Get me some more pills."

"No, Maggie," he said. "I can help you beat them now, because I realize what you've been going through. You've made a believer of me, Maggie."

"What did you see?"

"I saw Duff. Now I know there's been some kind of diabolical plot against you."

"You saw Duff, no one else?"

"That was enough. At first I thought—forgive me—that you were responsible for his body being there. Then I realized you couldn't possibly have opened his grave, broken the lock on the vault and lifted out the casket without help. Anyway, I called Mr. Nichols and he sent some of his men to get the body so it can be cremated."

"He isn't dead!"

"Maggie, he's been dead for weeks. You must have seen the condition of the body."

"He opened his eyes and smiled at me!"

"Maggie, Maggie . . ."

"Call your goddamn undertaker! Tell him I'll have him prosecuted if he goes into that house!"

He went away and came back in a little while.

"The men have been out there already," he said. "There was no body in the bedroom."

"They've taken him away so they can use him again."

"Not him, Maggie! It!"

She refused to argue. He asked some questions and she told him about going into the house with Jeff Duncan. He went away again and returned in a few minutes.

"I talked on the phone with the boy," he said. "He admits being with you, but he left because you were acting strangely. He says he didn't see anything out of the ordinary."

"They're using him too. He's General Caine now."

"Then what about Duff?"

"I don't think they need Duff anymore. I think they were telling me they can use him, if it becomes necessary, to make me submit to them."

"Duff is dead, Maggie, you've got to believe that. His soul has gone. Whatever you saw, or thought you saw, it wasn't the Duff you knew."

She thought about that for a while. It seemed logical that if they, through the power that controlled them, could make people become other people, it shouldn't be very difficult for them to make a dead body move and smile.

In a few days she was able to return to the routine of visiting Franny and sitting in front of the TV set. The priest went out to the farm and came back to report that Duff's body had seemingly been reburied. Or at least his grave had been filled in.

He is still imploring Maggie to take her daughter and leave the area, and she keeps promising to go very soon. He also says that since she had made him a believer in the existence of absolute evil, she has also strengthened his faith in an ultimate good.

Then the other day, since he wasn't making any headway with her, he drove out to the Duncan farm and suggested that the Duncans take their son and move somewhere else. Apparently Jeff's parents thought he was out of his mind.

He won't let Maggie use his car anymore, and he has told all the local rental agencies that she is an irresponsible driver who can't be trusted with their cars. Nevertheless there are ways.

Yesterday she walked out to the road that leads to the farm. She stood there for only a moment before Jeff Duncan came along. He opened his car door and asked if she would like a lift to the farm.

"Not today," she said, "but perhaps another day."

This afternoon the young priest came with the old priest and a strange priest. They put on their stoles and lit candles, and the young priest swung a thurible filled with fuming incense and the old priest shoved a crucifix in Maggie's face, while the strange priest intoned some prayers. Maggie Caine was only irritated, but Margaret Dorn was angry and began to curse them. Then she realized that was what they wanted so she was quiet again.

Later Margaret put a thought into Maggie's mind. If they can make Jeff become General Caine, maybe they can make him become Duff too. At first Maggie rejected that, because she was sure that Duff's soul was not available to them.

But you never know. Maggie is thinking now that maybe she ought to go out to the farm once more and see. She thinks that, as a mother, maybe it's her duty to do that.